ACCLAIM FOR KAT

"Fuller brings us compelling characters who stay in our hearts long after we've read the book. It's always a treat to dive into one of her novels."

—BETH WISEMAN, BESTSELLING AUTHOR OF *HEARTS IN HARMONY*, ON *THE INNKEEPER'S BRIDE*

"A beautiful Amish romance with plenty of twists and turns and a completely satisfying happy ending. Kathleen Fuller is a gifted storyteller."

—JENNIFER BECKSTRAND, AUTHOR OF *HOME ON HUCKLEBERRY HILL*, ON *THE INNKEEPER'S BRIDE*

"I always enjoy a Kathleen Fuller book, especially her Amish stories. *The Innkeeper's Bride* did not disappoint! From the moment Selah and Levi meet each other to the last scene in the book, this was a story that tugged at my emotions. The story deals with several heavy issues such as mental illness and family conflicts, while still maintaining humor and couples falling in love, both old and new. When Selah finds work at the inn Levi is starting up with his family, they clash on everything, but realize they have feelings for each other. My heart hurt for Selah as she held her secrets close and pushed everyone away. But in the end, God's grace and love, along with some misguided Birch Creek matchmakers stirring up mischief, brings them together. Weddings at a beautiful country inn? What's not to love? Readers of Amish fiction will enjoy this winter-time story of redemption and hope set against the backdrop of a beautiful inn that brings people together."

—LENORA WORTH, AUTHOR OF *THEIR AMISH REUNION*

"A warm romance that will tug at the hearts of readers, this is a new favorite."

—*THE PARKERSBURG NEWS & SENTINEL* ON *THE TEACHER'S BRIDE*

"Fuller's appealing Amish romance deals with some serious issues, including depression, yet it also offers funny and endearing moments."

—BOOKLIST ON *THE TEACHER'S BRIDE*

"Kathleen Fuller's *The Teacher's Bride* is a heartwarming story of unexpected romance woven with fun and engaging characters who come to life on every page. Once you open the book, you won't put it down until you've reached the end."

—AMY CLIPSTON, BESTSELLING AUTHOR
OF *A SEAT BY THE HEARTH*

"Kathleen Fuller's characters leap off the page with subtle power as she uses both wit and wisdom to entertain! Refreshingly honest and charming, Kathy's writing reflects a master's touch when it comes to intricate plotting and a satisfying and inspirational ending full of good cheer!"

—KELLY LONG, NATIONAL BESTSELLING
AUTHOR, ON *THE TEACHER'S BRIDE*

"Kathleen Fuller is a master storyteller, and fans will absolutely fall in love with Ruby and Christian in *The Teacher's Bride*."

—RUTH REID, BESTSELLING AUTHOR OF *A MIRACLE OF HOPE*

"*The Teacher's Bride* features characters who know what it's like to be different, to not fit in. What they don't know is that's what makes them so loveable. Kathleen Fuller has written a sweet, oftentimes humorous, romance that reminds readers that the perfect match might be right in front of their noses. She handles the difficult topic of depression with a deft touch. Readers of Amish fiction won't want to miss this delightful story."

—KELLY IRVIN, BESTSELLING AUTHOR OF
THE *EVERY AMISH SEASON* SERIES

"Kathleen Fuller is a talented and gifted author, and she doesn't disappoint in *The Teacher's Bride*. The story will captivate you from the first page to the last with Ruby, Christian, and other engaging characters. You'll laugh, gasp, and wonder what will happen next. You won't want to miss reading this heart-warming Amish story of mishaps, faith, love, forgiveness, and friendship."

—MOLLY JEBBER, SPEAKER AND AWARD-WINNING
AUTHOR OF *GRACE'S FORGIVENESS* AND THE
AMISH KEEPSAKE POCKET QUILT SERIES

"Enthusiasts of Fuller's sweet Amish romances will savor this new anthology."

—*LIBRARY JOURNAL* ON *AN AMISH FAMILY*

"These four sweet stories are full of hope and promise along with misunderstandings and reconciliation. True love does prevail, but not without prayer, introspection, and humility. A must-read for fans of Amish romance."

—*RT BOOK REVIEWS*, 4 STARS, ON *AN AMISH FAMILY*

"The incredibly engaging Amish Letters series continues with a third story of perseverance and devotion, making it difficult to put down . . . Fuller skillfully knits together the lives within a changing, faithful community that has suffered its share of challenges."

—*RT BOOK REVIEWS*, 4 ½ STARS, ON *WORDS FROM THE HEART*

"Fuller's inspirational tale portrays complex characters facing real-world problems and finding love where they least expected or wanted it to be."

—*BOOKLIST*, STARRED REVIEW, ON *A RELUCTANT BRIDE*

"Fuller has an amazing capacity for creating damaged characters and giving insights into their brokenness. One of the better voices in the Amish fiction genre."

—CBA RETAILERS + RESOURCES ON A RELUCTANT BRIDE

"This promising series debut from Fuller is edgier than most Amish novels, dealing with difficult and dark issues and featuring well-drawn characters who are tougher than the usual gentle souls found in this genre. Recommended for Amish fiction fans who might like a different flavor."

—LIBRARY JOURNAL ON A RELUCTANT BRIDE

"Sadie and Aden's love is both sweet and hard-won, and Aden's patience is touching as he wrestles not only with Sadie's dilemma, but his own abusive past. Birch Creek is weighed down by the Troyer family's dark secrets, and readers will be interested to see how secondary characters' lives unfold as the series continues."

—RT BOOK REVIEWS, 4 STARS, ON A RELUCTANT BRIDE

"Kathleen Fuller's A Reluctant Bride tells the story of two Amish families whose lives have collided through tragedy. Sadie Schrock's stoic resolve will touch and inspire Fuller's fans, as will the story's concluding triumph of redemption."

—SUZANNE WOODS FISHER, BESTSELLING
AUTHOR OF ANNA'S CROSSING

"Kathleen Fuller's A Reluctant Bride is a beautiful story of faith, hope, and second chances. Her characters and descriptions are captivating, bringing the story to life with the turn of every page."

—AMY CLIPSTON, BESTSELLING AUTHOR OF A SIMPLE
PRAYER AND THE KAUFFMAN AMISH BAKERY SERIES

"The latest offering in the Middlefield Family series is a sweet love story, with perfectly crafted characters. Fuller's Amish novels are written with the utmost respect for their way of living. Readers are given a glimpse of what it is like to live the simple life."

—*RT Book Reviews*, 4 stars, on *Letters to Katie*

"Fuller's second Amish series entry is a sweet romance with a strong sense of place that will attract readers of Wanda Brunstetter and Cindy Woodsmall."

—*Library Journal* on *Faithful to Laura*

"Well-drawn characters and a homespun feel will make this Amish romance a sure bet for fans of Beverly Lewis and Jerry S. Eicher."

—*Library Journal* on *Treasuring Emma*

"*Treasuring Emma* is a heartwarming story filled with real-life situations and well-developed characters. I rooted for Emma and Adam until the very last page. Fans of Amish fiction and those seeking an endearing romance will enjoy this love story. Highly recommended."

—Beth Wiseman, bestselling author of *Her Brother's Keeper* and the Daughters of the Promise series

"*Treasuring Emma* is a charming, emotionally layered story of the value of friendship in love and discovering the truth of the heart. A true treasure of a read!"

—Kelly Long, author of the Patch of Heaven series

AMISH GENERATIONS

Other Books by Kathleen Fuller

AMISH GENERATIONS

FOUR STORIES

KATHLEEN FULLER

ZONDERVAN®

ZONDERVAN

Amish Generations

Copyright © 2020 by Kathleen Fuller

This title is also available as a Zondervan e-book.
This title is also available as a Zondervan audio book.

Requests for information should be addressed to:
Zondervan, *3900 Sparks Dr. SE, Grand Rapids, Michigan 49546*

Library of Congress Cataloging-in-Publication Data
Names: Fuller, Kathleen, author.
Title: Amish generations : four stories / Kathleen Fuller.
Description: Grand Rapids, Michigan : Zondervan, [2020] | Summary:
   "Four sweet and funny Amish love stories, spanning four different
   generations. Love comes at all times and for all ages!"-- Provided by
   publisher.
Identifiers: LCCN 2019054487 (print) | LCCN 2019054488 (ebook) | ISBN
   9780310359548 (trade paper) | ISBN 9780310359555 (e-book) | ISBN
   9780310359579 (downloadable audio)
Subjects: LCSH: Amish--Fiction.
Classification: LCC PS3606.U553 A6 2020 (print) | LCC PS3606.U553
   (ebook) | DDC 813/.6--dc23
LC record available at https://lccn.loc.gov/2019054487
LC ebook record available at https://lccn.loc.gov/2019054488

Printed in the United States of America
20 21 22 23 24 LSC 10 9 8 7 6 5 4 3

To James. I love you.

Contents

GLOSSARY

ab im kopp: crazy in the head

aenti: aunt

appleditlich: delicious

boppli: baby

bruder: brother

bu/buwe: boy/boys

daed: dad

danki: thank you

dawdi haus: a small house built onto or near the main house for grandparents to live in

dochder: daughter

familye: family

geh: go

grandboppli: grandbaby

grosskinner: grandchildren

grossmutter: grandmother

gut: good

Gute morgen: good morning

Gute nacht: good night

haus: house

kaffee: coffee

kapp: white hat worn by Amish women

kinn/kinner: child/children

lieb: love

maedel/maed: young woman/young women

maam: mom

mann: man

mei: my

nee: no

nix: nothing

onkel: uncle

Ordnung: written and unwritten rules in an Amish district

schwester: sister

seltsam: strange

sohn: son

vatter: father

ya: yes

yer/yerself: your/yourself

yung: young

Young Love

CHAPTER 1

SUGARCREEK, OHIO

"Johnnie, you stop that right now," Fern Gingerich called to her seven-year-old charge. She didn't know what he planned to do with the pillowcase in his hands as he chased his five-year-old brother, Leroy—and she didn't want to find out. When the two boys made another circle in the living room, she grabbed both the pillowcase and Johnnie, immediately letting go of his arm as she blocked his way. "I meant what I said. Stop."

Johnnie looked up at her with vibrant, dark-blue eyes that reminded her of his *onkel* Dan, his face the picture of innocence. "I was just playin' around, Fern."

"He was gonna put that pillowcase over *mei* head."

Leroy kept his distance on the other side of the room as if unsure whether his brother would go after him again.

"*Nee*, I wasn't," Johnnie said, punctuating the point with a shake of his head.

"*Ya*, you were." Leroy scowled at him. "You've done it before."

Fern put two fingers against her temple and pressed against the throbbing point. Normally she could manage Johnnie and Leroy, but today she was having an arthritis flare, and all she wanted to do was lie down on the Klines' couch and take a nap. But she was here to babysit Alvin and Iva's children, and that's what she was going to do.

"How about we sit down and listen to a story?" she said.

"I wanna *geh* outside and play." Leroy scooted to the couch and climbed onto the back of it, then pointed out the picture window to the deep snow that covered the ground.

"Me too." Johnnie scrambled to perch next to him, and they both stared longingly out the window. The latest snowfall—the second one today, which wasn't unusual for January in Sugarcreek—had stopped half an hour ago. It also wasn't unusual for two young boys to want to play in the snow.

"Maybe in a little while." Fern's legs felt heavy as she stashed the pillowcase under the pile of magazines in the rack that also doubled as an end table. She made a mental note to retrieve it so Iva or Alvin wouldn't find a surprise there.

"But we want to *geh* now," the boys said in unison.

Fern stepped to the couch and looked out the window too. The blue curtains were drawn back to let more light into the living room, and cold air seeped through the glass. The boys didn't seem to care, but Fern shivered. "Look," she said, trying to distract them from wanting to go outside. "See the cardinal on top of that snowdrift?"

"The red bird by the driveway?" Leroy swiped his nose with the back of his hand.

"*Ya.*"

"That's a male cardinal." At Leroy's questioning look, she added, "It's a *bu*. And did you know the males are the only ones that sing?"

"Who cares?" Johnnie climbed down from the couch and left the living room.

Fern sighed. Normally it was the youngest child in the family who needed close supervision, but in this case, the roles were reversed. "C'mon, Leroy. Let's find *yer bruder* before he gets into something else."

"I like cardinals," he said as she took his small hand. He was meeker and calmer than his older brother, but not by much.

"Me too."

They moved in the direction Johnnie had taken and found him in the mudroom, putting on his boots.

"Excuse me," she said. She might be exhausted and having a bit of brain fog, but she would not put up with disrespect. "I never said you could *geh* outside."

"But I want to make a snowman."

Fern crouched in front of him and touched his boot. When he looked her in the eye, she said, "Take this off. Now."

"Aww." Johnnie pulled off the boot and then stuck out his lower lip. "I'm bored."

"*Nee* kidding," she muttered, although she was thankful she had won the battle of wills this time. Fern had arrived at the Klines' after school let out to watch the boys while Alvin and Iva traveled to a doctor's appointment in Akron. Fern didn't normally babysit for them, but when Iva mentioned she needed a sitter at lunch after church last Sunday, Fern volunteered. She'd thought it odd that no one else at the table offered. Then again, she'd forgotten what a handful Johnnie was. He wasn't a bad kid, but he did have a short attention span, and as she was finding out, a stubborn streak.

But she was glad she'd agreed to babysit. Because Alvin went with Iva to her appointment, Fern thought she might be pregnant with their third child. If she was, the two of them would definitely have their hands full, if they didn't already.

"Fern?" Leroy tugged at the sleeve of her navy-blue sweater. "Is Johnnie in trouble?"

"*Nee.*" She could forgive a little cabin fever, and

Johnnie had complied with her request when she was stern with him.

"He gets in trouble a lot," Leroy said.

"Be quiet," Johnnie snapped. He set the boot down and stood. "Why can't we *geh* outside?"

Because I can barely keep mei *eye on you two inside.* But she couldn't say that out loud. She wasn't about to admit any weakness to Johnnie Kline. He would take that information and run with it. She looked into the boys' expectant eyes. "We can't *geh* outside because I have a cold. And it's not *gut* to be outside in the cold when you have, uh, a cold."

God, forgive me for fibbing. But a fib was easier than telling the children her rheumatoid arthritis was acting up. They wouldn't believe her anyway. More than once she'd heard, "Isn't that an old person's disease?" It wasn't always, but right now she felt like she was eighty-four instead of twenty-four.

"You don't sound like you have a cold." Johnnie pinched his nose. "You should sound like this."

"*Ya*," Leroy said, imitating his brother, as he often did. "Like this."

Fern herded the boys from the chilly mudroom into the kitchen. "How about some hot chocolate and a cookie? Then I'll read you a story."

"I guess," Johnnie said.

The boys plopped into chairs next to each other and then watched Fern make the hot chocolate, which was more like lukewarm chocolate so they wouldn't burn their tongues. She poured it into sturdy plastic cups, then cut a sugar cookie in half, no doubt a leftover treat from Christmas. When she turned around the boys were pinching each other.

"Ow!" Johnnie said, then gave Leroy a pinch.

"Ow!" But Leroy laughed and pinched Johnnie again.

Fern had seen this game before. It was all fun until someone pinched too hard. She hurriedly put the cocoa and cookie halves in front of the boys. Then she dropped into a chair so she could rest while they had their snack. She glanced at the clock. Three. Alvin and Iva wouldn't be back for an hour or two. How was she going to keep these boys occupied for that long?

She heard a knock on the front door. "You two stay here." She started for the living room, then paused and moved Leroy's chair, with Leroy still in it, and his snack out of Johnnie's reach. *Better safe than sorry.* Then she hurried to answer the door. When she opened it, her heart skipped a beat at the sight of Dan Kline, all six feet two inches of him. He wasn't just the boys' uncle. He was her secret crush.

But that had been years ago. Okay, months ago. All right, she'd never fully stopped liking him, not even when he dated Miriam Lapp last year. But then they'd broken up when Miriam moved to Ashtabula with her family, and Fern's crush had intensified. Which was foolish, because Dan had never shown an inkling of interest in her.

She'd seen him at the feedstore yesterday while she was helping her father pick up food for their pigs. That exertion could be the reason she was so tired today, but she couldn't just stand there and not give her father a hand. Not in front of Dan. And then, like right now, her pulse had thrummed. That wasn't good at all.

"Hi," he said, taking off his woolen cap and shaking the snow from it. His striking eyes, childishly cute on Johnnie but mesmerizing on Dan, met hers. "I didn't know you were here."

Act casual. "I'm babysitting," she said, opening the door wider and forcing her heart rate to slow down.

"My condolences." But he winked as he spoke, which sent Fern's heart into overdrive again. She leaned against the door, which caused it to move a few inches, setting her off-balance.

He reached out and lightly touched her arm to steady her. "You all right?"

"Fine," she squeaked. *So much for casual.*

When Dan stepped inside, the boys burst into the living room, squealing as they ran to him. "*Onkel* Dan, can we *geh* outside and make a snowman?" Leroy said as he bounced on his tiptoes.

"Fern won't *geh* with us." Johnnie gave her a surly look before turning a pleading one on his uncle.

"I'm sure there's a *gut* reason for that." He turned to Fern and shut the door behind him. "Have you been here all day?"

9

"Just since school let out." She hoped she didn't look as tired as she felt. She also hoped neither boy would repeat her fib about having a cold.

Dan grinned. "Then you deserve a break." He put his cap back on his head of thick, honey-blond hair and looked down at his nephews. "Get *yer* coats and boots on, and we'll make the biggest snowman anyone's ever seen."

"Yay!" The boys sounded equally excited, and she couldn't blame them.

They all made their way to the mudroom, where the boys scrambled to get their boots on as Fern took their small coats from the hooks hanging by the door. She knelt and helped Leroy into his, then took a clean handkerchief out of her apron pocket and wiped the sugar cookie crumbs from his round little face. She always kept one or two handkerchiefs in her pockets when she babysat, just in case.

The boys were ready to go when Dan looked at her. "Are you sure you don't want to join us?"

A part of her did. There was a time when she could build snowmen and chase after young boys and not feel exhausted. Fortunately, some days she still could, but today was not one of them. "You *buwe geh*. I have a living room to clean up."

He nodded, then the three of them swept out into the cold.

Fern shut the back door and leaned her head against it. *Thank you, Lord, for Dan coming over.* Her quick prayer had nothing to do with her crush on him. Talk about an unexpected blessing. Hopefully he would tire out the boys before they returned.

She went into the living room and looked around at the mess of toys, crayons, coloring books, and regular books that littered the floor. She had to clean all this, but first she needed to rest for a few minutes. She sat down on the edge of the couch, then stretched out on it, her joints aching. She closed her eyes. *Just for a few minutes . . .*

~

Dan was more than happy to build a snowman with his nephews this afternoon. He just hadn't expected to have the opportunity. Today he'd finished with his last farrier customer, and since the man lived near his brother, he'd decided to ask Alvin what he was talking about at church last week when he mentioned a special project he wanted Dan to help with. Instead of Alvin, though, he found a weary Fern Gingerich and two young boys with obvious cabin fever. He felt a little sorry for her. He loved his nephews, but they both, especially Johnnie, always seemed to have ants in their pants.

This afternoon was no exception. Once they made half the snowman, the boys grew disinterested and wanted to make a snow fort. Dan suggested they make the fort around the snowman, and by the time they finished, Leroy was shivering. "Time to *geh* inside," Dan said, putting his mitten-covered hands over Leroy's red cheeks to warm them.

"But we still have to finish the snowman," Johnnie said.

"Y-ya," Leroy said. "W-we h-have to f-finish."

He had to admire their dedication. "You can," Dan said, smiling as he scooped up the smaller boy. "Tomorrow."

"Will you be here tomorrow?" Johnnie said, plowing through the wall of a snow fort that would fall over in a strong wind.

"*Nee.*"

"Aww." Johnnie kicked at the snow. "Why?"

"Because I have work to do." They trudged through the snow and into the house, where Dan let the back door close behind them and then set Leroy down. Expecting Fern to show up any second, he started helping Leroy out of his wet coat and boots while Johnnie got out of his. But by the time Dan had taken off his own boots and coat, Fern was still nowhere to be seen.

"Fern?" he called when he entered the kitchen. Silence.

Johnnie had already taken off for the living room. Dan and Leroy started to follow but halted when Johnnie rushed back. "She's on the couch," he said. "I think she's asleep."

Dan smiled. He wasn't that surprised. She'd looked in rough shape when he arrived. He put his fingers to his lips and then tiptoed to the living room, the boys imitating him. Sure enough, Fern was sound asleep, one arm dangling from the edge of the couch, her lips parted a tiny bit.

A little fascinated, he moved in for a closer look. He'd known Fern his whole life. They'd both been born in this community, they were the same age, and they'd attended school together all the way through eighth grade. She had been shy and a little on the mousy side, with the darkest hair of any girl he'd ever seen—along with the longest eyelashes. Her lashes captured his attention again as they rested against the top of her cheeks. She looked so peaceful, and, he had to admit, pretty.

Her attractive appearance was something else he'd noticed lately, which baffled him. After all, he'd sworn off interest in women—for a long, *long* time. That plan had been working for him, but for the past month he'd caught himself paying more and more attention to Fern. When he saw her at the feedstore yesterday, he'd felt a tug of attraction. More like a hard yank, if he was being honest—something more intense than he'd felt with Miriam despite dating her for several months.

"*Onkel* Dan, why are you staring at Fern?"

Fern's eyes, soft and chestnut brown, flew open. Then they grew round with alarm, and she bolted straight up. "Did I fall asleep?"

"*Ya*," Leroy said, biting the tip of his finger.

"And *Onkel* Dan was staring at you," Johnnie added.

Dan gave him a stern look. Johnnie was not only full of energy; he was smart, observant, and at times, like now, annoying. "You two get to picking up those toys. You've made a mess in here."

They both nodded and started working. Fern jumped from the couch and joined them. "Sorry," she said, grabbing a box of crayons and a coloring book. Then she pulled a pillowcase out from the magazine rack. That was a little weird, but he didn't ask any questions. "I should have had all this picked up by now," she added as she made her way around the room, straightening items as she went.

Dan noticed the boys had started playing with a toy car. He'd given it to Johnnie three Christmases ago, but they were acting like they'd never seen it before—a classic stalling technique.

"Fern," he said as he stepped to her side. He wasn't sure why he thought she needed reassurance. He just did. "It's fine. They're old enough to pick up their own stuff."

"But I'm the babysitter." She looked up at him, dark circles under her eyes. Then she knelt in front of the bookcase, wincing.

First she'd stumbled by the front door, now she seemed to be in some pain. "Are you okay?" Dan asked.

"I'm fine." She righted some of the books, then popped up like she was a jack-in-the-box. She turned and smiled. "Just great."

The under-eye circles and second wince told a different story, but his attention unwittingly shifted gears. Had she always had such a lovely smile? If so, why hadn't he noticed it until now?

He heard the back door open, and so did the boys, who

immediately took off. He followed them into the mud-room to see his brother and Iva standing there.

"Hey, Dan," Alvin said, his cheeks red from the cold. He frowned. "I must have forgotten you were coming today."

"You didn't forget." He explained as the boys swirled around Iva's legs, clamoring for her attention as she managed to remove her bonnet and coat.

"Gotcha," Alvin said as he sat down to remove his boots.

Fern looked in from the kitchen doorway. "Hello. Did *yer* trip *geh* all right?"

Dan didn't miss the loving look Alvin and Iva exchanged before they told Fern that, yes, the trip to Akron had been great. Alvin, who hated cities, would visit Akron for only one reason—because their obstetrician was there. His brother was having another kid. That would be nice . . . *for Alvin.* Dan loved his nephews, but he wasn't in any hurry for marriage or kids.

That had bothered Miriam, and when she told him her family was moving away, he knew she was giving him the chance to change his mind. But he couldn't bring himself to do it, and she ended their relationship that night. She left the week after, and Dan had to admit he hadn't thought much about her since, which only proved he'd been right. Even if Miriam hadn't moved away, they wouldn't have had a future together.

"Why don't you stay for supper, Fern?" Iva asked as she

removed her boots. "We're just having leftover meat loaf sandwiches, but you're welcome to join us."

Dan saw Fern's hesitation. If she didn't feel good, he didn't blame her for not wanting to stay. But to his surprise, her expression brightened.

"I would like that," she said, smiling. "How can I help with the meal?"

As Iva answered Fern, Alvin turned to Dan. "Before we eat, we can take a look at that project I mentioned."

"Sure." But Dan gave Fern one last look before he left with his brother. He was glad she'd decided to stay. Hopefully someday he could figure out why he was so drawn to her lately.

CHAPTER 2

Dan looked at the old-fashioned carriage in his brother's workshop. "How old is this?"

Alvin touched the ripped fabric on the back of one of the open vehicle's seats. "Early twentieth century. Two antique dealers found it in an old barn in Indiana. They heard we sometimes restore old cars, so they brought this one here. They call it a Stanley Steamer."

Dan walked around the rusty car, which was covered with a layer of dust. It had two seats—a lower one in the front and a higher one in the back, enough to seat four people. The Steamer didn't have a roof, and from what he could tell, it wasn't supposed to. The wheels, what was left of them, resembled thick, large bicycle tires without any tread. "I've never seen anything like this," he said, examining the steering mechanism.

"Neither had I or *Daed*." He strode to one of the workbenches and picked up a piece of paper. "Here's a picture of what these vehicles look like restored."

Impressed at what the simple car was supposed to look like, Dan nodded. Refurbished, it would be unique, more of a show car than drivable. Although he'd never learned how to drive a car, he did like the looks of some of the antique ones, especially the really old cars. "*Danki* for showing me this," he said, handing Alvin the paper.

"Like I said, I'm hoping you'll help me with it."

Dan looked at his brother, uneasiness coming over him. "You and *Daed* know I'm not interested in the buggy business."

"*Ya*, we both know," Alvin said, a touch of annoyance in his voice. "We're not talking about you joining the business. But you can see how much work needs to be done on this car, and *Daed* and *Mamm* are leaving for Sarasota in two days for their yearly vacation. The undercarriage needs to be taken off and repaired, if not outright replaced. There's plenty of body work to do too."

Dan glanced at the vehicle again. He wasn't just a farrier; he was also a blacksmith, and from what his customers said, he was a good one. He also had welding experience. He'd started his own business two years ago, building it from the ground up, and he preferred to work exclusively with iron and metal. "When is it supposed to be finished?"

"In a month."

He frowned. "Why didn't you tell them that isn't enough time?"

"Because I can use the work, Dan." He touched the torn, dusty fabric again. "Business is slow in the winter—you know that yourself. Also, I'll soon have another mouth to feed."

"I figured that's why you and Iva went to Akron. But you aren't in financial trouble, are you?"

Alvin shook his head. "*Nee*. But the dealers are paying top dollar for the short deadline. And"—he grinned, spreading his arm out over the car—"Look at this beauty. We'll never have the chance to work on a vehicle this old again."

Dan didn't miss how his brother had already assumed he would agree to help. But Alvin was right. This was not only a chance to do something different and unique, but Dan's farrier and blacksmith businesses were also slow right now. Besides all that, Alvin needed his help in more ways than one, and Dan wasn't going to let him down.

"All right," he said, kneeling and inspecting the undercarriage of the vehicle, which was dented and warped with flaking paint. Then he stood. "I'll help you."

Alvin clapped him on the back, looking relieved. "*Danki*, Dan. I think this will be a great project."

"I agree. But after that, I'm back to *mei* own businesses." He had to make it clear that he wasn't going to join them, no matter how his father and brother kept trying to convince him to do it.

"Understood."

They discussed the car a little longer and cared for their horses, and by the time they walked into the kitchen, supper was on the table. Turning after washing his hands at the kitchen sink, he saw Fern seated between Johnnie and Leroy, which was a smart move on her part—as long as she didn't mind being a human buffer. More than once he'd witnessed the boys trying to irritate each other during a meal, and Alvin always reprimanded them. But just like Alvin and Dan at their age, his nephews never failed to push the edge of that envelope whenever they could.

Dan sat down across from Fern as Alvin and Iva took their places at the opposite ends of the table. After prayer, they all passed around the food and started eating, Fern taking the time to cut Leroy's sandwich into four pieces the size of a five-year-old's hand.

Alvin looked at Johnnie, who was stuffing a huge spoonful of mashed potatoes into his mouth. "I want you to practice *yer* reading after supper."

"Mff fffm mmm?" Johnnie said around the potatoes.

"Don't talk with *yer* mouth full," Iva said. "Swallow those potatoes before you speak."

Johnnie complied, then looked at his father. "Do I have to?" he repeated.

"*Ya.* You have to."

Dan sympathized with his nephew. He'd disliked school from the time he started until he completed the last year for every Amish child—eighth grade. Except for recess.

He enjoyed recess. He guessed Johnnie might be more like him than he thought.

"Practice will help you improve *yer* grade." Iva held up a plate of pickled eggs toward Fern. "Would you like one?"

"*Danki.*" Fern took an egg and placed it next to her open-faced meat loaf sandwich.

Dan thought back as he watched her cut the sandwich precisely in half. Unlike him and Johnnie, she had always been a good student. That gave him an idea. "Fern, do you do any tutoring?"

She glanced up, looking surprised. "*Nee. Nee* one's asked me to."

"Would you consider it?"

"I'm . . . not sure." She looked as uncertain as her statement indicated. "I guess I could . . ."

"Are you thinking about Fern tutoring Johnnie in reading?" Alvin asked. When Dan nodded, Alvin looked at Fern. "That's a great idea, if it's something you're interested in."

"What's tutoring?" Johnnie asked.

"It's extra help with *yer* reading schoolwork." Iva smiled at Fern, who still appeared a little confused.

"Yuck." Johnnie swirled his potatoes with his spoon. "I don't want *nee* tutoring."

Now Dan was having second thoughts. Maybe he shouldn't have asked Fern about this in front of Alvin and Iva. He'd put her on the spot without meaning to. Johnnie was a challenge, possibly one Fern didn't want to take on.

Alvin put his hand on Johnnie's, stopping him from making a bigger mess on his plate. "What do you say, Fern? Will you tutor *mei sohn*?"

∼

Fern didn't know what to say. She was still so tired, and it was taking all the energy she had not to fall asleep or rub her sore knees under the table. She should have just gone home, but she didn't want to be rude by turning down Iva's invitation. Besides, she liked Alvin and Iva, and, for the most part, their children. And she had to admit, Dan being here might also have had something to do with her decision.

She glanced at him, wondering why he'd brought up tutoring. It was ironic, because she had always wanted to become a schoolteacher. But Dan wouldn't know that. She'd never told anyone other than her mother and sister, and she'd never applied for a teaching job because of her illness.

Fern looked at both Alvin and Iva. They seemed eager for her answer. While she preferred time to think about something this important, she didn't want to keep them waiting. "I'd like to," she said, meaning it. She was confident she could manage one student for a short period of time. She would enjoy tutoring, and although Johnnie would be a reluctant pupil, she was up for the challenge. At least she would be once her RA flare was over and she got some sleep.

"Terrific. How about starting tomorrow?" Alvin said.

"I think we can hold off until next week," Iva said with a gentle tone. "Is that okay with you, Fern?"

She nodded, relieved that she would get a few days rest before meeting with Johnnie.

When they'd finished their meal, Alvin excused himself to finish the chores outside. Fern offered to help clean up, but Iva refused. "We've kept you long enough," she said, glancing out the window. It was already dark, and snow had started to fall again.

"I can take you home," Dan said.

Fern's heart seemed to flip. Dan was taking her home. Even though his offer was nothing more than a nice gesture he'd make to anyone, her brain and heart weren't paying attention to that truth. How should she answer him? She didn't want to appear too eager, but she didn't want to turn him down either. He might actually withdraw the offer, and she didn't want to miss this opportunity to be alone with him.

Wait. She was going to be alone with Dan? She glanced down at her dress, wishing she'd worn something a little newer—

"Fern?"

She looked up. Dan was standing in front of her now. He was nearly half a foot taller than her, and, as usual, she noticed his strong build. Especially his arms, which were well developed from working in the forge. But she tried not to notice that and focused on his eyes. That wasn't much better since their mesmerizing blue hue was turning her aching knees to jelly.

"Hello? Fern? Did you hear me?"

Dan tapped her on the shoulder, and she blinked, then came to her senses. *Get yourself together.* "Oh *ya . . . danki . . .* I'll take the ride home . . . it's nice of you to offer . . . *danki.*" Her words blended together in one weirdly blurted sentence.

He gave her an odd look. "Okay, then. I'll get *mei* buggy hitched up."

When he walked into the mudroom, her shoulders slumped. Why did she have to act like a fool in front of him? He probably wished he could take back the tutoring idea.

She felt a tug on the hem of her skirt and looked down to see Leroy gazing up at her. He had a small piece of banana bread in his little hand. She crouched in front of him and smiled, temporarily forgetting about her embarrassing exchange with Dan, bracing against the pain in her knees. "*Ya?*"

"Here." He handed her the sweet treat.

She took it, her heart filling with joy. He was such a nice boy, even if he'd already taken a bite out of the bread. "That's very generous of you, Leroy," she said, brushing fine light-brown hair off his forehead before rising to her feet. When she turned around, she found Johnnie leaning against the table, his arms crossed over his chest.

"Good-bye, Johnnie," she said. "I'll see you next week."

"I don't want *nee* tutoring."

"I know."

"I don't like reading."

She moved closer to him. "I know that too. And you don't have to like it, but you do have to get *gut* grades. I'm going to help you do that."

He seemed to relax a bit, although his arms were still crossed. Then he dashed out of the room, without giving either Fern or his mother another look.

"I think you'll have *yer* work cut out for you," Iva said as she carried a stack of dishes to the kitchen counter. "Are you sure you want to do this?"

Fern nodded as she gathered utensils, the least she could do. "I'm sure. I'll try *mei* best to help him."

"Alvin worries a bit too much," Iva said. "He remembers what he and Dan were like in school, and he doesn't want Johnnie to be the same way."

Fern had never thought Dan was a problem in school. Then again, she'd noticed only his good qualities. Alvin was several years older than they were, and she hadn't paid much attention to him. "Johnnie will be okay," she said, believing it.

"I know. God is in control." Iva smiled as she scooped up the last of the dinnerware on the table. "*Danki* for helping us this afternoon and for being willing to tutor Johnnie."

"You're welcome," Fern said, then glanced out the kitchen window. A few flakes had stuck to the glass. "I shouldn't keep Dan waiting." She told Iva good-bye, then went to the mudroom to put on her coat, bonnet, and boots, trying to hide the effort it took to do so in case anyone walked into the room. Sitting for so long at the table had made her limbs stiff, and the cold weather didn't help.

As she stepped outside, the snow was falling steadily, the air crisp and filled with the smoky scent of burning wood from the fireplaces in the surrounding houses. She didn't live that far from Iva and Alvin, but it was nice not to have a cold, snowy walk home tonight, especially when she was so exhausted.

Her joints loosened a bit as she moved to the passenger side of Dan's buggy. She started to climb in, and without warning, her legs suddenly gave way, causing her to slip on the buggy's step and fall on her backside in the snow.

"Are you all right?"

Fern looked up to see Dan rushing toward her. The snow seeped through the skirt of her dress, and she shivered. Great. What a way to start a nice, private ride home with him. "I'm fine," she said, trying to get up. Her hips hurt. She moved slowly, but she still lost her balance again.

"Here." He put his arm around her shoulders and helped her up off the ground, almost lifting her completely. After he set her on her feet, he removed his arm.

"*Danki*," she mumbled. Her body always betrayed her when she was this tired and cold. When she started to climb into the buggy again, Dan held out his hand. Under normal circumstances she would have been thrilled by the idea of holding his hand, but this wasn't a normal circumstance. *Because I'm not normal.*

Reluctantly, she accepted his offer. Her gloves were still in her pockets, and she felt the warmth of his hand, which was twice the size of hers. Despite her embarrassment, her heart sparked again. He pulled back the winter shield and helped her into the buggy, then climbed in on the other side.

Dan handed her a thick blanket. "This will warm you up."

She took it and wrapped it around her legs, then snuggled into it up to her chest. The blanket smelled good, like Dan—fresh and clean and comforting.

"Sometimes that step can get icy." He tapped on the reins, and his horse moved forward.

Fern nodded, but she didn't say anything, her mood dipping again. There was no ice on the step, and they both knew it.

~

Dan glanced at Fern as he drove her home. Even though the winter shield protected them from the cold, wind, and snow and made the interior of the buggy darker than usual, all the streetlamps lining the route to her house allowed him to see that she was asleep again. *That was fast.*

He smiled. He could tell she was still exhausted, and

he was glad she felt comfortable enough after that spill to catch a few winks.

He stared straight ahead, his mind thinking about the strangest thing—how Fern's hand had felt in his.

Before, he'd noticed she was walking slowly, her movements stiff, and it wasn't the first time he'd seen her move that way. Still, he was surprised when she fell, and he'd offered his hand to her because he didn't want her to fall again. But when he held her hand, he got another surprise. Something shifted inside of him, and for a split second, he hadn't wanted to let her go. Her hand was cold, but it was also delicate, and her skin was soft.

Shaking his head, he turned left onto Fern's road. She'd laugh at him if she had any idea where his thoughts were going. Or she'd be offended. With Miriam, he never knew which mood she'd be in next, and he got tired of guessing and being wrong. He couldn't imagine Fern being that fickle.

When he pulled into her driveway, he stopped the buggy, then gently tapped her on the shoulder. She murmured something and snuggled deeper into the blanket, making him wish he didn't have to wake her. He put his hand on her small shoulder and gave her a harder nudge.

"Ow." She jolted, the blanket slipping from her upper body.

He drew back. He didn't think he'd pushed her hard.

She blinked. "Did I fall asleep?"

Dan nodded. "As soon as we hit the road."

Fern pulled off the blanket and handed it to him, frowning a little. "I'm sorry. I didn't intend to nap."

"You must have been really tired. *Mei* nephews can wear a person out. Just ask their parents."

She let out a weary chuckle. "They had a huge case of cabin fever today for sure. *Danki* for taking them outside."

"*Nee* problem. I enjoy spending time with them."

"I could see that." She glanced at the house in front of them, wide awake now. "I better get inside. *Mei* parents are probably wondering what's kept me so long."

As she started to get out of the buggy, he scrambled around it to help her. She looked at his outstretched hand and paused, then slipped her hand into his again.

Jolt. There was the feeling again, stronger this time. He tried to ignore it, but when she set foot on the ground, she was close to him, enough that he could put his arms around her and hold her tight. At that moment, he really, really wanted to do just that.

"*Danki*," she said, then yawned, her mouth forming a big O shape. "Sorry. Guess I'm still tired."

"Don't be sorry." He pulled his hand from hers before he held on to it longer than necessary—or worse, gave in to his instincts. "I'm the one who's sorry. I didn't mean to hurt you."

She frowned. "You didn't."

"You said *ow* when I nudged you awake."

"I did?" Her eyes widened under the lamplight. Snow

caught on her long, thick eyelashes, and she blinked it away. "I don't remember."

He could stare at her all night, he realized, but it was too cold for that. He almost offered to walk her to her front door, but he pulled back. This wasn't a date, although it was starting to feel like one.

"It's getting colder," he said, at a loss for words—at least any that wouldn't make him sound like an idiot.

"*Danki* for the ride home." She started to turn, then looked at him again. "What made you come up with the idea for me to tutor Johnnie?"

He shrugged. "I just remembered how *gut* you were at schoolwork. You used to help the teachers grade papers during recess, which I thought was a little *seltsam*."

"You remember that?"

"*Ya.*" He suddenly remembered other things, like how happy she was the one time she'd hit a home run while they were playing baseball during recess. Little did she know that he had whiffed catching the ball on purpose while playing shortstop, knowing she was fast enough to run the bases. That had been in fifth grade, and now he remembered she'd started staying inside during recess the following year. Was she always grading papers? He didn't know.

"You have a *gut* memory."

"Sometimes. Other times I can't remember where I put *mei* shoes."

She smiled, sharing that sweet little laugh of hers. Then

she gazed up at him. "I'm glad you suggested it. I'm happy to tutor Johnnie."

"You might change *yer* mind after next week."

She started to walk away. "Or I might change his. You never know. He may end up liking reading."

"He's a Kline. None of us like reading."

"We'll see." She waved at him but didn't turn around as she made her way to the front door, taking the porch steps slowly. He knew she was tired, and the fall couldn't have helped.

He watched until she was inside. It wasn't that late, but Fern's father was a farmer, and their whole family were early risers. When the light in the picture window went out, he finally climbed into his buggy but didn't leave until he had one last look at her house.

Dan shook his head. Something strange was going on with him. First, he agreed to help his brother with the Stanley Steamer, something he normally wouldn't do, and now he had these inexplicable feelings for Fern. That bothered him the most. He'd been set on not getting involved with another woman after Miriam. Now it was clear his mind was changing . . . along with his heart.

CHAPTER 3

"Okay, spill it."

Fern looked at Clara as they were peeling apples in her kitchen. Her two nieces and three nephews were at school, and her brother-in-law, Joseph, was at work, so the usually bustling household was quiet. But leave it to her sister to spoil the silence.

"I don't know what you're talking about," Fern said, sliding the paring knife through a juicy Gala apple. "How many bushels of these did you guys pick, anyway?"

"Only ten."

"Ten?"

"Joseph came with us, and you know he can pick apples faster than anyone." Clara dropped her freshly peeled apple into a large bowl. "Now, stop dodging the question."

"I don't recall you asking me a question." Fern smirked.

Clara shook her head. "How about this, then. Fern, will you please tell me why you are so happy this morning?"

Fern picked up another apple, unable to keep from beaming. Dan had driven her home two days ago, and while she was annoyed with herself for falling asleep in his buggy, she still savored the short interaction they'd had when he pulled in front of her house. She couldn't believe he noticed that she liked school and remembered that she used to stay inside at recess and grade papers. At the time, she'd felt self-conscious about missing so many recesses. That was also around the time she and her mother had started pursuing a diagnosis for her symptoms. Since she had enjoyed helping their teacher during the last few years of school, she hadn't missed going outside too much. But she never imagined Dan would have paid attention to anything she did in school.

Meanwhile, that Dan would trust her to help Johnnie meant a lot. He was close to his family, and anyone could see how much he loved and doted on his nephews.

"Fern?" Clara tapped her on the shoulder. "Are you in there somewhere?"

She blinked, then looked at her sister. "*Ya*. I'm here," she said, aware her tone was a little too dreamy.

"Oh brother." Clara sat back in her chair. "Who is he?"

"Why do you automatically assume I'm thinking about a *mann*?"

"Because the only other time I've seen you like this was when you were crushing on Dan Kline."

Fern started peeling another apple, refusing to look at her. "How would you know anything about that? You were already married by then."

"Just because I was married didn't mean I wasn't paying attention." She got up from the table, then rinsed off her hands before pouring two glasses of fresh apple cider. She put one in front of Fern. "Besides," she said, picking up the conversation, "a little birdie might have mentioned it to me a time or two."

Sighing, Fern began peeling her apple faster. "I should have never said anything to *Mamm*."

"She only told me," Clara said, sitting back down. "*Nee* one else. But let's get back to what we were talking about."

Fern scowled. "Let's not."

"I haven't seen you this distracted since Dan . . ." Fern looked up just in time to see Clara's eyes widen. "It *is* Dan, isn't it?"

Fern trained her eyes on her apple and didn't say anything.

"You still have a crush on him?" Clara chuckled. "Talk about loyalty."

"What's wrong with loyalty?"

"Didn't he have a steady girlfriend at one time?"

Why did her sister have to bring that up? "Miriam," Fern said, her tone tight.

"Right. Miriam Lapp. She moved away around the same time they broke up, if I remember correctly."

"You do."

Clara grinned. "He's been single for a while, then."

Fern rolled her eyes. Her sister had a mind like a steel trap, and she rarely forgot anything. "*Ya.* He's single. Which doesn't matter."

"It does if you still like him."

She knew it would be foolish to deny how she felt to Clara. Besides, she didn't like lying to her family—or to anyone else. Then there was the fact that Clara would pester her until she got an answer. "I don't have a crush on Dan. It's more like . . . a passing interest." Okay, maybe a little downplaying was required, because if her sister found out how she really felt about Dan, she would never leave her alone about it.

"Uh-huh." Clara gave her a knowing look. "Passing interest doesn't last ten years."

"Eleven." Fern winced. So much for downplaying.

Clara smiled. "So, tell me all about it. Are you two serious about each other?"

Fern scoffed. "Of course not. All he did was give me a ride home."

"I see." Clara beamed.

"And the reason I'm happy is that I'm going to be tutoring his nephew starting next week. Johnnie."

"You are?" Clara's smile widened. "That's wonderful. Are you reconsidering becoming a teacher?" When Fern shook her head, she added, "Why not? You'd be a wonderful teacher."

Fern placed another peeled apple in the bowl. They

would be making applesauce and apple butter when they finished preparing the rest of the fruit. "You know why," she mumbled.

"Because of *yer* arthritis?" Clara shook her head. "I thought you have more *gut* days than bad."

Fern didn't respond. It was easy for Clara—and anyone else on the outside looking in—to think she was fine. And while her sister was right, that often she was okay, when a flare hit like it had at the Klines' the other day, it hit hard. And that was the reason she couldn't be trusted to oversee a classroom full of children. That wouldn't be fair to the students.

"Fern?"

She looked at her sister. Gone was the teasing and the smile. Clara's dark-brown eyes, the same shade as her own, were filled with concern. Although she was nine years older than Fern, and three siblings had been born between them, she had always felt closest to Clara. "I'm not going to be a teacher," she said. "I made that decision a long time ago, and nothing has changed."

Clara pressed her lips together. "I just thought . . . *Mamm* said you were on a new medication . . ."

Fern would have to talk with her mother about keeping things to herself—although she knew she wouldn't think mentioning medicine or Fern's condition would be gossiping or revealing a secret. The entire family knew about Fern's diagnosis of RA, and they also knew not to discuss it beyond immediate family. Still, Fern would like to keep a few things to herself. "The medicine is helping, but not enough to where I could run a classroom."

"Maybe you could be an assistant?"

She shook her head. "I'm too unreliable."

Clara nodded. "I continually pray for *yer* healing. You know that, *ya*?"

"I do." Just like everyone else in her family. Just like Fern did, every day. And every day she woke up hoping that was the day God would heal her completely. But that hadn't happened, and while she said the prayers, she also had come to terms with the reality that she might not be healed. God had a plan for everyone, and it was possible that his plan for her was to have RA for the rest of her life. Having a chronic illness was difficult, but it wasn't the end of the world. *Just the end of* mei *teaching career . . . before it even began.*

"That's great that you're tutoring Johnnie." Clara took a sip of her cider. "I take it that was Dan's idea?"

Fern nodded and told her what happened.

"And then he took you home." A twinkle appeared in Clara's eye. "Sounds romantic to me."

"It was dark and cold and snowing," Fern replied. "Dan's a courteous *mann*. Of course he would offer me a ride home."

"What did you talk about?"

Fern's cheeks warmed. "I, uh, fell asleep."

"You fell asleep? The *mann* you've had a crush on for over a decade takes you home, and you fall asleep?"

"I was tired. Really tired."

"Oh." Clara nodded, ceasing her teasing. "Still, maybe there's a chance he'll show up at Alvin's again and offer you a ride home."

"You're assuming he's interested in me."

"Why wouldn't he be? You're pretty, smart, sweet, and unattached." She placed another peeled apple in the bowl. "Most importantly, you like him."

"But I don't know if he likes me."

"One way to find out." She grinned.

"Clara, I can't tell him how I feel."

Clara scoffed. "I'm not saying that. Just invite him out for *kaffee* or something."

She shook her head. "I'm not like you, Clara. You basically asked Joseph to marry you."

"Because he was dragging his feet."

"I thought it was because you were impatient." Fern smiled.

"That too. Anyway, you've nursed this *passing interest* for a long time. Maybe it's time you found out if there's anything between you. Or maybe it's time to move on."

Fern didn't say anything, and fortunately her nieces and nephews arrived home from school. That saved her from Clara's continuing lecture. But as she walked home after supper, she thought about what Clara said—and what she didn't say. Was Dan the reason she was still single? Other single men lived in her district, although none of them had shown any interest in her. But she hadn't made herself available either. She didn't attend singings, and when she went to frolics and fellowships after church, she stayed close to her girlfriends or to her family. Were her feelings for Dan keeping her from dating other people? Or was it her illness?

She shook her head as she turned into the driveway. While she had come to terms with her RA and her decision not to pursue teaching, she still grappled with dating and marriage. It would take someone special to understand that some days she wouldn't be able to do much but get out of bed and take care of herself. That sometimes she would be in a lot of pain. What man would want only half a wife?

No, she wouldn't take Clara's advice. Even on the outside chance that Dan felt something for her—which she doubted—she wouldn't pursue a relationship. It wouldn't be fair to him.

~

The next Monday, Dan showed up at his brother's house, ready to work on the Steamer. Their mother and father had already left for Sarasota, and a part of Dan wished he was going with them. He enjoyed swimming in the cool, salty waves of the ocean and feeling the hot sand between his toes. He thought of that as he got out of his buggy and a blast of cold air hit him. Maybe next winter he would take a vacation to Florida. But right now, he had promised to help his brother with the car.

He entered the workshop, where Alvin was already at work, slicing the torn upholstery from one of the seats. He had removed the wheels from the car, and the chassis was standing on blocks high enough that Dan could wiggle underneath if he needed to. "Are we taking this entire thing apart?" he asked, removing his coat before hanging it on a peg on the wall near the door.

"*Ya*. I've done a drawing of the car, so I remember where the pieces are supposed to *geh*." He walked to his worktable and then brought a single sheet of paper to Dan.

Dan reviewed it. "*Gut* job. You might have missed *yer* calling as an artist."

Alvin chuckled and took back the paper. "I don't think so. Besides, I'd miss out on doing projects like this." He turned and looked at the car with a satisfied expression.

While Dan had never driven a car, he knew Alvin had before he joined the church. "Do you miss driving?"

Alvin touched the Steamer's dented body. "I'd be a liar if I said I didn't. But when I was baptized, I made a promise to the church and to God to live a simple life." He turned to Dan. "Working on cars is enough for me."

Dan nodded and turned to a large toolbox to look for a regular wrench and a socket wrench too. As he shuffled through the tools—Alvin and *Daed* weren't tidy when they worked—he heard more ripping of fabric behind him.

"What made you think about Fern tutoring Johnnie?" Alvin said above the cutting noise of the knife.

Wrenches in hand, Dan returned to the car. "Just an idea I had."

"That doesn't answer *mei* question."

Dan slipped under the front of the car. Just as he thought, the nuts were rusted. They would be either too difficult to remove or they'd crumble as soon as he started turning the wrench. He said a little prayer asking that they would come off decently, then went to work. "If I didn't think she would do a *gut* job, I wouldn't have suggested it. Can you give me a hand here?"

Alvin walked over and knelt in front of the car, putting his hands on the bar connecting the two wheels. "It seemed so out of the blue."

"What did?" He twisted the wrench. Nothing, as he feared. Well, at least he didn't have to worry about the bar crashing down. He tried another nut, and this one moved a bit.

"Fern. *Yer* tutoring idea?"

Dan quickly twisted off the nut, then shimmied out from under the Steamer on his back. He flipped over to his knees, then took the bar from Alvin and gently released it before turning to his brother. "It's been a while since we worked together. Do you always talk this much?"

Alvin smirked. "Only when *mei* wife wants me to be nosy."

"Ah. I should have guessed. What does Iva want to know?"

"If there's something between you and Fern."

Dan paused. There wasn't, but he hadn't been able to get Fern off his mind since he took her home the other night. They hadn't had church this past Sunday, which meant he hadn't seen her since, and when he wasn't thinking about her, he was trying to figure out why he couldn't stop thinking about her. He'd never been this preoccupied with Miriam.

"I'm guessing *ya*, there is, since it's taking you so long to answer."

Before Alvin could notice that his face was heating, Dan jumped to his feet. "Do you have any WD-40?" He strode to one of the workshop walls, where a tall shelving unit stood with cans of paint, turpentine, oil, mineral spirits, and other chemicals.

"Wow," Alvin said, moving to stand next to him. He handed him a can with the label missing. "You really are interested in her."

"Look," he said, about to deny it. Then again, maybe his brother would have some good advice when it came to his feelings for Fern. "I . . . I might be interested in her . . . as more than a friend. But," he said, holding up his hand, "that's not why I suggested she tutor Johnnie. She was always a good student in school, and I think she can help him."

"She can't make things worse." A shadow passed over his brother's face.

"Johnnie will be fine." He clapped Alvin on the shoulder. "We made it, didn't we?"

"Drove *Mamm* and *Daed ab im kopp* in the process."

Dan laughed. "I guess you're getting a taste of *yer* own medicine, then."

"*Yer* time will come." Alvin snickered.

"Not anytime soon, that's for sure." But the words rang hollow this time.

Alvin nodded. "I'm just glad you've finally moved on from Miriam."

Frowning, he looked at his brother. "I moved on from her a long time ago."

"Oh. I just figured the reason you hadn't dated anyone else was that you were still hung up on her. She did move away."

"*Ya*, but we had broken up by then."

"You never mentioned her after that."

He turned and faced Alvin. "She was out of *mei* life. What was there to talk about?"

"You've got a point." He paused. "And now you're interested in Fern."

"Like I said, I *may* be interested in her." But there really wasn't any maybe about it.

"Look, if you like her, ask her out on a date. You're twenty-four years old, and it's not like you've never gone on a date before."

But this was different. Still, his brother was right. When Dan wanted something, he went after it. And there was no more hemming and hawing about it. He wanted a date with Fern.

Alvin clapped him on the back. "Now, are we going to keep talking like a couple of hens? Or are we going to get back to work?"

Dan nodded, then lifted a small torch from the bottom shelf along with a pair of safety glasses. He put on the glasses, then lowered himself under the chassis again. First he'd oil the nut, then carefully apply low heat, which would take care of the rust. He had to force himself to focus on the task, though. As a blacksmith, he was used to being around fire and keeping his mind free of distractions. Right now, Fern was a big distraction. But the next time he saw her, he would ask her out on a date.

~

"Bat," Johnnie said, bending his elbow and leaning the side of his head against his palm.

Fern nodded, then showed him another vocabulary card.

"Cat." He yawned. "I know all these, Fern."

"Then we should get through them quickly." She flipped over another card.

"Rat. Mat. Pat." His shoulders slumped. "How long do we have to do this?"

She had anticipated his reluctance. After she'd come home from Clara's, she'd taken some of her mother's blank recipe cards—with her permission, of course—and made two sets of flashcards. She pulled the second set out of her tote bag and shuffled both stacks. Then she started laying the cards facedown on the table. The word *recipe* was at the top corner of each card, along with seven thin red lines.

Johnnie perked up a bit. "What are you doing?"

"Putting cards on the table." She hummed as she finished arranging them in a set of six down and six across. Then she looked at him. "Have you ever played concentration?"

He shook his head. "What is it?"

"A fun game." She turned over one of the cards. "What does this say?"

"Cat."

"Right. Now you have to find the matching word and read both of them out loud. But you only get one chance per turn to find the other word."

"Oh, I've played this, only with pictures." He started to turn over a card.

"Wait. Close *yer* eyes. *Nee* peeking." While he closed his eyes tightly and put his hands over them, she shuffled the cat card back into the group. "Now it's *yer* turn."

He quickly turned over a card. "Bat." He frowned. "Can I have another turn?"

"Not yet. Now it's *mei* turn." She turned a card over, and they continued to play the game until all the pairs were matched. Johnnie had won by one pair, and he had read all the words correctly. Maybe she had started too easily with him, but he did enjoy the game. She would have to put some harder words in the deck next time. She made a note to go to a discount store in New Philadelphia to purchase some index cards and other teaching materials.

They worked on the reading schoolwork he didn't complete in class for the next fifteen minutes, and she realized she wasn't going to keep Johnnie's attention much longer than that. When he finished the assignment, she said they were done for the day. He ran off as Iva came into the kitchen. "How did it *geh*?"

"*Gut*. He doesn't like sitting still. I think that's his biggest problem."

She sighed. "I know. Alvin and I have talked to him about that, but what we say doesn't seem to be getting through. He's just like his father." She smiled. "Which means he'll be a fine *mann* when he grows up . . . if I live through his childhood."

Fern laughed and put the cards into her tote bag. "I'll be back next Monday."

"That sounds *gut*. We'd like you to stay for supper again."

"I'm sorry, but I can't today. I will next week, though."

Iva nodded. "We'll plan on it."

Fern said good-bye to Iva, then left through the front door of the Kline house. She saw a familiar buggy in the driveway and realized it was Dan's. She hadn't known he was going to be here. She guessed he was working in the shop with Alvin. Iva had mentioned something about a new car project, but Fern had been only half listening as she tried to get Johnnie settled in his seat. She paused, looking at the shop, which was behind the house and to the side, where she could see it from the driveway. She wished she had an excuse to see Dan, but anything she came up with seemed too obvious. Instead, she turned and started for home.

"Fern?"

She spun around at the sound of Dan calling her name. Surprised, she waited as he jogged toward her. "Hey," he said, wiping his hands on an old rag before he shoved it behind his back. "Alvin and I are fixing up a Stanley Steamer," he said, a little sheepishly. "Messy work right now, tearing it apart."

"What's a Steamer?"

"A very, very, *very* old car. This one doesn't even have a steering wheel." He shrugged. "I know you don't want to hear about that, though."

"Actually, it sounds interesting."

His brow lifted. "Really? We can show it to you when it's finished. Right now, it's just a bunch of metal and nuts and bolts. Oh, and some really dirty upholstery."

"I'd like to see it." She stood there for a moment, suspecting he wanted to say something else. When he didn't speak, she said, "I better *geh* home. It's *mei* turn to cook supper tonight."

"I won't keep you, then." When she started to leave, he said, "Fern, wait. I want to ask you something."

She froze as she met his gaze. *Keep calm. It's not like he's going to ask you out on a date.*

"Would you like to *geh* sledding with me Saturday afternoon?"

Chapter 4

Fern's jaw dropped. "Sledding?"

"*Ya*. Work gets slow during the winter, and I'm usually finished by lunchtime." He kicked at the snow with the toe of his boot, then looked at her again. "I haven't been sledding in a while, and I wondered if you'd like to come with me."

"I, uh . . ." She didn't know what to say. Did he mean with him, alone? Or with him and other friends? Would it be rude to ask?

"If you don't want to, that's okay." He took a step back. "In fact, you can forget I mentioned it."

"Dan . . ." She should say no. She hadn't been sledding in years, and she wasn't sure if she'd be able to. And if she had a flare that day, she'd have to cancel without giving him the real reason, and that would be not only rude but a lie.

"I guess it was a silly idea." He gave her a little wave and started to turn around. "I'll see you later."

What am I doing? She was actually considering turning him down. After eleven years of waiting for this moment, she was hesitating. She could hear Clara's voice in her head. *Don't be an idiot. If you give up this chance, it won't come again.*

"Wait," she said, stepping toward him. When he faced her again, she said, "I'd like to *geh*. It sounds like fun."

Dan grinned, and she almost dissolved into a giddy puddle on the driveway. His face lit up like a kid's at Christmas, and she was so thankful that she hadn't gone with her gut instinct and turned him down.

"I'll pick you up at one," he said, still smiling.

"*Mei* sled and I will be ready." She didn't have a sled, but her father still had one she and her siblings used when they were children. She was sure he wouldn't mind her using it.

He nodded, the grin still on his handsome face, then he turned and hurried back to the buggy shop.

Fern grasped her tote bag and squealed into the handles. Even if this wasn't a date and every single unattached person would be sledding with her and Dan, she didn't care. She would also put the worry about having a flare out of her mind. Dan had asked her out, and she was determined to savor that fact.

~

Dan couldn't help but whistle as he drove to Fern's house on Saturday afternoon. When he'd glanced out the shop window the other day and seen her leaving the house, he jumped into action. Sledding had been the first thing to pop into his mind, weirdly enough. He'd never been sledding with Miriam, who would have scoffed at the idea anyway. Miriam liked quiet activities, like reading and doing jigsaw puzzles. Nothing wrong with that, but he hadn't been ready to act like an old married couple right off the bat.

When he saw the excitement in Fern's eyes when she said she wanted to go sledding, he knew he'd suggested the right activity. In school, their teacher had occasionally let them sled at recess, and he remembered how much Fern had seemed to enjoy it.

Although there was that moment when he thought she was going to turn him down. She wouldn't have been the first woman to turn him down for a date, but the idea disappointed him more than he thought possible.

He pulled into her driveway. It had snowed again last night—two inches or so on top of the few inches that had already been on the ground—but it was cold, and the snow would pack easily. That made for good sledding down the steep hill close to the school, and he was determined to make sure they both had a fun time today.

When he knocked on the front door, first noticing a

sled leaning against a pole on the porch, he expected one of her parents to answer. Instead, Fern came right out, bundled in her coat, bonnet, a heavy scarf, and snow pants and boots. She was carrying a thermos and a small canvas tote bag. "I hope you like hot chocolate. I also brought a couple of sandwiches."

"Perfect." He was also thinking about how perfect Fern was. Her cheeks and nose were instantly rosy from the cold, and she gave him a shy smile that reached clear to his heart.

He picked up the sled for her, then they walked to the buggy, and he noticed she climbed inside without any problem. She even seemed to have a pep in her step she didn't have last week. *I'll take that as a good sign.*

He handed her the same thick blanket, and she put it on her lap. So far, so good. But as he drove to the hill, he suddenly clammed up. He was rarely at a loss for words, but right now his mind was blank. His palms started to sweat, and he took off his gloves and gripped the reins. Finally, he asked, "Have you ever thought about becoming a schoolteacher?"

Fern paused, then said, "Why are you asking me that?"

He cringed. Maybe the question was too personal. "Alvin mentioned that Iva noticed how *gut* you were with Johnnie during *yer* tutoring session. She said you seemed like a real teacher."

"I thought about it," she said softly. "But then I realized it wasn't for me." Quickly, she asked, "How is work on the car going?"

"Pretty *gut*." Since she seemed a little touchy about the teaching subject, he was glad for the change of topic. He told her they had removed the chassis, and he thought he would be able to save the entire metal mechanism. "I wasn't sure at first, once I got into the project. But I think we'll make the deadline."

"That's *gut*." She paused. "Why do they call it a Stanley Steamer?"

"The company that produced the car was started by twin brothers whose last name was Stanley. Steamers were cars that ran on steam. There's a boiler under the seat that's fueled by gas or kerosene, depending on the model. Alvin knows all about how that works. He brought me on board to help with the bodywork."

"Do you enjoy doing that?"

"Sometimes. I wasn't interested in making and repairing buggies. I liked blacksmithing better, so I decided to start *mei* own business. Still, Alvin and *Daed* ask me to help them with a project every once in a while—usually bodywork. Alvin's the mechanic in the family." He pulled the buggy to a halt. "We're here," he said, glancing at her, more relaxed now that she had started a conversation. "Ready to sled?"

Her eyes lit up. "*Ya*," she said. "I can't wait."

Fern tried to control the swirling in her stomach. The butterflies were out of control, and for good reason. She could sit there and gaze at Dan all day long. But she was also excited about sledding. When she woke up this morning, she felt better than she had in weeks. She not only had the will but also the energy to enjoy herself.

Leaving the hot chocolate and sandwiches in the buggy for later, she got out. Dan had tied his horse to one of the hitching posts in the school parking lot, and he was putting a horse blanket over him so he wouldn't get too cold. Then he pulled out both of their sleds, which he had managed to fit behind the buggy seat. Fern glanced around. No one else was in sight, and the hill was white and pristine. She turned to Dan. "Are we the only ones here?"

He stilled, looking unsure. "*Ya*. Were you expecting anyone else?"

She shrugged. "I wasn't sure if this was a group gathering or not."

"Oh. It's not." He looked into her eyes. "It's just me and you. Is that all right?"

More than all right. She nodded, trying not to appear too eager. But inside she was thrilled.

They walked to the top of the hill, which was a few feet from where he'd parked the buggy. Then he put his sled down on the edge of the precipice. A light snow had started to fall, and he motioned to her. "Ladies first," he said.

She placed her sled next to his. She didn't know how to steer the sled with her feet, so she lay on her stomach on top of it. He did the same on his sled, and she turned to him. "Race you down the hill?"

"Exactly what I was thinking." He put his hands on both sides of the rod that steered his sled. "One . . ."

"Two . . ." she said.

"Three!" they shouted together.

Fern pushed off with the toe of her snow boot, and soon she was speeding down the hill. The sled moved faster than she remembered as a kid, and she fought to steer. Dan was way ahead of her, but she barely noticed as she heard a cracking noise coming from the front of her sled. The wood gave way and split into pieces, sending her skidding down the hill.

CHAPTER 5

Dan was just getting up off his sled when he heard the cracking noise behind him. He spun around and watched in horror as Fern's sled broke apart and she went flying wildly down the rest of the hill, coming to a stop in a lump several yards away. "Fern!" He ran over and knelt in the snow next to her, his heart pounding.

She turned over slowly, looking up at him, bits of snow covering her face. Without thinking, he took off his glove and brushed the clumps of flakes off her cheeks. "Are you okay?" he asked in a breathless panic. "Can you move *yer* legs?"

Fern nodded. "Just . . . got the wind . . . knocked out of me."

He blew out a relieved breath, and when she started to move, he instinctively put his arm around her shoulders and helped her sit up. "Are you sure that's all?" He couldn't believe she wasn't more seriously injured after her petite body had flown around like that.

She moved her legs and arms. "*Ya*," she said. "I'm okay." She looked around. "But *mei* poor sled. It's in pieces everywhere."

"Don't worry about that." He turned her chin, so she was facing him, wanting to make sure she wasn't just saying she was okay to reassure him. "All I care about is that you're all right."

Fern blinked, her chestnut-colored eyes never leaving his face. "I'm okay, Dan. I really am."

He believed her, but he kept his arm around her. It wouldn't take much effort to pull her into his lap and kiss her. But he didn't. Something more intimate had formed between them, though. He felt it, and he saw a spark of attraction in her eyes. The fact that she wasn't trying to get away from him or protesting that he was crossing the line also convinced him that she was interested in him. But he wouldn't take advantage of any woman in this situation. Especially Fern.

Dan moved his arm from around her shoulders and got to his feet. He held out his hand, and she took it. After he helped her stand, she brushed the snow off her dress and pants. "I guess I better pick up what's left of *mei* sled," she said, sounding slightly breathless.

"I'll help."

They gathered the pieces and met back at the landing

point at the bottom of the hill. "How old was this sled?" Dan asked, looking at the wood. He could see it was partly rotted, something he should have noticed when he picked it up at her house. But he'd been too busy paying attention to Fern.

"I don't know," she said. "It was *mei Daed*'s from when he was a *kinn*." She frowned. "I hope he doesn't get mad that it's ruined."

"I think he'll be glad you weren't hurt." He glanced at his sled. "We could take turns using *mei* sled, if you want." The thought that maybe they could sled together—an idea that really, really appealed to him—ran past him, but he'd be asking for trouble by getting that close to her.

She looked at the hill, this time a little less excited, then back at him. "Okay."

They sledded down the hill two more times, but he could tell she wasn't as enthusiastic about it as she'd been at the beginning. When she walked back up the hill the third time, he noticed she was moving much slower than she had the first time they went down.

"I don't know about you," he said, "but I'm getting cold. Can we break open that hot chocolate now?"

She nodded, and her eyes filled with what looked like relief. They made a beeline back to the buggy, and Dan took off Crabapple's warming blanket and feed bag, then unhitched him. The horse needed to move around after standing in the cold, and they could sip hot chocolate and eat sandwiches while he sauntered toward Fern's house.

By the time he'd put his sled and what was left of hers behind the front seat, Fern was already in the buggy and had poured the hot chocolate into the lid of her thermos. He climbed in, and she handed him the drink. He took a sip. It was still nice and warm. *"Appleditlich."*

"I put miniature marshmallows in it, but they melted." She rested her hands on her lap.

He looked at her. "Aren't you having any?"

"I meant to pack it, but I left *mei* mug at home."

"Here," he said, handing her the lid, which was still half filled with the drink.

She shook her head. "I can't drink *yer* hot chocolate."

"We can share it." He gave her a long look before picking up the reins.

She nodded and took a sip. *"Danki."*

He maneuvered the buggy out of the small school lot and headed for Fern's house, letting the horse move at the slowest pace possible.

"Would you like a ham and cheese sandwich?" she asked.

"I would. I'll hold the cup while you get it."

She gave it to him, and he noticed her wince when she bent down to get the sandwich from the tote bag on the floor. He frowned, concern building up in him again, along with a little irritation.

"Fern, why didn't you tell me you were hurt?"

~

Fern cringed as she picked up the tote bag. She set it on the seat this time, which is what she should have done in the first place. Her body ached all over, and it wasn't all because of the tumble she took from the sled. She was familiar with this pain, with the stiffness overcoming her as she sat in the cold buggy. She should have known her body would betray her.

She glanced at Dan, seeing the concern in his eyes. How could she explain this to him? She hadn't been hurt in the accident, but she was hurting now, probably from going up and down the hill so many times. Why couldn't she do a normal, fun activity without feeling like she was ninety years old? But she had to tell him something.

"I guess I didn't realize it at the time," she said, not looking at him. She quickly unwrapped the sandwich, which she'd made with fresh, soft bread she'd baked last night and the good Swiss cheese her father always got as a treat from the Walnut Creek Cheese store. "Here you *geh*," she said, mustering a smile. "One ham and cheese sandwich."

He gave her a dubious look but took the sandwich. She stared straight ahead, feeling like she'd spoiled their time together. What had started as a great afternoon had come to a grinding halt. She should have checked the sled. It hadn't been used since she was a young kid, and when she found it in the shed, she had to wipe dust and cobwebs off it.

Dan ate his sandwich but didn't say anything on the

way to her house. He also didn't ask for more hot chocolate. As for her, she had lost her appetite.

When he pulled to a stop in her driveway, she scrambled out of the buggy with her tote the best she could, her limbs stiff and sore. "*Danki*," she said, not looking back at him, and then she hurried into the house, trying to hide both her physical and emotional pain. When she got inside, she leaned against the door, tears of frustration streaming down her cheeks.

Mamm came into the living room. "You're back so soon? *Yer* note said you'd be gone all afternoon . . ." Concern crossed her features as she walked toward Fern. "Oh, *lieb*, what's wrong? Did something happen?"

She closed her eyes. "Another flare. A bad one. I'm going to bed."

~

On the drive to church the next day, Dan was still concerned about Fern. He hoped she was okay. She had shot out of his buggy like a wounded, fearful animal, in contrast to the vibrant, joyful woman he had picked up two hours earlier. He was certain she was hiding some sort of injury from him, but he didn't know what it could be or why she would do such a thing. It wasn't her fault the sled had broken.

When he arrived at the Miller place, he immediately looked for Fern on the other side of their barn, where the service was being held. He didn't see her, and throughout the service he kept glancing around to look for her. Once church was halfway over and she still hadn't arrived, he realized she wasn't coming. His concern shifted to worry. Had she sprained an ankle? Broken a bone? Thrown out her back? He could barely concentrate on the rest of the service.

As soon as church ended, he sought out Fern's father, who happened to be talking to Alvin near the front bench. Dan waited until they finished their conversation, then gave his brother the *get lost* look. "I can take a look at that wheel for you this week," Alvin said. "Just drop it by when you get a chance."

"Will do," Melvin said.

Alvin frowned at Dan, then walked away. As soon as his brother was out of earshot, Dan blurted, "Is Fern all right?"

Melvin tilted his head, a confused look in his eyes. Then it disappeared and he smiled. "She's a little under the weather, but she's fine."

Dan blew out a breath. "Glad to hear it. I was worried about her, considering the wreck with *yer* sled."

Her father frowned. "What are you talking about? I know you and Fern went for a ride yesterday, but she didn't say anything about sledding." His jaw dropped. "Did she use *mei* old sled?"

Now Dan knew he'd stepped in it. "Um, *ya*." He explained what happened, including how Fern had insisted she wasn't injured.

Melvin's expression grew impassive. "If she said she wasn't injured, then she wasn't injured. I'm sure she just has a cold."

"*Gut.* I mean, it's not *gut* she has a cold, but *gut*—"

"I know what you mean, Dan." He paused. "Don't worry. She'll be all right."

Dan could only take the man at his word. He went home, declining to stay for lunch with the members of his community. He didn't go straight into the house but to his shop. He looked at the broken sled pieces Fern had left in his buggy. He picked up a sliver of wood, still confused not only about her behavior but also about her father's reaction once he'd heard about the accident. He couldn't shake the feeling that something was going on. *Something that isn't* mei *business.* But Fern didn't owe him an explanation, and neither did Melvin. He and Fern didn't have that kind of relationship . . . even though he wished they did.

He went into the house, so quiet with his parents in Sarasota. He never minded being alone, and sometimes he preferred it. But right now, he longed for some company. Fern's company, to be specific. He threaded his fingers through his hair. *Lord, I don't understand this. I've known this woman all* mei *life, and I had never given her much thought. So why am I falling for her now? Why is it that when I think about the future, she's always right beside me?*

None of it made sense to him. Then again, he couldn't think of a time when his relationship with a woman had. For a brief period, he'd thought Miriam was the one for him. And look how that turned out. But Miriam hadn't consumed his thoughts and invaded his heart like Fern did. Maybe this was one of those things he wasn't meant to understand.

~

Fern rolled onto her side, the covers on her bed shifting as every muscle in her body ached. Her joints were swollen and felt hot. She had taken her medicine and used warm compresses, but she hadn't been able to go to church yesterday morning. Today she felt slightly better, but she wasn't in any condition to meet with Johnnie today, and she'd called Alvin's business phone and told him she had to cancel.

She'd been in bed most of the day yesterday and half of today, and she couldn't stand lying there anymore. She winced as she sat up and rubbed her knees, which were hurting the most. She never should have agreed to go sledding with Dan, and once her sled broke, she should have stopped sledding. She could have watched Dan sled without her. She'd cheered enough people from the sidelines before.

But her pride got in the way, and now look where she was. Sore, tired, and sure Dan Kline wouldn't want anything more to do with her. She hadn't even truly thanked him for the afternoon, just run off with her tail between her legs, embarrassed that she couldn't keep up with him.

Fern slipped on her dress and braided her hair, then pinned on a yellow kerchief. She glanced in the small mirror above her dresser and frowned at the dark circles under her eyes and the weariness on her face. Over the black tights she'd also donned, she put on her socks and slippers to keep her feet warm. That often helped with her symptoms in the winter. Then she grabbed her compresses and went downstairs.

Her mother was in the kitchen baking bread for the week. She looked up from the dough she was kneading as Fern walked into the room. "Glad to see you up," she said, brushing the flour off her hands. "How are you feeling?"

"Lousy. But a better lousy than yesterday." She smiled weakly as she went to the sink. She rinsed out the compresses and then laid the cloths on the dish drainer.

"Just a few more minutes, and I can put these in the bowls to rest. Then I'll make you something to eat," *Mamm* said.

"I was thinking about a peanut butter and jelly sandwich, and I can make that." PB and J might be a kid's food, but to her it was comfort.

Mamm put one of the large dough balls into a bowl and covered it with a damp towel. "I plan to *geh* to the grocery store in a couple of hours, after the bread is done. But there's some milk left if you want some."

Fern moved to the gas-powered fridge, then pulled out the milk. It took her a little longer to make the sandwich than it would have if she'd felt better, but a short time later she had her sandwich and a glass of milk on the table. She closed her eyes and said a silent prayer, thanking God for the food. *And I know this may sound selfish, but I hope Dan doesn't think too poorly of me. Or think I'm weird. If you can make that happen, I would appreciate it.*

She opened her eyes and started to eat. But after a few bites she pushed the sandwich to the side.

Mamm was cleaning the excess flour from the table. "You're not hungry?"

She shook her head. She wasn't only feeling bad about Dan. She also felt guilty about Johnnie. She'd tutored him only once before she had to cancel because of her health. She'd given Alvin her usual excuse when she was having a flare—that she had a cold. But she felt so irresponsible.

Her mother shook out her cloth in the sink and then laid it over the dish drainer next to Fern's compresses before sitting down at the table. She patted Fern's hand. "I'm sorry you have to deal with this."

"It's not *yer* fault." She stared at the partially eaten sandwich. A drop of strawberry jelly dripped onto the plate.

"I know, but it hurts *mei* heart to see you in so much

pain." *Mamm* paused. "Is it only the arthritis that's bothering you?"

Fern looked at her. "*Ya*. What else would it be?"

"You were so upset when you came home Saturday afternoon, and I assumed it was because *yer* arthritis flared again. Then yesterday at church, Dan asked *yer vatter* if you were all right and told him about the sledding accident. But did something else *geh* wrong? Between you and Dan?"

She shrugged, averting her eyes.

"Clara told me you're still interested in him."

"Neither of you can keep a secret, can you?" she muttered.

"I didn't realize *yer* feelings for Dan were a secret."

She picked at the edges of the sandwich. "It doesn't matter anymore. I made a mistake. I shouldn't have gone with him."

Her mother frowned. "I'm confused. Dan is a nice *yung mann*. When I read *yer* note saying you two were spending the afternoon together . . ." She paused. "I guess I assumed it was a date."

"I know you're eager to get me married off." Fern heard the bite in her tone, but she couldn't help it.

Mamm sighed. "Fern, we've talked about this. Do *yer vatter* and I want you to get married and have a *familye*? *Ya*, we do. But only if that's what will make you happy."

"What if I said being single makes me happy?" Fern met her eyes.

Mamm's brow lifted. "Then I would say you're lying, because I don't think a desire to be single is the reason you're single."

Fern tried to wrap her head around her mother's logic. She wasn't sure if it was her brain fog or her mother's convoluted words, but she wasn't sure what she was saying. "I don't understand."

"I think you're afraid." *Mamm* lifted her chin. "Afraid to admit to anyone other than our family that you have a chronic disease."

That concept Fern did understand, and she couldn't deny it. "Who wants a wife like me?"

"Maybe Dan does?"

Fern shook her head. "Even if that were true, he wouldn't want me after what happened on Saturday." She told her mother how she'd immediately had pain and stiffness following the sledding accident and had made it worse by climbing the hill twice after that. "I was so embarrassed," she said, running her fingers down the side of her glass of milk.

"Why? Because he saw you in a weak moment?"

"*Ya.*" Fern was starting to get irritated. "You don't understand what it's like to not be able to do what you want to do."

"*Nee* one gets to do everything they want to do, Fern."

"I know that. But this is different. I can't even sled down a hill without a problem."

Mamm gave her an incredulous look. "*Yer* sled broke. It's a *gut* thing you weren't seriously hurt when you tumbled down that hill."

"But I hurt just the same." She looked at her mother. "Because of this disease, I ruined a date with Dan, and I had to cancel tutoring with Johnnie today." *And I had to give up* mei *dream of teaching.* That stuck in her craw the most, because she thought she had accepted that reality. Apparently, she hadn't.

Mamm frowned. "I'm surprised at you. You've never been one to throw a pity party for *yerself.*"

Her brow lifted. "I'm not."

"*Ya*, you are. If Dan is so shallow that he can't understand you have an illness that sometimes knocks you off *yer* feet, he's not worth *yer* time. And if you can't be up-front with Alvin and Iva about *yer* illness and that you might have to cancel tutoring Johnnie every once in a while, you shouldn't be tutoring him." She shook her head and got up from the table. "We all have our crosses to bear. *Yers* happens to be RA. You can let it get you down, or you can manage it and live *yer* life the way you want to."

"What about teaching?" Fern said, a lump in her throat. "I can't be a teacher, and that's all I ever wanted to do."

"You're the only one who said you couldn't." She looked at Fern intensely. "You can do anything you want to do if it's God's will. If you're meant to teach, he'll make it happen. But you have to do *yer* part. How will you know if you give up before you even try?"

Daed came into the room. The front of his clothes was grimy from his work on the farm. "Dan's here," he said to Fern. "He's asked to see you."

CHAPTER 6

Dan paced in the living room as he waited for Fern to arrive. He'd second-guessed himself all the way over here from Alvin's, but when he found out Fern had canceled her tutoring session with Johnnie, he had to make sure she was okay.

Melvin came back into the room. "She'll be here in a minute," he said. Then he motioned to the couch. "Have a seat. Do you want something to drink?"

He shook his head and perched on the edge of the couch. "I'm fine."

Melvin nodded and sat down across from him. He looked at Dan for a long moment, but he didn't say anything.

Dan squirmed under the older man's scrutiny. "I'm

sorry about the sled," he said, grasping for any kind of conversation.

"It was pretty rickety. Had that thing ever since I was a kid. I should have taken better care of it. I thought I might pass it down to *mei grosskinner*, but their parents already bought them sleds. If I'd known Fern was planning to use it, I wouldn't have let her." He looked at Dan with the same curious expression.

Dan couldn't take it anymore. "Is something wrong?"

"I'm just a little surprised you're here. Surprised and curious. This is the first time you've come to see Fern."

"Melvin, don't pry."

Both men turned as Fern's mother entered the living room. She stopped beside her husband and tapped him on the shoulder. "Let the two of them have some privacy."

"I wasn't prying," Melvin said, getting up from the chair and giving Dan an intense look. "I was just stating a fact."

Fern's mother rolled her eyes, and then they both left the room.

Dan waited another minute, and he was about to stand and pace again when Fern came into the room. She was wearing a light-blue dress and a blue cardigan sweater, and she had a yellow handkerchief in her hair. The bright color looked good contrasted with her dark hair. When she was closer to him, he could see how tired she looked. Now he felt like a heel for bothering her.

"Hi," she said in a soft voice.

"Hello."

She sat down across from him in the chair her father had vacated and folded her hands in her lap. "*Daed* said you wanted to see me?"

Dan's heart thumped. Even tired, she looked lovely. He noticed she was walking a little slowly, but not as if she were seriously injured. "I was just checking to make sure you're all right. You missed church yesterday, and then when you canceled tutoring Johnnie, I thought something must be wrong. *Yer* father told me you might have a cold, but . . ."

She shook her head. "I'm fine."

He frowned. While she wasn't in as bad a shape as he'd imagined, she wasn't fine either. "Fern, I can tell something is wrong." He moved closer to the edge of the couch, keeping his gaze locked on hers. "I'm worried about you."

"There's *nix* to worry about." She smiled.

His breath hitched a bit at her attractive smile, even though he was sure she was still holding back from him. He asked himself again if he had the right to interfere with whatever was going on with her, but he couldn't help it. "Are you sure? If you've got a cold, *mei mamm* has a *gut* recipe for some salve. I still have some at home. I could get it and bring it back to you."

She shook her head, her brow furrowing. Then she sighed. "It's not a cold."

~

Fern's stomach turned as she looked at Dan. His worried expression touched her. His kindness was one of many traits she had always liked about him. He genuinely cared about people, and right now she had the feeling he cared about her. And that made her hold back from following her mother's advice and telling him about the arthritis.

"I don't have a cold," she said, "but I did twist *mei* ankle a little bit on Saturday." She bit her bottom lip at the lie. Why had she told him that?

"Oh. Did it swell up?"

"*Ya*," she said, cringing inside as she made the lie worse.

"Then you should probably be propping it up. I sprained *mei* ankle two years ago. Hurt something awful. It did feel a little better when I kept it elevated." He pushed the coffee table closer to her. "Why don't you put it up on this?"

Not having a choice, Fern put her right foot up on the table, glad her black tights covered her legs.

Dan stared at her ankle. "Looks like the swelling has gone down. Mine looked like a grapefruit when I sprained it."

"It has gone down a lot," she said, biting the inside of her cheek.

He looked relieved. "Then you're on the mend. I wish you would have told me about it. I wouldn't have suggested we continue to sled."

"It didn't hurt as bad then."

Dan nodded. "I have to say, the afternoon didn't turn out the way I planned."

Guilt churned inside her. "I'm sorry."

"Hey, it's not *yer* fault the sled was on its last legs." He turned toward her. "How about we try it again? Not the sledding, but the date."

Her mouth went dry. "A date?"

"*Ya.*" His voice grew husky. "Last Saturday was a date. You knew that, didn't you?"

Not wanting to look like she was *seltsam* for not realizing it, she nodded. "And you want a second one?"

"Of course I do." He chuckled. "I can't believe we didn't do this sooner. We've known each other forever."

"You did have a girlfriend for a while, Dan."

"Don't remind me. Besides, if I'd known how much I . . ." He paused, but his eyes continued to hold hers. "How about we *geh* on a sleigh ride?"

He'd given her an opening. This was the time she could tell him they shouldn't date. Then she would never have to reveal her secret to him. He would find someone else and she . . . wouldn't.

"Fern?" he said, frowning again. "This is the second time I've asked you out and the second time you've hesitated. If you're not interested, you can tell me." His mouth tightened. "I'd rather you be honest with me than *geh* out with me if you don't want to."

She'd already lied to him once. How could she lie to him again? "A sleigh ride sounds wonderful."

His expression relaxed, and he smiled. "If *yer* ankle is still not one hundred percent, we can find something else to do."

"I'm sure it will be fine." She gripped the edge of the chair.

Dan stood. "I'll pick you up around two o'clock on Saturday, if that works for you." After she nodded, he said, "I'm glad you're giving me another chance. And don't bother getting up. I'll see myself out."

Her heart squeezed as she watched him go to the front door, turning to smile at her once more before he left. He hadn't been gone more than a minute before *Mamm* came in, as if she'd been lingering just outside the living room. "So? What happened?"

"I thought you said not to pry." *Daed* walked in behind her, but Fern could see the curiosity in his eyes.

She tried to smile, to be enthusiastic about seeing Dan again on Saturday. But what was the point? It wasn't as if they were going to have any kind of long-lasting relationship. She wasn't about to say that in front of her parents, though. Instead, she mustered a half grin, the best she could do. "Dan and I are going on a sleigh ride this Saturday."

Mamm gently smiled, but *Daed* frowned a bit. When *Mamm* noticed, she said, "It will be fine, Melvin."

Finally, her father nodded. "You have fun," he said. "But not too much fun."

"We won't."

After her parents left for the kitchen, Fern moved her foot off the coffee table. Then she straightened her shoulders. This would be the last date she would have with Dan, because after their sleigh ride, she would tell him about her RA. But she wouldn't let that stop her from having fun, even if it was just for a little while.

~

On Wednesday, Fern took a taxi to her rheumatologist's office in Geauga County for her checkup, which would involve some blood work. Her mother used to go with her on these visits, but for the past several years she'd made the trip alone.

When she walked into the office, she signed her name on the clipboard at the receptionist's desk and then turned to sit down. The door to the office opened, and Miriam Lapp and her grandmother walked in.

Fern froze. What were they doing here? She hadn't seen Miriam since she and her family moved to Ashtabula over a year ago. Miriam seemed just as surprised to see her. Her grandmother, Ruth, hobbled over to Fern, using a cane to help her with balance.

"Hello, Fern," she said, the creases in her skin deepening as she smiled. "Fancy seeing you here."

Miriam moved to stand next to her. "Hi, Fern."

"Hello." Fern had never liked Miriam too much, and not because she'd dated Dan. She was a year older than both her and Dan, and she had been the smartest girl in school. Trouble was, she knew it. Miriam wasn't overtly prideful, but sometimes she would make snide comments about other people that rubbed Fern the wrong way. Yet Dan had seen something in her. Otherwise, he wouldn't have dated her for almost a year.

"Who are you here with?" Ruth asked.

Fern panicked. She still felt bad for lying to Dan, and God had pricked her conscience about that. She didn't want to pile more guilt on herself. "*Nee* one," she said in a low voice. "Dr. Ripa is *mei* doctor."

"I had *nee* idea you saw a rheumatologist," Ruth said.

Miriam turned to Ruth. "I'll sign you in, *Grossmutter*, and I'll apologize for being late."

"*Danki, lieb.*" She turned to Fern. "Let's sit down. These legs aren't what they used to be."

They both sat down on the light-green office chairs. At first, Fern kept one eye on Miriam, who was chatting with the receptionist, but then she relaxed. Miriam and her family, including Ruth, didn't live in Sugarcreek any-more, which meant Fern didn't have to worry about them telling anyone they'd seen her here. Her secret was still safe—until she told Dan, of course.

"Isn't Dr. Ripa a wonderful doctor? She's done won-ders for *mei* rheumatism."

Fern nodded but didn't say anything.

"What do you see her for?"

Ruth asked the question just as Miriam sat down on the opposite side of her grandmother.

"An autoimmune disease," Fern said quietly, suddenly realizing she didn't have to be specific. Dr. Ripa saw patients for all kinds of chronic conditions, not just RA.

"Aren't you *yung* to have something like that?" Miriam said, giving her a dubious look.

"Chronic illness can affect all ages," Fern said, a little irritated. Did Miriam think she was lying? For once lately, she wasn't.

"I had *nee* idea." Miriam picked up a magazine and opened the cover. "By the way, how's Dan doing?" she said as she leafed through the pages.

"He's fine."

"He's such a *gut yung mann*," Ruth said, with a reminiscent smile. "I wish the two of you could have worked out, Miriam."

Miriam looked up from her magazine and straight at Fern. "Me too."

"Ruth Beiler," a nurse called.

"That's me." Ruth slowly got up from her chair and grabbed her cane. "Lovely to see you again, Fern. Tell *yer familye* hello for me. I do miss Sugarcreek, but Ashtabula is very nice too."

"I will."

Miriam set down the magazine and turned to Fern. "Tell Clara that Phoebe says hello. She really enjoys getting her *letters*." Then she followed her grandmother back to the exam rooms.

Fern leaned against her seat and blew out a breath. Then she frowned. Why had Miriam given her such a pointed look when they were talking about Dan? And why had she stressed Clara's letters to Miriam's older sister, Phoebe? Clara and Phoebe were good friends, and Fern wasn't surprised that they wrote to each other. But Fern had detected a biting undertone to Miriam's words, which was strange.

Unless . . .

Fern's stomach dropped. *Surely Clara didn't.* Her sister had promised not to say anything. But she knew better than anyone that Clara had loose lips, and she wouldn't put it past her to also have a loose pen.

When she was finished with her appointment and had filled her new prescription, she had her driver take her straight to Clara's house. After paying him, she marched up the porch steps and knocked on the door. When Clara opened it, she barged in, whipping off her bonnet and coat before dropping them on a chair.

"Good afternoon to you too." Clara frowned and shut the door. "Is something wrong?"

She clenched her fists. "I just saw Miriam and Ruth Beiler at Dr. Ripa's office."

"Really? What were they doing there?"

She took a step toward her sister, ignoring her question. "Did you tell Phoebe there's something going on between me and Dan?"

Clara looked bewildered. "*Nee*, I didn't say anything—" Her face turned pale. "Wait. I might have mentioned that the two of you had become a little friendlier lately. But that was it, I promise."

"I guess Phoebe told Miriam." Fern sank down on the couch. "Why can't anyone mind their own business? You, *Mamm*, Phoebe . . ."

Clara sat down next to her. "I'm sorry. I wasn't thinking when I wrote that, other than I was happy for you. I don't see why it would matter to Miriam one way or another whether you and Dan are friends or . . ." She shook her head. "You're right. I shouldn't have said anything. Can you forgive me?"

She studied Clara's eyes and saw genuine regret there. "Of course I do," she said, weary. Then she told Clara what Miriam said, emphasizing how Miriam had agreed with her grandmother, wishing she and Dan had worked out. "Maybe I read more into her words than was there."

"It sounds like you might have. I wouldn't worry about it. If they were meant to be together, they would be." She patted Fern on the knee. "How did *yer* appointment *geh*?"

Glad for the change of subject, she said, "*Gut*. I told Dr. Ripa about *mei* pain and exhaustion—and about the sledding accident." She glanced at Clara. "I'm sure *Mamm* mentioned that event to you."

"Um, *ya*."

"Of course she did." Fern sighed. "Dr. Ripa said to

take it easy for the next couple of weeks, and she increased *mei* medicine dosage, even though I didn't want her to."

"Why not?"

"I'd rather not be taking medicine at all. I know it helps me, but sometimes it upsets *mei* stomach. I also have to watch out for upper respiratory infections because of it. But lately, while I've been on the smallest dose of medication, *mei* symptoms have been bothering me more. At least Dr. Ripa said she'll adjust the dose again if she needs to."

"I'm glad you agreed to her recommendation."

Fern paused. Maybe she shouldn't be so upset that her mother was talking to Clara. If she put herself in *Mamm*'s shoes, if she had a child with a chronic illness, she would need to talk to someone too.

"Do you think it helps *Mamm* to talk to you?"

"*Ya*," Clara said, without hesitation. "It definitely does. And it helps me to talk to her."

"Then I'm glad you have each other to talk to." She told herself not to be so hard on them in the future. She was the one living with her illness, but it also affected her loved ones. She had to remember that.

Clara's eyes shone. "*Danki*. That means a lot." She added, "Since you're here, why don't you stay for supper? The *kinner* will be home from school soon, and I know they'd love to see their *aenti* Fern."

She was tempted, as she did enjoy being with her nieces and nephews. But she was also tired from going to her appointment, and she was determined to follow doctor's orders to the letter. "I'll have to take a rain check. And instead of walking home, I'll call another taxi."

"I understand. Do you want a cup of *kaffee* while you wait on *yer* ride?"

"That would be nice."

While Clara started the percolator going, Fern slipped on her coat and trekked to the phone shanty. The snow had been falling in spurts all day, which made her think about her sleigh ride with Dan on Saturday. Now she wasn't sure if she should go. A sleigh ride wouldn't be strenuous, but she would be spending more time out in the cold, and that could aggravate her symptoms, something her doctor had emphasized during her visit. "Keep yourself as warm as possible in this cold weather," she'd said after she made out the prescription and handed it to Fern. "That will help with the pain."

She called for a taxi, and the driver showed up just as Fern was finishing her coffee with Clara. Instead of instructing him to take her home, though, she gave him Dan's address. But she asked him to pull up in front of his mailbox instead of into the driveway. Searching her purse, she found a scrap piece of paper and scribbled a note on it. She rolled down the window and tucked the note into the mailbox. "I'm finished here," she said. "You can take me home."

As the driver pulled away, she looked at Dan's house, regret washing over her. She saw his buggy there, which meant he was home. She told herself she didn't want to bother him while he was working in the forge, but that wasn't the reason she'd put the note in his mailbox. She hadn't wanted to face him when she canceled their date. She was a coward—another reason he was better off without her.

CHAPTER 7

After a long day in the forge, Dan closed his blacksmith shop and stepped outside. Although it was early in the evening, the sun had gone down, and the cold air was welcome even though he was wearing no coat. His shop had been hot.

He hadn't had a chance to check the mail yet, something he normally did at his lunch break, so he strode down his driveway to do it. He opened the mailbox lid and was pulling out some envelopes and fliers when he saw a piece of folded paper floating out. It landed on the ground. He snatched it up from the snow but waited until he got inside the house to read it. He turned on the gas lamp in the kitchen, and it hissed to life. He opened the paper.

Dear Dan,

I'm sorry, I can't make it on Saturday.

Fern

He crumpled the paper in his hand, disappointed and partially annoyed. If she'd had enough time to drop off the note, she'd had enough time to tell him to his face. Better yet, if she wasn't interested in him, she should have said so from the start, like he'd asked her to.

He tossed the paper and his mail on the table. Fine, he got the message. He wouldn't bother asking her out again.

He'd been starving when he stopped working, but now he wasn't hungry. Wandering around the house, he tried to put Fern out of his mind, but he couldn't. *Lord, just let me be free of* mei *feelings for her.*

~

For the rest of the week, Dan worked in his shop, shod a few horses, and helped Alvin restore the Stanley Steamer. By the time he got home each night, he was past tired. Even so, he had trouble sleeping, unable to stop thinking about Fern and whether he had done something to upset her. But by Saturday afternoon, he realized he couldn't go on like this. If Fern didn't want him, he'd have to accept that.

Trouble was, his heart wasn't listening, and by Sunday afternoon he could no longer stand not knowing why Fern had canceled their date. Iva had even seen her looking fine at the discount store during the time they were supposed to be on their sleigh ride, so she couldn't have canceled on him because she was sick.

He hitched up the buggy and drove to her house, determined to find out what was going on once and for all.

When Fern answered the front door, she seemed shocked to see him.

"Can we talk?" he said, trying to hide the bitterness from his voice.

She opened the door wider and nodded. He stepped inside and took off his hat and boots but didn't remove his coat.

"Would you like some tea?" Her voice was wobbly, but he noticed that she looked fine to him too. No, more than fine. She looked beautiful.

He shook his head. "I need to know one thing, Fern, and then I won't bother you again." He swallowed. "Why don't you want to *geh* out with me?"

~

As the blood was surely draining from her face, all the guilt and regret Fern had been carrying from the time she'd left Dan that note overwhelmed her. He had every right to be mad, and even though she could tell he was trying to hide it, she saw anger flaring in his eyes. There was some hurt there, too, which pierced her heart. Canceling the date had been the right thing to do, but she had gone about it in the worst way possible. "I'm sorry," she said.

"That's not an explanation."

"I know." She looked at her feet, covered in brand-new woolly socks and slippers. She was wearing thermal underwear under her dress too. But while her body felt warm, inside she was icy cold. Dan deserved more than she was giving him. They both knew that.

"Can we sit down and talk?" she said.

He hesitated, then nodded, but he kept his coat on. They sat down on opposite ends of the couch. "Iva said she saw you at the store yesterday," he said. "During the time we were supposed to be on our sleigh ride."

She grimaced. "I had to, uh, purchase some new socks."

He hung his head, gave it a shake, and looked at her. "Why can't you be honest with me? I don't like to play games. I've been down that road before, and I won't do it again. If you don't like me, just tell me." He heaved in a breath. "Put us both out of our misery."

His words broke a dam inside her, and she knew she couldn't keep the truth from him any longer. She'd been unfair to him, and that had to stop. "I like you, Dan," she said. She sighed. "I've liked you for a long time, even when you were with Miriam. I'm not proud of that, but it's the truth."

His brow furrowed. "Then why did you cancel our date?"

"Because I'm ill."

He looked confused. "I knew you weren't feeling well last week, but you seem fine today."

"I usually do look fine. It's only when I feel awful that I look sick. That's part of the problem with *mei* disease. I can look *gut* on the outside, but on the inside I feel terrible." She took a deep breath. "I have rheumatoid arthritis."

Dan looked shocked. "Aren't you too *yung* for that?"

She shook her head. "It can strike in *yer* twenties, or any age, really. I was finally diagnosed last year, but they think I've had symptoms since sixth grade. *Mei* joints are swollen, and I've been in a lot of pain lately, which is why you noticed I didn't seem well. *Mei* symptoms are usually worse in the winter." She held out her hands. The knuckles in the middle of her fingers were red. "I probably shouldn't have gone sledding with you the other day."

"Then why didn't you say so? We could have done something else. I wouldn't have minded."

"Because I wanted to be normal for a change." Tears welled in her eyes. "I wanted to have fun like I used to when I was a *kinn*. I loved to sled and skate and play outside in the snow, and I can't do that the way I want to anymore."

Compassion entered his eyes. Or was that pity? "I'm sorry," he said.

She held up her hand. "Don't. I can't stand for someone to feel sorry for me." The tears were threatening to fall, and she couldn't bear to have him see her like this. "*Danki* for coming by," she said, then stood from the couch ready to hurry upstairs.

But he touched her arm, stilling her. "You don't have to run from me, Fern."

"It's better for both of us if I do."

"How? You just said you liked me. And I definitely like you. Very much." His smile was soft and understanding. "Not just recently either. I've always thought you were sweet, even in grade school."

Stunned, she said, "Why didn't you say anything?"

He shrugged. "I also thought you were a little out of *mei* league. You're smart, I'm not. You were a *gut* student, I was a troublemaker. And when we finished school, Miriam started hanging around. I wasn't attracted to her at first, but she wore me down. I truly did like her at one time. But not as much as I like you."

Her heart skipped a beat. "I never knew any of that."

"I guess we've both been keeping secrets." He took her hand. "Fern, I've got to admit I'm a little floored about *yer* illness, but it also explains some things. I don't think it should stand in the way of us having a relationship, though."

"But I haven't told you everything." Her voice grew thick. "I can have a flare at any time, and when I do, I can't do much. I hurt and I'm tired, and sometimes it's all I can do to get out of bed."

"We can work through that. I can bring you tea and read you a bedtime story."

She couldn't help but chuckle. "You're saying that

now, but it will be different when we make plans to *geh* somewhere and I can't make it."

"Then we'll have to be flexible." He squeezed her hand. "I'm willing to at least try, but I need you to meet me halfway. Are you willing to do that?"

Was she? Could she set aside her fear and worry to make a relationship between them work?

She met his eyes, and warmth flooded her soul. She had cared about this man for years. How could she let anything come between them? "*Ya*," she said, meaning her words. "I am."

"Does that mean we can *geh* on that sleigh ride next Saturday?" He winked. "I'll make sure you stay nice and warm."

Laughing, she nodded and said, "I hope you do."

EPILOGUE

EIGHT MONTHS LATER

The season's first snow fell as Fern looked out the window of her new house, the one she shared with Dan, now her husband. Their second date had turned into a third, then a fourth, and then they lost count and were soon engaged. She gazed at the snow outside, feeling a little bit like Johnnie and Leroy when they had cabin fever. She still tutored Johnnie once a week, along with two other students, and she found that she enjoyed working with children on a one-on-one basis. Teaching an entire schoolroom of children would be too much for her, but she was more than satisfied helping students who needed extra attention.

She also kept herself busy with other activities, although she'd overdone it the other day while working at an auction to raise money for a missionary group. She'd spent the last two days in bed. Dan hadn't minded, as he'd had plenty to keep himself occupied in his shop. But now she felt better and wanted to go outside.

As if he'd read her thoughts, Dan came up behind her and wrapped his arms around her shoulders. She leaned back against him as he pressed a kiss to her temple. "Feeling better today?"

"Much."

"*Gut.* Then I have something to show you in the shop." He helped her into her coat, and she put on her boots and wrapped a scarf around her neck before following him outside. Once inside the shop, she saw a sled on the table.

"Where did you get that?"

"Do you recognize it?"

Moving closer, she realized it was her father's sled. "You put it back together," she said, grinning.

"Yep. Do you like it?"

"Of course I do." She turned and kissed him. "It looks like it did when I was a *kinn*, although much better."

"How about we test it today? If you feel up to it, obviously. I made it a little longer so we can both use it."

A short while later they were at the top of that same hill by the school where they had their first date. She sat down on the sled, and he nestled behind her, his arms around her waist.

"Ready?" he asked.

"More than ready."

Then, together, they flew down the hill.

LONG-AWAITED LOVE

CHAPTER 1

~~~~~

MIDDLEFIELD, OHIO

Jemima Kurtz peered through a raindrop-stained window as her bus pulled into the Ashtabula bus station. Away from home for nearly a year, she'd been taking care of a younger sister's family after Julia had become seriously ill with the chicken pox. It was a miracle she survived, and the illness and its aftereffects had been tough on her. Jemima had been glad to help, but now that she was sure Julia would be all right and had regained enough strength to care for her husband and children, she was glad to be home.

She stepped off the bus and grabbed her suitcase from the porter, then walked to the pickup area and looked around. Her father had said he would have a taxi waiting for her, but she didn't see one. *The driver must be running late.* She hoped nothing was wrong with him.

She heard a large hiss behind her, then the groan of her bus as it pulled away. After a few minutes of pacing, she sat down on the single bench beneath an awning and waited. This was one of the few times she wished she had a watch. She'd wait a little while longer, then go inside the station and call a taxi herself. *I hope* Daed *didn't forget about me.*

Behind her another bus pulled in, but she didn't pay it any mind. Instead, she closed her eyes and focused on the faint sound of birds twittering. She'd missed that during the long winter months she'd spent in Maine with Julia and her family.

During most of the bus ride, she'd thought about her future, and those thoughts were still with her now that she was almost home. *I'm going to find a job.* She couldn't even say the words out loud yet, but inside she was ready to pursue that goal. After spending most of her thirty-four years helping to care for her ten younger siblings, who were all married now, she was ready to live her own life.

"Jemima?"

She opened her eyes and looked up at the man standing in front of her, shielding her eyes from the setting sun that obscured his face. "Yes?"

"I thought that might be you."

When he stepped aside, Jemima could see him more clearly, and her breath caught. She couldn't believe the last person she ever expected to see again was standing in front of her. Her throat tightened, but somehow she managed to be polite. "Hello, Everett."

He had the nerve to grin at her, and she noticed that although ten years had passed since they'd last seen each other, he was still as handsome as ever. Even more so, because instead of a wiry twenty-five-year-old, the man in front of her was broad shouldered and well built.

Ugh. How could she pay any attention to his physique after what happened between them?

"Mind if I sit here?" He pointed to the empty spot on the bench next to her.

She shrugged but didn't reply.

The grin slid off his face, but he sat down. As he set his suitcase beside hers, she had a quick moment to take him in. Not only was his bag plain black with no distinctive markings, similar to hers, but with a typical Amish straw hat set firmly on his head and his suspenders, broadfall pants, and boots, no one would mistake him for anything but the Amish person he'd always been. His bright-blond hair was now a darker, sandy-blond color, brushing the top of his collarless, yellow, short-sleeved shirt.

She looked away just before he turned to speak. "Where are you headed?" he asked, his tone as friendly as the first day they met.

"Home."

"Me too. Well, it used to be home."

She could feel his gaze on her, but she stared straight ahead even though she desperately wanted to know why he was back after all these years. This was one aspect of her personality she didn't like—the tendency to hold a grudge. It wasn't Amish or Christian, yet she couldn't help it. And if anyone deserved to have a grudge held against him, it was Everett Wengerd.

~

Everett gave up. He shouldn't have even bothered trying to start a conversation with Jemima, who was practically pretending she didn't know him. Not that he could blame her after what happened. But when he saw her sitting there on the bench, her eyes closed, thick brown eyelashes resting on her cheeks, he knew he had to try.

But first he had to gather himself, and he took that time to gaze at her face. Although she looked older, as expected after a decade, she was still the prettiest woman he'd ever seen.

Immediately, the memories he'd tried to forget over the years washed over him. Apparently, she hadn't forgotten her memories either.

He sat back on the bench, lost in thought. He didn't want to be back in Middlefield, but after living in Shipshewana for ten years and working himself up to manager at an RV factory, the factory had closed. He was out of work.

And that happened at precisely the same time his mother wrote asking him to come home. He'd thought long and hard about it—and had prayed just as much. Returning home meant more than just facing his father.

But his mother said *Daed* was eager to see him, something new. Her words also seemed to have an underlying urgency, and he decided he couldn't refuse her request. If his father's heart had softened, the least Everett could do was meet him halfway.

Yet while he was prepared to see his father, he hadn't expected to run into Jemima Kurtz so soon. *Lord, you have an interesting sense of humor.*

A silver four-door sedan pulled up in front of them. He'd arranged for a taxi to pick him up before he left Shipshe, and he wondered if this was the car. He grabbed his suitcase and glanced at Jemima again. Maybe the taxi was for her.

The driver stepped out. "Hi, Jemima," he said as he strode over to her.

She stood, ignoring Everett and lifting her suitcase. "Hi, Max."

"Sorry I'm late. Your dad called about an hour ago and asked me to come get you."

Jemima looked relieved as she smiled. "Thank you."

Surely she hadn't thought her father would forget she was here. Then again, Jemima had always been an afterthought when it came to her family. That had been part of the problem between her and Everett.

The driver switched his gaze to him. "You must be Everett."

Surprised, Everett nodded. "That's me."

"Louis, the guy you called this morning, had to cancel because of an emergency. He asked if I could pick you up. Since I was coming out here anyway, it wasn't a problem . . . until I had a flat tire."

"Oh *nee*," Jemima said.

Everett wasn't sure if she was upset about Max having a flat tire or the possibility of sharing a cab. Max had already popped the trunk and was reaching for Jemima's suitcase. She handed it to him, then she glanced back at Everett.

He wasn't about to call another taxi and wait an hour or more. If she was out of sorts because of him, she would have to deal with that on her own. He hefted his suitcase to the trunk and dropped it in. Max shut the lid, then shook Everett's hand. "Nice to meet you. Are you new to Middlefield?"

"Not exactly," he said, glancing at Jemima as she climbed into the back seat. "It's been a while since I've been here, though."

"Well, welcome back. I'm sure you'll find some things have changed, but most have stayed the same." He grinned and then stepped to the driver's side and climbed into the car.

As Everett passed Jemima's window, he glanced at her.

She was staring straight ahead. When he got into the car and looked at her over his shoulder, she didn't meet his eyes, as if she were looking right through him. Fine. He turned and faced the front. *She's as stubborn as ever.*

CHAPTER 2

H*e's as friendly as ever.* Jemima kept her eyes focused on the back of the front passenger seat, barely listening to the chatter between Everett and Max. Max had been providing rides for the Amish for years, and she knew him quite well. He was friendly, and she often chatted with him whenever he shuttled her around.

Everett's friendliness had appealed to her at one time. Now she found it annoying.

"How was Maine?" Max asked, glancing at her in his rearview mirror.

His question jerked her out of her thoughts. "Good," she said.

"You had a cold winter, I heard. Record low temps." He paused. "I'm glad Julia recovered."

"Me too."

"What happened to Julia?" Everett asked.

Jemima hesitated. Of course, he would be concerned about Julia, but the last thing she wanted was to engage in conversation with him.

"Chicken pox," Max said. "A real bad case too. Everyone was praying for her, including my church."

That touched Jemima. Max attended a nondenominational church. Learning that people she didn't know took time to pray for her family softened her heart a little. "Thank you, Max."

She could see him smiling in his mirror. "You're welcome. God is good, all the time."

A lump developed in her throat as Jemima glanced out the window. God was good, and she needed to remember that more often. She could be pessimistic at times, and after Julia recovered, she made a vow to be more grateful. She and her sister had grown closer as Jemima had cared for Julia and her family. They'd had some long talks, and through them Jemima had gained some perspective about her life. Now she hoped she could get her family to understand that she'd changed. She wasn't the same Jemima who left months ago.

"I'm glad she's okay too," Everett said. He was talking to Max, but Jemima heard him. "I remember she was a nice kid."

She looked out the window, her heart hardening upon hearing Everett talk about her family as if they were all still close. Her gratitude was already being tested, and she couldn't wait to get out of the car.

But at the same time, hearing the concern in Everett's voice had sparked an ember of warmth in her heart, based on her memories of better times they'd had together. Everett had always been a thoughtful man, even when they were teenagers. Which had made what he'd done to her even more awful. She clenched her teeth, pain shooting through her jaw.

Fortunately, Max took her home first. She scrambled out of his vehicle as fast as she could, then waited impatiently while he took her suitcase out of the trunk. She paid him and grabbed the case. "Thanks," she said, then hurried to the house. As she opened the front door, she heard the car pull out of the driveway.

She blew out a breath, her heart hammering. Everett shouldn't be affecting her like this after ten years.

Her mother rushed out of the kitchen to greet her. "Jemima! I'm so glad you're home," she said, giving her a big hug. "We're having the *familye* over tomorrow for supper. They're all eager to see you after all this time." She clucked her tongue. "I just wish Julia and Gabe weren't so far away. If only they would move back here, our family would be complete again."

"They like it in Maine."

"It is beautiful there. But I miss *mei dochder*." She looked at Jemima. "Are you all right? You look pale."

"I'm fine." She gave her mother another quick hug and said, "I'm going to take *mei* bag upstairs and unpack."

"All right. But supper is ready and nearly on the table. *Yer vatter* will be inside any minute. He's finishing up a few things in the garden. He finally got that summer squash planted this year."

"That's *gut*." Her mother returned to the kitchen, and Jemima climbed the stairs to her room. She put her suitcase on her bed and glanced around. Everything was exactly the way she'd left it, not that she'd expected it to change. She'd lived in this room all her life and had shared it with her sisters until they each married. Now she, the oldest, was the only one left after Jessica married last year. Thirty-four years old and still living with her parents. *That has to change.*

But first she had to get organized. She unzipped the top of her suitcase and opened it. She was stunned when she saw men's shirts, a black toiletry bag, and a pair of church shoes tucked against one of the sides. "What is this?"

Then her stomach sank for the second time. This wasn't her suitcase. It was Everett's.

~

"We're so glad you're home, Everett." *Mamm* put another helping of sweet potatoes on his plate, next to the one he hadn't finished. "We've missed you so much. Haven't we, Steven?"

His father didn't look up as he scraped the side of his spoon across his plate.

"You know he's a *mann* of few words." *Mamm* pressed her lips together as she took a sip of iced tea.

That was true, but once Everett had seen his father, he knew only one of his parents was glad he'd returned home. If his father didn't want him here, though, why had his mother thought he did? While he'd kept up correspondence with her over the years, and she'd been to visit him in Shipshe, he hadn't spoken with his father or exchanged a single letter with him. *Daed* and Jemima were neck and neck when it came to holding grudges, although Everett had to admit he was deserving in both cases. But in both cases, he wasn't the only guilty party.

"Would you like some more rolls?" *Mamm* said, holding up the basket.

Everett pointed to the two rolls already on his plate. "These are enough, but *danki*." As usual, she'd made more food than three people could eat. She'd always made more food than needed, having been raised in a large family. He knew *Mamm* had wanted one of her own, but God had other plans, as she always said, and Everett was his parents' only child. *And then I left them.* He'd had a good reason, but the guilt had never completely gone away. He'd especially felt it when he saw other families together in the district where he lived in Shipshe.

"What are *yer* plans now that you're home?" *Mamm* asked, setting the basket next to her plate.

"To work. To get a job."

Both she and his father stared at him. Then his *daed* picked up his plate and stood. He put the dish in the sink and then strode out of the kitchen. They heard the back door shut.

"Didn't take long for him to get mad at me." Everett tore a chunk off one of the rolls and jammed it into his mouth.

"He's not mad." But his mother's mouth was tugged into a frown, and she didn't look at him. "He's, um, surprised you're here."

Everett swallowed and then frowned too. "Surprised? You didn't tell him I was coming?"

She lifted her gaze partway. "Not exactly."

"Why not?"

Mamm pushed her plate of half-eaten food away, something she never did. "I was waiting for the right time."

"You told me he wanted me to come home." He clenched his napkin in his fist.

She sighed. "I might have overstated that a bit. Everett, how are you and *yer daed* ever going to reconcile if you don't talk to each other?"

"So that's what this is all about." He tossed the napkin back on the table. "I can't believe you lied to me, *Mamm*."

Wringing her hands, she said, "Don't be upset."

He paused, then blew out a breath. "I'm not." That wasn't true. He just didn't want to upset her more than she already was. Then he noticed tears filling her eyes. *Too late.*

"Did you come back only because I begged you to?" Her hands were tightly clasped together now.

His heart squeezed, and he shook his head. "*Nee.* That's not the only reason. I wanted to see you. You know I've missed you."

"Not enough to come home."

"There wasn't anything for me here," Everett said, a lump in his throat. At least there hadn't been, not for a long time.

"Except *yer familye.*"

But their family was almost nonexistent. Unlike other Amish families, the Wengerds didn't have a network of aunts, uncles, and cousins to depend on. His parents were in their sixties, and they were both the youngest in their families. All their siblings had died or moved away to live with their children. The Amish were more mobile now because of farmland prices and job opportunities. But his parents were firmly planted in Middlefield. They had found the family they wanted and needed through their community, even if that family wasn't biological.

He knew what his mother meant, though—his parents were his family. And he loved them, even his father. But he hadn't been back in Middlefield for more than an hour before he realized nothing had changed. Jemima was still mad at him, and his father was still resentful. *What am I doing here, Lord?*

"I made *yer* favorite dessert." *Mamm* jumped up and hurried to the counter. She was thin, wiry, and full of energy, rarely sitting still. She turned and held a plate with a cake cover over it. Smiling, she brought it to the table.

Everett's emotions tempered. He loved his mother, and she was trying so hard to make things right with him and *Daed*. Even through her cheery expression, he could see the strain on her face, and he didn't want to be the reason for it. He grinned and rubbed his palms together, the way he had when he was a kid and she baked something special for him. "I wonder what it could be."

"Triple chocolate cake!" She pulled off the cake cover to reveal a perfect chocolate Bundt cake. Definitely his favorite.

"*Danki, Mamm.*" He got up from his chair and gave her a tight hug. "For everything."

She hugged him back, and he heard her sniff. "I'm so glad you're home."

He pulled away and sat down. As his mother got a knife to cut the cake, he figured he'd hear her say that several more times this week, and he was fine with that. At least somebody wanted him here, and now that he was home, he realized how much he'd missed his mother. He'd hurt her when he left, but she still supported him. He wouldn't be able to live with himself if he hurt her again.

She had just started to cut the cake when they heard a knock on the front door of the small house. He looked up at her. "Are you expecting someone?"

Mamm shook her head. "Maybe *yer daed* is, but I think he went to the barn."

Everett was sure he had. The barn was his father's place to escape, and when he was troubled, he would sit on a hay bale in the back and whittle. He'd taught Everett how to whittle when he was little, something Everett hadn't done in a long time.

Mamm started to set down the knife, but Everett held up his hand. "I'll get it." She nodded and continued to cut the cake as he stood. Once in the living room, he opened the front door, and his jaw dropped when he saw Jemima standing there.

"This is *yers*." She set a suitcase on the threshold. "Now give me mine."

When she was snippy like this, he wondered how he'd ever found her attractive. "Our suitcases got mixed up?"

"*Ya.* I'll wait for mine here."

"Who is it, Everett?" *Mamm* stepped into the room and then halted, obviously surprised. "Jemima! I didn't know you were back from Maine."

Jemima nodded and smiled. "I arrived just a little while ago."

Mamm came closer. "How's Julia faring? She must be better."

"She's doing well. She's still a little weak, but she's

back taking care of her *familye*. You know how stubborn she can be."

Everett believed stubbornness ran in the Kurtz family.

"I was willing to stay a little while longer," Jemima continued, "but she insisted I come home."

"You were there for almost a year," *Mamm* said.

A year? That was a long time to care for her sister. Everett hadn't realized how ill Julia had been. Thank God she'd survived her illness.

"Don't just stand there, Jemima." *Mamm* waved her hand. "Come in. I was just cutting some triple chocolate cake." Her eyes twinkled. "I remember how much you liked it."

Jemima's mouth formed an O, and for the first time since he'd seen her again, she looked uncertain. Jemima and *Mamm* had been close at one time, and he could tell his mother really wanted her to stay.

Apparently, Jemima did, too, because to his surprise she said, "Okay."

"I'll get *yer* suitcase," he said. "It's in *mei* room."

But she was already following *Mamm* to the kitchen as if they were still close friends. As if they were almost mother and daughter.

At one time, they almost had been.

CHAPTER 3

Jemima forced herself to take a bite of the moist cake in front of her. Lucy had given her a huge piece, not a surprise since the older woman was well-known for her overcooking and large portions. She did love Lucy's triple chocolate cake, and normally she would have dived in. But her stomach was turning too much to enjoy it.

"Imagine that, you and Everett having the same suitcase." Lucy chuckled as she cleared some dishes from the table.

Realizing they'd just had supper, Jemima stood. "May I help you clean up?"

"*Nee*, I've got it. But *danki*. You've always been so thoughtful."

Jemima lowered herself back into her chair as Lucy turned from the sink and walked back to the table.

When Everett came in, he glanced at the piece of cake next to hers, and Jemima realized his mother had seated her next to him. The sweet woman had a sneaky side to her.

Everett sat down and tucked into his cake as if they had all gone back in time to when everything was happy and normal between them—more than ten years ago. Her stomach turned again.

"Not hungry?" Everett pointed at her piece with his fork.

"Not really. I just ate." That wasn't true, though. As soon as she realized the suitcases had been mixed up, she'd taken the family buggy over here, telling her parents she had to see a friend. She didn't want Everett's belongings at her house any longer than necessary, and fortunately, her parents hadn't questioned her about which friend or why.

Her eyes widened as she stared at her plate. Everett acted like the mix-up was a surprise to him, but had he looked inside her suitcase? Had he riffled through her clothes . . . *her unmentionables?* Her cheeks heated at the horrendous thought.

"Don't be shy, Jemima." Lucy sat down at the table in front of her own piece of cake. "Dig in."

She picked up her fork and sliced off a small amount, then took the bite. Oh, this was as good as she remembered. She had avoided eating this cake at gatherings whenever Lucy brought it. It stirred up too many memories, not to mention the cake had a lot of calories. She frowned. Had she really forgone this dessert for a full decade? Because of Everett? She started to gobble up the cake, feeling ridiculous for denying herself anything on account of him.

"Slow down, Jemima," Everett said.

She rolled her eyes at him and shoveled another large bite into her mouth. Then she swallowed . . . and the cake lodged in her throat. She reached for the first drink she saw in front of her, a half-full glass of tea, but she couldn't get a breath.

"Jemima?" Lucy said, her eyes growing wide with alarm. "Everett, I think she's choking."

He rose and put his arms around her waist, lifting her from the chair like she was a rag doll. Trying hard to breathe, she barely felt his arms encircle her body under her ribs and yank upward.

A ball of chocolate flew out of her mouth and dropped onto the table. She gulped in air, her eyes watering. Her legs weak, she leaned against him as he continued to hold her up.

"Are you okay?"

Everett's voice was low in her ear, and for a split second she relaxed, feeling safe and cared for. The way he used to make her feel. Then she came to her senses and jumped away from him. "I'm fine," she croaked.

"Goodness, I didn't know someone could choke on chocolate cake," Lucy said.

"You can if you shovel it in like a bulldozer."

Jemima shot a look at Everett. He may have just saved

her life, but he was still a jerk. Then she saw his mouth twitch, which irritated her even more. How dare he tease her? She'd never minded his teasing in the past, but now she wanted to dump the rest of her cake on his head.

Lucy handed her a napkin and led her back to her seat. "Can I get you a drink?"

"She already grabbed mine," Everett said, the teasing glint in his eye gone. "She can have it." He glanced at her, then added, "I'll put *yer* suitcase in *yer* buggy."

"That's a great idea." Lucy dabbed at Jemima's forehead with a napkin.

Her anger at Everett subsiding, Jemima wanted to crawl under the table. She'd never been so embarrassed, and she didn't want Lucy hovering over her. "I should get going," she said, her voice raspy.

"Do you want me to wrap up the rest of *yer* cake?" Lucy asked.

"*Nee.*" She didn't want to see another triple chocolate cake for the rest of her life. She got up from the table.

"All right, dear." Lucy looked up at her, worry still evident in her eyes. "It was nice to have you over again."

Jemima forced a small smile. What Everett did wasn't Lucy's fault. "*Danki.* It's nice to see you too."

"Don't be a stranger," Lucy called as Jemima left the kitchen.

When she went outside, she found Everett patting her father's horse. She hurried to the buggy, stopping halfway to clear her throat, both guilt and dread slamming her.

She at least owed him a thank-you, even though all she wanted was to race away from him. "*Danki*," she said quickly, climbing into the buggy.

"For saving *yer* life?"

Of course, he had to rub it in. "*Ya*. For saving *mei* life."

"You know what this means?" he said with a lackadaisical tone as he stepped backward, still facing her.

"What?" she asked, even though she knew she should ignore him.

"It means you owe me one." Then he turned and sauntered toward the house. He never looked back as he pushed open the door and went inside.

She rested her forehead against the heel of her hand. She'd said thank you. What else did he want? *He didn't want you enough to stay.* The resentment burned inside her, and she snatched up the reins. He could say whatever he wanted. She knew the truth. She didn't owe him anything.

~

Everett exited the house through the back door and headed to the barn. Its door was wide open. His father hadn't come out, even though he'd surely heard a buggy arrive and leave. That wasn't a good sign. But at that moment his mind wasn't on his father. He'd panicked when he saw Jemima choking on that piece of cake, and he was glad he knew the Heimlich maneuver, having learned it in a Saturday CPR class he'd taken on a whim a few years ago. Once he knew she was safe, he couldn't help but tease her, like he used to when they were together. But he'd immediately regretted doing it.

Ten years ago, she would have sparred with him, a game they both enjoyed. When she was away from her family, she'd been able to relax and joke with him. But he'd fallen into that old habit without realizing it, and that had been a mistake. Even though it was dark out by the buggy and he couldn't see her expression very well, he could tell she was still angry.

He paused before entering the barn, then crossed the threshold. He stopped, listening to the breathing of his parents' new horse—at least new to him. Earlier that year *Mamm* had written that their old horse, Faithful, had passed away, and Everett had grieved for him. He'd known the horse his entire life, and oddly enough, Faithful's death caused him to reevaluate some things. He hadn't returned to Middlefield only to appease his mother. Although he was irritated with her deception, he knew she was right—he had to reconcile with his father. He also knew *Daed* wouldn't make it easy.

He took a deep breath and walked toward the back of the barn, glancing at the stall where the new mare, Loyalty, was kept. He was tempted to stop and meet her. But talking to his father was the priority. As he neared, he could hear the faint scrape of a knife blade against wood, and he halted a few feet from his father. *Daed* was sitting on the same old hay bale, dented from years of use as a seat. Clumps of hay littered the floor. His thin shoulders were hunched, and Everett could imagine him often staring at a hole in the wood, deep in thought.

After a few moments, he said, "*Daed.*"

His father didn't turn around. "What?"

At least he spoke, and Everett decided to capitalize on that. He stepped closer and stood in front of the hay bale, leaning against the double doors usually open three seasons out of the year to let in fresh air. "Can we talk?"

"Don't see as we have anything to say to each other." *Daed* cut a long strip of birch from the project he was whittling, which was starting to take the shape of some sort of animal. He was especially good at animals. His father was a talented carver, but he did it strictly as a hobby.

"It's been ten years." Everett shoved his hands into his pockets. "We have a lot to say to each other."

Daed finally glanced at him, peering at him over his glasses. "Maybe *you* do."

Everett paused. His father had changed, at least physically. His hair was almost all gray, matching his gray beard, which reached the top of his chest. The hands that gripped the knife and wood were covered in age spots, and his knuckles were swollen. And at the supper table, Everett had noticed a stoop to his posture He looked older than sixty-two. Far older. Once again, guilt made an appearance. "Will you at least listen?"

Daed paused, whittled away a strip, then gave one short nod.

"I'm sorry. I shouldn't have left the way I did. I was wrong to take off and move to Indiana without telling you first."

"Yep."

Everett was about to point out that it wasn't completely his fault—his father had been pushing him to oversee the restaurant in the future, which Everett absolutely hadn't wanted to do. He'd already worked in the place since he was eight, and the thought of spending the rest of his life dealing with rude customers, filling in for cooks, and even washing dishes when the diner was extra busy had made his nerves raw.

He tried telling *Daed*, but his father wouldn't listen, pointing out that owning a business, especially an Amish restaurant that had been successful for over twenty years, was more stable than jumping from job to job.

"You done?" *Daed* said, still not looking at him.

He tamped down his resentment of his father's blame. First, it wouldn't do any good, and second, God had pointed out that this wasn't about blame. It was about reconciliation. "I want to work for you again." There, he said it. And it hadn't been as bad as he thought.

His father's head shot up. "What?"

"You and *Mamm* asked me what *mei* plans were. I told you I wanted to find a job. You left before I finished explaining where I planned to work." He drew in a deep breath. "I want to learn how to manage the restaurant." He swallowed. He wasn't any more interested in the restaurant than he'd been ten years ago, but it was clear this was the only way he could make up for what he'd done— and open the door to making up with his father.

His *daed* looked at him, unblinking. "Why?"

"Because I believe it's what I'm supposed to do."

Daed's gaze narrowed. "That's not much of an answer."

Everett's anger sparked, as it always had when he talked to his father, especially in the month before he left. "Does it matter why? I'm here, and I'm offering. This is what you've wanted all along, *ya*?"

"At one time." He got up from the hay bale, much slower than he used to, and set the knife and wood on the bale. "Not now."

"Are you saying you don't want me to work for you?"

His father didn't answer right away. Everett shifted his feet, wondering why he'd even bothered. He could find a job in Shipshe, one he would like a lot more than working at the restaurant. His father didn't even want him here, obviously. What had been so clear to him before—returning home and offering to take the job his parents always wanted him to have—was turned on end. *Have I made a mistake, Lord?*

"*Yer mamm* told me you were a manager at that RV place," *Daed* said.

Everett nodded. "For three years."

"Did you like the job?"

He couldn't lie. "I don't have a problem being a manager. It was—" He stopped himself before he ruined everything. "*Ya.* I liked the job."

Daed's expression was inscrutable as he stared at Everett. Finally, he spoke. "If you want to work for me again, you have to start at the bottom. Dishwasher/busser. That will be *yer* job."

Everett balked. "I already know how to do those things."

His father turned and started to walk away. "That's the position available. As always, we'll leave at three thirty, sharp. If you're a second late, you're fired." *Daed* moved past him and left the barn.

"Great," Everett muttered, plopping down on the hay bale. He picked up the birch wood, which only had a couple of grooves whittled in it. He'd expected his father to give him a hard time, but he hadn't anticipated this, making him start from the bottom. And *Daed* didn't mean they were leaving at three thirty in the afternoon. The restaurant served only breakfast and lunch, and his father liked to be there far earlier than necessary.

He glanced up at the barn rafters, still holding the wood. He wasn't going to back down now because the circumstances didn't suit him. He wasn't the same young kid he'd been when he left for Indiana, and there was only one way to convince his father of that. But, boy, did he hate washing dishes.

CHAPTER 4

The next morning, Jemima and her mother walked into the Morningstar Diner at seven. When *Mamm* suggested having breakfast together, she thought she meant at home. But then she mentioned the diner, and Jemima had been tempted to say no even though the food there was delicious. But at least she didn't have to worry about seeing Everett. He'd always despised working at his parents' restaurant, and she had never held the Wengerds responsible for what happened between her and Everett. That had been 100 percent his fault.

She had hoped she and her mother could spend some time alone together, so she could talk to her about looking for a job. They couldn't have that conversation in public, that was for sure. But *Mamm* seemed set on eating breakfast here, so Jemima had reluctantly agreed.

A familiar niggle ate at her as they sat down at a table near the back of the diner. The place was seat yourself unless it was busy, which it usually was the latter part of the week. Even though she was sure Everett wouldn't come within one thousand feet of this place, the diner still reminded her of him. And for some reason, the thought that perhaps he might not have been completely to blame for the end of their relationship entered her mind. She had wondered about that shortly after he left, only to spend the rest of the last ten years blaming him completely. He was the one who left, not her.

"Gute morgen." Sarah Detweiler looked at Jemima. "Welcome home. I heard Julia is doing well. I'm so glad about that."

"Danki." Jemima shoved Everett out of her mind and smiled at Sarah, a young woman she'd known since she was born. On the buggy ride over, *Mamm* told her she suspected Sarah might wed soon—to Andrew Miller, someone else Jemima had known his whole life. Jemima had frowned at the news, but not because she wasn't happy for the couple. She wished them well. But it was one thing to see her friends and younger siblings all get married and quite another to see kids she'd known from their birth planning their weddings.

"Would you like to start with some *kaffee*?" Sarah asked.

"Ya. And *nee* need for menus. We'd both like the short stack, with sausage links." *Mamm* grinned.

Jemima nodded, but she felt a little off-balance at her mother ordering for her, even though she'd always done it when they came here. She liked the short stack and sausage, but maybe this time she wanted something different. Or at the very least to order for herself.

"I have some news for you," *Mamm* said, lowering her voice. She placed a napkin over the skirt of her light-purple dress, which was the same color as Jemima's. "Susannah is having another *boppli*. I haven't even told *yer vatter* yet." She sat back, a satisfied grin on her face. "That's the seventeenth *grosskinner*. God has blessed our *familye* once again."

"That's wonderful." But she wasn't as enthusiastic about the announcement as she should be. Everett suddenly came back to mind. If he hadn't left her, would they have *kinner* now?

Sarah placed the coffees in front of them and looked at Jemima. "Sugar and—"

"I'll just have cream."

Sarah placed a small bowl with individual creamers on the table. "*Yer* breakfast will be up shortly."

"*Nee* sugar?" *Mamm* gave her a skeptical look as Sarah walked away.

"I'm trying to cut back."

Mamm smiled. "That's an excellent idea. You should particularly watch *yer* weight at *yer* age. The pounds creep up fast." She took a sip of her black coffee. "Oh, I forgot to tell you this. Priscilla would like you to watch the *buwe* tomorrow afternoon while she and Miriam *geh* to the flea market. She would take them with her, but you know how they are at that age. They would be pulling things off the shelves. It will be much easier on her for you to watch them."

"Uh, sure. I'll keep them." Her brow furrowed. Both her mother and sisters just assumed she would be available to babysit right after being gone for nearly a year. And what was that crack about her weight? She glanced down at her dress. It had become a little tighter over the months she was in Maine, but she hadn't thought anyone else would notice.

"Also, I haven't had a chance to scrub the floorboards because I've been so busy working on dresses for Irene and Susannah's *dochders*, and I have an appointment this afternoon to get *mei* eyes checked. Would you mind cleaning them for me?"

"*Nee*, I don't mind," she mumbled, staring at the bowl of creamers.

Mamm grinned again. "I'm so glad you're home." She pushed the bowl toward her. "Better add this before the *kaffee* gets cold."

Jemima picked up one of the creamers and slowly opened it. Scrubbing the floorboards, babysitting, breakfast at the diner—she barely had time to catch her breath. Not to mention she hadn't slept much last night. Despite her vow not to think about Everett anymore, his words echoed in her mind. *You owe me one.* She didn't like being in debt to anyone, especially to Everett. Now she couldn't seem to keep her mind off him.

Sarah brought their food and a bottle of pure maple syrup. The Wengerds didn't scrimp on their servings, so their plates were full. After she said a silent prayer of thanks, she opened her eyes and lifted her head—and saw Everett on the other side of the restaurant, gathering dirty dishes from an empty table. He put them in a bin, and when he turned his head, his eyes grew wide as they met hers.

She couldn't believe what she was seeing. Was he working here? How could that be possible? And as a busboy? *Correction. Busman. If that's even a thing.* The one task he couldn't stand to do, and here he was doing it.

Mamm looked at her, then turned to glance over her shoulder. Her eyes filled with surprise. "Everett's here?" She whirled around and faced Jemima. "Did you know he was in town?"

Jemima slowly nodded as Everett lifted his own head in a short nod and then hurried to the kitchen.

"Why didn't you say anything? How long is he here for? And is he back working at the diner?"

Ignoring her mother's questions, she reached for the bottle of syrup and flipped open the top. She'd cut back on how much she ate after breakfast today, but right now she wanted to drown her pancakes in plenty of sweet goo. "How many more dresses do you have to make for the *maed*?"

"Don't change the subject, Jemima Anne."

Jemima winced at the use of her full name. She'd dropped the Anne when she was in school, and her family had followed suit—most of the time. She poured syrup on her pancakes and set down the bottle, then looked at *Mamm*. "I don't want to talk about him."

Mamm rolled her eyes. "It's been ten years. Don't you think it's time to forgive him? Not to mention that you already should have."

She gripped her fork, her appetite gone. She knew she was supposed to forgive Everett and move on, but whenever she thought about what he did, the pain returned. The hurt hadn't been as sharp as when he left, yet seeing him again had honed it to a new razor point. "I have forgiven him," she said through gritted teeth.

"It doesn't look like it to me."

Jemima shoved the syrup bottle toward her mother, hoping she would focus on her pancakes and not on her daughter's lack of forgiveness. But before *Mamm* could reach for it, the bottle hit the edge of Jemima's plate, syrup spilling on the table—and all over the skirt of her dress.

"Oh *nee*," *Mamm* said, quickly handing her some napkins from the holder on the table. Then she stood and yelled across the entire restaurant. "Sarah! Jemima's had an accident!"

"Everett!" Sarah hollered into the kitchen. She was carrying a tray of food. "Clean up!"

Jemima glanced around the restaurant, which had

filled with patrons since they arrived. She dabbed at the sticky syrup, shrinking into her seat, wanting to disappear yet again as she saw Everett coming toward her.

~

Everett had been on the other side of the restaurant wiping a table when Sarah called his name, making him cringe. He'd also heard what Jemima's mother said. The woman hadn't meant to embarrass her daughter, but he knew in her own usual and clueless way, she had. And now he had to clean up the mess, which would bother Jemima further. But he had no choice. This was part of his job.

He slipped into the kitchen, where he dodged the cook and his mother, who was making pies for the lunch crowd. Grabbing a fresh cleaning cloth, he rinsed it in water at the sink and wrung it out, then headed toward the sticky mess.

"Goodness. I think half the bottle spilled out of there," June Kurtz said as Everett approached the table.

"It wasn't that much," Jemima muttered, rubbing a napkin against the syrup stains on her dress.

June was exaggerating, but it was a pretty large amount, and syrup was a problem no matter how much spilled. He wiped the table as quickly as he could.

"Oh, Everett, hello," June said. "Welcome back home."

"*Danki*," he mumbled, not looking at either of them

for his sake as much as for Jemima's. He wasn't thrilled that she was seeing him working as a busboy, especially since she'd heard him complain so much about the restaurant. He could only imagine what she was thinking now. Here he was, age thirty-five, bussing tables and mopping up syrup. And she probably didn't even know he was formerly a manager in an RV plant. *Makes perfect sense.*

Some of the syrup had dripped onto the floor, and he'd have to get a bucket of water and a mop to clean it. He didn't mind hard work, but mopping floors was as high on his list of distasteful tasks as dishwashing and bussing were. Yet he'd made a vow to himself and a promise to his parents this morning that he would do the job and do it right. Which meant mopping under Jemima and June's feet.

Then he made the mistake of glancing at Jemima, who looked miserable. His heart went out to her, which it had no business doing. But although she was thirty-four, at that moment she looked like the shy, serious girl he'd met in school when he and his parents moved here to take over the restaurant. He found out she had a passel of younger siblings, and it wasn't long before he also learned that she had a lot of responsibility when it came to those siblings. More responsibility than she should have, he'd thought at the time.

"I think it's wonderful that you're working here while you're in town," June said, oblivious to Jemima's misery and Everett's aloofness. "How long will you be here?"

"Indefinitely," he said, pulling his gaze from Jemima and moving her plate to the side so he could finish cleaning. His arm brushed against her shoulder. "Sorry."

She looked up at him, confusion in her eyes. Of course she'd be confused. She knew more than anyone how much he'd disliked working here.

"I'll be back in a minute to finish," he said, then retreated to the kitchen. He deposited the cloth near the sink, where the dishes were already piling up for him to attack. They had an electric dishwasher, along with all the appliances needed to run a restaurant while also making sure they didn't violate the community *Ordnung*. But his father had insisted on the smallest dishwasher possible, and it didn't keep up with the daily breakfast and lunch rush. Plenty of handwashing always needed to be done.

When Everett came out with the bucket and mop, June was chattering away between bites of pancakes, but he could see Jemima hadn't touched her food. Her mother wasn't a bad person, or a cruel one. Oblivious was a more apt description, along with a little self-absorption. The Amish certainly weren't perfect.

Because June had so many kids in succession after Jemima was born, Jemima had always been her little shadow. When she and Everett were together, he'd never been able to convince her she was too involved with her family—to the point that she put them above everything and everyone else, including him more than once. But her loyalty had been one of the many things about her he'd fallen for. Still, there was loyalty, and then there was letting yourself be used. He often thought Jemima's family had let her fall into the latter category, depending on her so much that she didn't have a life of her own.

"Are you going to clean the floor?" Jemima snapped at him, yanking him out of his thoughts. He hadn't realized he'd been standing there looking at her.

"Jemima Anne!" Her mother shook her head. "There's *nee* need to be rude."

Oh, but there is. Obviously, she hadn't told her mother everything said between them before he left. Or she had and her mother didn't realize how deeply he'd hurt her daughter. That could go either way when it came to June.

"Sorry," he said again, and then he quickly mopped up the sticky mess. Jemima stared at the plate in front of her, and he saw the embarrassed blush on her cheeks.

Then her gaze lifted and landed on her mother. To his surprise, he saw a spark of resentment there, and for once it wasn't directed at him. His brow lifted. Was she finally seeing the light?

He halted his thoughts. Why was he so concerned about how Jemima felt and her relationship with June? That had been his concern at one point, a concern he had the right to have. Now it wasn't any of his business.

He finished cleaning, and after saying a quick goodbye, he pushed the bucket and mop back into the supply room. He washed the mop outside, behind the restaurant, before tilting it against the wood fence rail so it could dry in the sun. Then he went back into the kitchen and quickly took care of the stack of dishes before his father could direct him to. He and *Daed* had been keeping their distance all morning, and he wanted to keep it that way.

When he went back into the dining room to bus more tables, Jemima and June were gone. He removed the dishes from their table and saw they had left Sarah a nice tip. He put it in the pocket of his half apron to give to her when she wasn't busy. The breakfast rush, populated with the English who liked to sleep in late, had just begun, and she was hustling, as was his father, who was also taking orders. One thing he'd give to *Daed*—he was a hard worker.

As he dumped most of Jemima's food into the bottom of his bin, he spotted a small, folded piece of paper on the table. He picked it up and opened it, making sure one of the women hadn't left something important.

Sorry. Thank you.

Jemima. She didn't sign it, but he recognized that handwriting. He smiled, tucked the note into the pocket of his pants, and finished clearing the table.

The rest of the workday went quickly, and Everett fell into the routine of his job, which hadn't taken him long to do. When his father turned the Closed sign around on the front door, he was tired but not exhausted like he thought he would be. He enjoyed chatting with the customers, who had welcomed him back home and, of course, asked how long he was staying. He gave them all the same answer he'd given June—indefinitely. In his mind, he knew he would be here until he'd reconciled with his father—or until God nudged him to move on.

An hour later he'd finished mopping the dining room floor, had cleaned a second mop, and had brought the mop he'd used to get up the spilled syrup back inside. He was ready to leave, but as always, his father was staying to work on the books. The restaurant was within walking distance of their house, and his mother had left two hours earlier, as she always had. When it came to the Morningstar Diner, not much had changed over the years.

As he left the restaurant, he noticed that his father had put a sign in the front window. *Waitress wanted.* They had only two waitresses, Sarah and Beulah. He wondered which one was leaving. They were both young, and usually when they lost help, it was because someone was getting married. His father hired only Amish waitresses, so the turnover had always been steady.

He headed home, Jemima on his mind again. She'd been away from her family for almost a year, but nothing had changed, at least that he could see—probably because she'd still been the babysitter, cook, and housekeeper for her sister Julia's family. That was obviously needed since Julia was so sick. And he knew Jemima wouldn't have hesitated to help her. But when would Jemima live for herself?

Waitress wanted.

He halted his steps right before his driveway and groaned as a thought came to him. *Nee. That's a bad idea. A terrible idea.* One that might help Jemima but would open a gigantic can of worms for him. He was already facing an uphill challenge with his father. Why was he coming up with another problem?

But a still, small voice spoke inside him. He recognized that voice, and he groaned again. Then he turned on his heel and headed for Jemima's house.

CHAPTER 5

Jemima wiped her brow with the back of her hand, then sat back on her knees and tossed the washrag into the bucket of water sitting beside her. Washing floorboards wasn't a piece of cake, but hard work had never bothered her. And she'd done it dozens of times. After her mother had humiliated her at the diner that morning, though, her asking Jemima to wash the floors stuck in her craw. No, it was more than that. Her mother seemed eager to dump the chore on her, and with every swipe of the wet rag, she grew more resentful.

She chastised herself. Her mother wasn't that hard of a taskmaster, although she didn't like to do housework. Jemima had always preferred things neat and tidy, so growing up she often did the chores her mother didn't enjoy—sweeping the floors, dusting the furniture, washing the walls. But scrubbing floorboards was something neither of them liked. On top of that, when she left for her eye appointment, *Mamm* informed her she would be visiting Jemima's cousin Ruth before coming home.

She yanked the rag out of the bucket and wrung it out, then continued to clean the boards as quickly as possible while still doing a thorough job. She was almost finished when she heard a knock on the front door. She got up from the floor, her knees creaking a bit, and dropped the rag in the bucket. She arched her back a little as she went to the door, then wiped one hand on her apron before opening it.

"Hi, Jemima."

Great. This was all she needed, a visit from *him*. "Everett."

He put his hands behind his back. His clothes were stained as if he'd walked here straight from work.

"What do you want?" The words flew out of her mouth, and she pressed her lips together. While she'd been grateful that he hadn't made her feel bad about spilling the syrup, and she had thanked him by writing a note, that didn't mean the past was instantly erased.

"Pleasant as always." He shook his head. "I'm sorry. I shouldn't have said that."

She agreed, but kept her mouth shut.

Then he looked directly at her. "May I talk to you about something? I promise it won't take long."

She should just slam the door in his face, but she

couldn't bring herself to do that. Instead, she nodded and stepped out on the front porch, shutting the door behind her. The wood planks warmed her bare feet, but she didn't move more than a couple of steps from the threshold, even though she couldn't help noticing once again how handsome Everett was—even more so than when they were younger. Never mind that his clothes were covered in food stains and he smelled like grease, onions, and bleach. He was by far the most attractive man she'd ever known.

Jemima drew in a sharp breath, reining in her thoughts. He wasn't welcome here, at least by her. From the way her mother acted around him, it was obvious she had long ago forgiven Everett for what he'd done to Jemima. *If only I could do the same.* Then again, she'd never told her mother any details about what happened.

She crossed her arms over her chest, forcing herself to be curt. "I'm listening."

"*Daed*'s advertising for a waitress."

"Okay."

He blew out a breath. "I thought you might want the job."

She dropped her arms. After the initial shock, she squinted at him. He'd smashed her heart into a thousand pieces, and now he was offering her a *job*? "Why would you think I'd ever, *ever* want to work with you?"

He hung his head, then lifted his gaze to her. "Technically, you wouldn't be working with me. You'd be working above me."

She frowned. "Huh?"

"A waitress gets paid more than a busboy." His lips flattened. "Between the wage and tips, you can make decent money."

"Do I look poor to you?" she snapped, then guilt washed over her. Being poor or rich wasn't supposed to matter to her as an Amish woman. But her pride rose up anyway. "I don't need charity."

"This isn't charity. It's a job." He scowled. "I see you're still the mixed-up *maedel* you always were."

"Mixed up?"

"You're so beholden to what *yer* parents and *familye* want from you that you don't know who you are. Or what you want." He shook his head. "I would have thought by now you'd be married—or at least living *yer* own life."

Anger boiled within her. "How dare you say that to me, after what you did? You don't know me, Everett Wengerd. You never have." She unfolded her arms and clenched her hands into fists. "You can take *yer* job and . . . and . . . Ugh!"

She whirled around and went inside, slamming the door in his face—which should have felt good since she'd imagined doing something similar all these years.

But it didn't.

She leaned against the door, a lump forming in her throat. She wasn't mixed up. Was she? She loved her family, and she had always wanted to be there for them. She'd been her siblings' second mother, her mother's assistant. And even her father had depended on her when he and *Mamm* decided to take a trip to Michigan with her sisters three years ago. She'd made all the meals, cleaned the house, tended the garden, cared for her nieces and nephews . . .

Jemima closed her eyes. Those three weeks had been exhausting.

Another knock sounded at the door. Soft, as if whoever was on the other side was unsure if knocking was acceptable. "Who is it?" she asked, her eyes still closed.

"Everett."

Her eyes opened a little. "Now what?"

"If you won't take the job because of me, I'll quit the restaurant."

She paused, letting his words soak in. He'd quit once, and it had caused a rift between him and his father. Now he was willing to do it again. *For me.* Which didn't make one bit of sense.

She gave her head a quick shake. Whatever Everett did was his business, not hers. But she wasn't going to be the reason he left the restaurant again. She wasn't about to be his scapegoat. "You're not the reason."

"But you're angry with me."

"I'm . . ." She frowned. Why couldn't she admit how she felt? He'd already guessed anyway. But somehow she couldn't say the words out loud, couldn't say them to him.

"Or is it that you're angry with *yerself*?" Before she

could reply, he added, "Don't get in *yer* own way, Jemima. You did that once before."

Now she was furious. He was always telling her how she should feel, what she should do—and she was tired of it. From him, and from everyone else. Balling her hands into fists again, she shouted, "Just *geh*, Everett!" When she didn't hear anything, she turned to open the door and yell at him again. But a second later his footsteps faded away.

She took in a deep breath and straightened, his words echoing in her mind. Angry at herself? She had no idea what he was talking about, and she was sure he didn't either. He hurt her, not the other way around. He left, she stayed. Why would she be mad at herself for that?

Then she realized he'd offered her the exact thing she'd planned to find when she returned to Middlefield—a job. But working at the diner? No matter what he said, she would see him there.

No, she was right to tell him to leave. And now that she thought about it, maybe she didn't need a job. In Maine, when she and Julia had discussed her finding work outside the house, her sister had thought it was a great idea. "It's *yer* turn," Julia said. "Don't let *Mamm* and *Daed* stop you from doing what's best for you."

"They haven't stopped me," she'd said. But hadn't they? Over the years, when her brothers and sisters had various jobs, her mother always said, "You don't need a job. There's plenty here at home to keep you busy."

She spied the bucket across the room. *Like the floor-boards, for example.* Was that all her life was going to be? Being available to her parents and siblings whenever they asked? She was single and had never planned to get married after Everett left, even though that's what was expected of Amish women. She wasn't the first person to break up with a fiancé. But she vowed not to go through that heartache again. That plan had come to fruition, leaving her free to live her life without worrying about a husband or children. But was this the life she wanted?

"Don't be ridiculous," she said out loud, then marched over to the bucket to finish scrubbing. Everett had always thought her parents treated her like a personal maid and babysitter. He'd made no secret of his feelings where that was concerned, especially after telling her about a job in Shipshewana he wanted.

"I want to take you away from all that," he said.

"But I love mei familye." She was torn. How could he even consider leaving Middlefield and moving to another state? She couldn't imagine being that far from her parents and siblings.

"I know you do. But I've also told you they sometimes take advantage of you." He brushed the back of his hand over her cheek. "You and I can have our own familye. I thought that's what you wanted."

"It is. But why can't we stay here?" She took his hand and squeezed it. "Why can't you work for yer vatter like he wants you to?"

"Because I can't." He let go of her hand.

"Can't? Or won't?"

The lump in her throat tightened at the memory. He'd changed the subject by kissing her—and he was an amazing kisser—and for the next two days she'd forgotten the conversation. Then he was gone. Without a word or a note. Nothing. And she learned from his mother a week later that he had moved to Indiana, their engagement effectively broken.

She squeezed her eyes shut, forcing the past out of her mind. She'd wanted to marry Everett and have a family more than anything, and she'd thought he wanted the same thing. Apparently, that wasn't true, and she'd found out in the worst way possible. Now her family was all she had.

She got up from the floor and took the bucket into the kitchen, where she dumped the dirty water into the sink. Then she washed out the bucket and rinsed out the rag before putting them both in the mudroom. She would wash the rag later this week when she did the laundry. Her mother didn't enjoy doing laundry either.

Jemima had just sat down on the couch to take a quick rest before starting supper when she heard another knock on the door. But before she could get up and answer, her sister-in-law Abigail breezed inside, carrying two plastic bags. "Hi," she said, setting the bags on the coffee table. "Devon told me you were back. Wonderful news about Julia. We're all thrilled."

Nodding, Jemima got up from the couch, glad for some

company to keep her mind off Everett and the past. "I was just about to start supper," she said. "But I can make us a snack, and there's already some lemonade made."

"Oh, I can't stay." Abigail smiled, her gaze flitting to the door. "I've got to get home and start supper myself. You know *yer bruder* and his appetite, especially when he gets off work." She gestured to the bags. "Could you hem the *buwe*'s pants for me? Two of Amanda's dresses are in there too. They're only half finished, but I just don't have the time." Her smile turned sweet. "Besides, *yer* stitches are always perfect."

"Uh, I—"

"*Danki*, Jemima. I can always count on you for help. I need those by Saturday, though. Earlier if you can. Maybe next week you can come over for a visit. Just not on Monday, Wednesday, or Thursday. I'm busy those days with company. Oh, and Tuesday is also out. But Friday will definitely work." She opened the door and left.

Jemima stared at the bags, then at the closed door. She'd been home less than twenty-four hours, and the chores and babysitting were already piling up. She'd go through the clothes after supper and see how much sewing she was in for.

An hour later, when her supper of pork chops, sauerkraut, and potatoes was nearly done, *Mamm* finally came home.

"Oh terrific. You started supper," she said as she entered the kitchen. "Smells *gut*."

"Actually, it's almost ready," Jemima mumbled. She put a bowl of pickled beets on the table.

Mamm smiled. "I meant to be home earlier, but time gets away from me sometimes." She patted Jemima on the arm, then removed her bonnet. "Did I tell you how much we missed you?"

Just as her mother sailed out of the kitchen to put away her bonnet and purse, *Daed* entered the room. He poured himself a glass of iced tea and sat down at the table. "Where's *yer mutter* been?" he asked.

"She just got back from Ruth's. She went there after her appointment."

"I shouldn't be surprised she spent the rest of the day there. She loves to visit."

As she placed the rest of the meal on the table, she waited for him to ask how her day had been. But *Mamm* had told him about going to the diner for breakfast when he came home on his lunch break from his job helping Phil Beiler run his furniture store one street over. Then before he left again, after eating a lunch Jemima had prepared for him, she'd started washing the floorboards in the living room. She'd just worked in the house most of the day, and he knew it. Still, being asked would be nice.

Mamm came back into the kitchen and greeted *Daed*, then they all sat down and said prayer. When they opened their eyes and *Mamm* started passing serving dishes, she buzzed about her visit with Ruth and a few other friends who'd been there, telling them the latest news in the district. Then she said, "I saw two bags of clothes in the living room. *Kinner* clothes."

"Abigail dropped them by." Jemima explained her sister-in-law's request.

"You do such nice work," *Mamm* said, finishing off the last bite of her beets.

The compliment should have made her feel good, but for some reason it rang hollow. "I wish she would have asked me first, instead of dropping them off and assuming I had time to do it."

Mamm put down her fork, her brow furrowing. "But what else would you do, Jemima? You have plenty of time on *yer* hands. *Yer* siblings are busy with work and *kinner* and their extended families. It's a blessing to them that you're able to help."

Jemima yanked at the pocket of her apron, feeling the stitches split apart. Great, now she'd have more mending to do. But would she even have time to mend her own clothes? Or would her family continue to assume that she had no life and could be at their beck and call? Would they always expect her to bless them without giving a single thought to the possibility that she might also have plans? Hopes? Even dreams?

Everett had smashed those dreams, though. Or had he? *Don't get in* yer *own way, Jemima.*

"What if I had a job?" she blurted. "That would give me something else to do."

Mamm's fork clattered onto the table, and even her

father stopped eating long enough to stare at her. "A job?" *Mamm* said. "You have a job?"

"You've never had a job before," *Daed* said, pointing out the obvious. "Not a real one."

"I can't believe you have a job," *Mamm* said. "When did this happen?"

"It hasn't—yet," she said in a low voice, her stomach churning.

"Oh." *Mamm* looked relieved and continued eating. Her father did the same.

Jemima gaped at her parents. "Why are you so surprised that I would consider taking a job?"

"Because you don't need one," *Daed* said, scraping up the pork chop gravy with a bit of bread. "You have everything you need here."

"And *yer vatter* and I don't need extra money."

Jemima agreed with their last point. When her siblings were younger and had jobs, they'd contributed to household expenses. But now with just the three of them here . . . Yet the more she thought about it, the more she realized she didn't have everything she needed. Something was missing. It had been missing all along.

"Enough of this job nonsense," *Mamm* said.

"It's not nonsense. *Mei bruders* and *schwesters* all had jobs."

"We needed them to work at the time." *Daed* looked at her. "And *yer mamm* needed you here to help with the little ones and around the *haus*."

"You don't need a job, Jemima," *Mamm* repeated, then looked at her. "Oh, and if you're sewing tonight, would you mind darning *yer vatter*'s socks?"

A few more stitches popped from her apron pocket as her future flashed in front of her. Her life would always be like this. She would always be taken for granted. Humility was a key trait among the Amish, but that didn't mean she had to be a doormat. Her wants and feelings counted. At least she hoped so. Having a job would give her some independence. She would be doing something other than cleaning and watching children.

But she had to consider something else about taking a job at the restaurant, something even bigger than her urge to change up her life. Everett. Maybe it was because her family was showing its selfish side at the moment, but it suddenly sank in that maybe he'd been sincere when he offered to quit his job so she would take hers. She didn't know what to do with that.

Then there was the plain fact that seeing Everett every day would remind her of the heartbreak that had scarred her so deeply. Could she manage that and still do the job to the best of her ability? She wasn't sure she could.

"Jemima, did you hear me?" *Mamm* said. "Can you darn *yer daed*'s socks tonight?"

Every fiber of her being urged her to say no. But that would lead to more questions, and she was already confused. Or mixed up, as Everett had called her. "*Ya,*" she said, weary. "I can."

"And the dishes tonight. I'm working on a quilt for Mark and Juanita's new *boppli*. I'd like to finish it before next week."

"*Ya*." Jemima's fingers relaxed around the pocket of her apron. If she couldn't take the waitressing position, she would have to look for another job. But if her parents found out she was looking for one, they would discourage her until she gave up the search. Everything Julia had urged her to do—be more independent, find a job, live her own life—was growing further out of reach.

Daed got up from the table. "*Gut* supper, Jemima. I really missed *yer* cooking. Can't wait to taste what you come up with tomorrow night." Then he left the room, *Mamm* following him.

She stared at the table in front of her and thought about the dishes that needed to be done, the leftovers that had to be put away, the sewing she would work on until late tonight because she didn't want to disappoint anyone. Her parents were right. She didn't need a job, at least not just to stay busy. They and the rest of her family made sure of that.

CHAPTER 6

Everett unlocked the diner's back door and entered the kitchen. He'd decided to get here early this morning, partly because he wanted to make sure everything was ready for opening but also because he couldn't sleep. What had he been thinking, offering to quit this job for Jemima? That would have set him way back in making amends with his father. *Daed* would never believe that Everett was leaving a job he disliked for Jemima's benefit. He'd always think it was an excuse for Everett to get out of the work, even though it wasn't.

Fortunately, she hadn't agreed to his suggestion, which he would have followed through on. Over the years, he'd learned to be a man of his word, something he hadn't been in the past, his relationship with Jemima a prime example.

He'd made a commitment to her, and when he didn't get his way, he bailed. He deserved her derision, that was for sure. Even so—even knowing that the idea of seeing her every day would cause problems for both of them—he had hoped she would agree to take the job. He shouldn't have been surprised when she nixed it.

He turned his focus on work, and his parents arrived a half hour later. His father didn't say a word about Everett arriving early, although his mother questioned him about it.

"I wanted to get a jump start on the day," he said. "I used to get to work early at the RV place too."

"Oh." His mother nodded. "All right. That's very responsible of you." She smiled and went to work baking the biscuits that were so highly requested for breakfast.

The day went smoothly, and he and his father continued to ignore each other except when it was necessary to interact. A half hour before closing time, when Everett was washing the last of the dishes, his mother approached him. "I thought you'd left already," he said, up to his elbows in suds.

"I was on *mei* way out. But you won't believe what happened."

Noticing the confusion in her eyes, he turned off the water and pulled his hands out of the sink. "Is something wrong?"

"I don't think so." Now she looked downright perplexed. "Jemima came in. She asked to interview for the waitress job."

Everett's heart performed a little leap. "She did?" He couldn't help but grin.

"*Ya.*" His mother frowned. "I'm surprised you're so happy about it."

He schooled his features and turned the water back on. "If it's something she wants, then I'm happy for her."

"Hmm." *Mamm* didn't say anything for a moment, and Everett kept his eyes on his task. Finally, she said, "I'll see you at home."

Everett rinsed off his hands and forearms as the water swirled down the drain. So, Jemima had changed her mind after all. He wondered why, but he would keep his curiosity to himself. Whatever it was wasn't any of his business. But she must have really wanted the job if she was willing to work in the same building as him. Fortunately, they could keep somewhat of a distance from each other since Sarah would train her. This morning he'd learned she was the one who had put in her notice, but she'd also agreed to stay long enough to show the new waitress the ropes.

He finished cleaning the kitchen and even straightened up the pantry. That wasn't part of his job, but the mess had been driving him crazy all day. Although their cook and junior cooks were excellent, they weren't the neatest people. Once he finished that job, he removed his apron and started to head out the back door.

"Everett."

He turned at his father's voice. "*Ya?*" he said, expecting to be given another job, like cleaning the outside of the building with a toothbrush.

"I hired Jemima Kurtz as the new waitress."

"I see." There was that heart flip again. He'd thought he wouldn't have any reaction to her after a decade of being apart. *You thought wrong.*

"She doesn't have any job history, which I thought was odd. But we hired her anyway." His father's gaze bored into him. "Is that going to be a problem?"

"*Nee.*"

"*Gut,* because you'll be training her."

"Me?" He stepped away from the door. "Why me? Sarah needs to train her."

"You said you'd do any job I gave you."

"But this one?" His stomach sank. "There's *nee* reason for me to train her."

"*Ya,* there is." *Daed* turned on his heel and left without further explanation.

Everett ran his hand through his hair. His father was driving him *ab im kopp.* Or maybe this was some sort of punishment. Oddly enough, Everett hadn't thought twice about his father hiring Jemima since he knew her, and he'd liked her when they were together. But knowing how Everett had left her, why would his father put Jemima through training with him?

Then again, this wasn't about Jemima, and he knew that. He suspected the reason his father had made this decision was so Everett could prove that he was serious about reconciliation. He didn't appreciate his father dragging his ex-fiancée into their private matter, though. Or maybe he was trying to get Everett to quit—an idea that wasn't too far from his mind at this point.

Everett shook his head. He wasn't going to let his father off the hook that easily. He'd train Jemma well and with minimal discomfort on her part. His father wasn't going to push him away. *You're not the only stubborn one in this* familye, Daed.

Jemima showed up at the restaurant ten minutes before six, her starting time for today. Everett's father, Steven, had said that after her three-day training period, she would have to be here at five, which wasn't a problem. She'd always been an early riser. As she knocked on the back door, where Steven had told her to enter, butterflies flitted in her stomach. Not only was she nervous about being in Everett's proximity but she was worried about not being up to the job. Last night, over supper, her parents hadn't instilled much confidence in her when she informed them she had a waitress position.

"We said you didn't need a job." *Daed* grimaced, his fork poised over a plate full of chicken and rice.

"I know." Jemima looked at her mother, whose eyes were also filled with disappointment.

"Who's going to help me out here?" *Mamm* exclaimed. "And what about *yer* siblings?"

"You all managed while I was in Maine," she said, baffled that her mother sounded so helpless. Jemima had known they wouldn't be happy with the news, but her mother's reaction seemed a little over the top.

"But that was temporary. Is this a part-time job?"

She shook her head. "Full time. From five a.m. to two thirty."

"Oh." She let out a relieved breath. "Then you'll be free the rest of the afternoon. I guess that will be okay."

"Where is this job?" *Daed* had said, his eyebrows knitting together. "It's not very far away from home, is it? It better not be."

She pressed her lips together. "Morningstar Diner."

"But Everett's there," *Mamm* said, frowning again.

Jemima nodded.

"Why would you want to work with him?"

She went on to explain that she wouldn't be, not directly. They questioned her further, but she had started clearing the table at that point, and this morning she'd left before they were up, which made her thankful for the early start time. She hadn't wanted to listen to another round of why she was making the wrong decision.

Lucy opened the door. "Hi, Jemima," she said, her smile bright as usual. "Come in. Everett's in the dining area."

"Everett?"

"*Ya*, he's training you." Lucy's smile stayed in place, but there was a tiny bit of doubt in her eyes. "I can take *yer* purse and put it in the office. And don't worry about bringing *yer* lunch anymore. You can eat whatever you want on us."

"O-okay," she mumbled, still trying to take in that Everett was training her. Steven hadn't said anything about that after he hired her yesterday. If he had, she might have had second thoughts—or more like third or fourth. She'd been filled with some level of doubt ever since Everett had shown up.

She stepped into the dining area, where Everett was setting up chairs. The room had tables that sat either two or four people, and booths lined one side of the wall. A small counter was on the opposite side, with all the tables in the middle. After setting down one of the chairs, Everett looked up. His gaze met hers, and she could see the uncertainty in his eyes. That gave her pause. He seemed as doubtful about this as she was, which was unusual for him. He'd always been so sure of himself—the exact opposite of her most of the time. Often, she'd wished she had his surety about life.

Finally, he moved toward her. "*Gute morgen*," he said. "Sorry about how the training is set up, but *Daed* insisted." He met her gaze, and the confidence she recognized returned. "We'll get through it."

Despite everything, she believed him, although she still didn't trust him. "What do you want me to do first?"

He moved behind the counter and pulled out a name tag and a neatly folded white apron. "Put these on." After she complied, he said, "I'll show you around the kitchen. When you're not taking orders from customers or serving them or checking on their needs, you'll be in the kitchen helping get the plates ready."

She followed him, and he introduced her to the cook, Bertha, her assistant, Martha, and Beulah and Sarah, the waitresses. Unlike the rest of the staff, she learned, Beulah didn't live in their district, but she did live in a community nearby. "You'll be taking Sarah's place," she said. "She's getting married soon."

Sarah's cheeks turned rosy. "I'm glad to work with you for a little while, Jemima."

"Me too." She hid the fact that she already knew about Sarah's impending marriage. Steven had told her.

Then Lucy came over. "If you have some time later, I can show you how I make *mei* special pies." She grinned. "They're top secret. Everett just loves the cherry one, remember?"

"Maybe another time, *Mamm*," Everett said, guiding Jemima away from her. "Today will be busy."

As Everett continued to show her around, Jemima was impressed by his demeanor. It was as if he was already in charge of the restaurant and hadn't been gone for ten years. That must be because of his experience managing the RV plant where he'd worked in Shipshe. Even though she'd done her best to avoid Lucy telling her about Everett all these years, at church one day she'd managed to eagerly tell her how well he was doing there.

"Jemima?" Everett said, pointing to a closet door. "Did you hear me?"

She snapped to attention. "Uh, sorry."

"This is where we keep the cleaning supplies. *Yer* main job is waitressing, but you'll have to do some cleaning as well, especially when we're busy."

She had plenty of experience with that, and they both knew it. Everett didn't point that out, though, and she appreciated it.

"Customers are starting to come in. I'll let you shadow Sarah in a little while. But I want you to get familiar with the menu first. It doesn't change too often, but we do have different breakfast and lunch specials every day—except for Sunday when we're closed, of course."

She followed him out of the kitchen and behind the counter again. Several English customers walked in and sat down, greeting Sarah and Beulah as if they were regulars. Everett handed her the menu, and she started to study it, suddenly caught up in the realization that this was her job. Her first job outside of helping her parents and family. She couldn't help but smile a little. Even though her parents tried to convince her otherwise and Everett training her wasn't ideal, she was starting to believe she'd made the right decision.

Everett thought his coaching Jemima had run smoothly, considering this was her first day at her first job. Maybe her being a bit older than most of their waitresses had been why, but he barely had to train her before letting her shadow Sarah. And by the end of the day, Jemima was already taking orders on her own. Then again, he shouldn't have been surprised. She took everything she did seriously, and when it came to hospitality and caring for others, she was top-notch. Her gifts in that area partly explained why her family had hung on to her so tightly.

When his father turned the Closed sign around, Sarah and Beulah stayed to help *Mamm* in the kitchen. She'd fallen behind on the pies, and a few still needed to bake. The cooks were cleaning the stove and grill, and it was time to mop the dining room floor. He retrieved the mop and bucket from a supply closet and handed them to Jemima. "Cleanup time."

She nodded, then started mopping near the kitchen while Everett wiped down the four-and two-top tables and put the chairs on top to clear the floor. Then he wiped down the booth tables, Jemima now working behind him. When he turned around, he slipped on the wet floor, landing on his backside.

"Everett!" The mop handle clattered onto the floor as Jemima ran to him and knelt. "Are you okay?"

"I'm fine."

"I should have used less soap." Her pretty brow knitted

together with worry. "And I'm sure I didn't wring out the mop enough."

Everett wanted to reassure her. "I'm really okay."

"But—"

Unable to help himself, he touched her soft cheek. "Jemima, this isn't the first time I've slipped, and it won't be the last." Then he jerked his hand away and got up. When Jemima didn't rise, he held out his hand.

CHAPTER 7

Jemima stared at Everett's hand as if it were a foreign object. She knew he was just helping her up from the floor, but she couldn't stop thinking of his gentle touch a moment ago. When he touched her cheek, she'd been transported into the past, to when they'd been happy together and in love. When she thought he would never hurt her and that their life would be perfect.

Now she was gaping at his hand and trying to collect herself. It was her fault he slipped. She knew better than to put that much soap in the bucket, but she was so tired she hadn't paid attention. She was glad he was okay.

"All right." He pulled his hand away, and she met his gaze. Was that disappointment flickering in his eyes? Then he started to turn away, and she was sure she'd imagined it.

As she started to get up off the wet, slippery floor, her foot slid out from under her. Suddenly Everett's arm circled her waist and steadied her on her feet.

"That was close," he said. "You almost repeated *mei* trick."

She looked up at him, and her breath caught. He had crow's feet at the corners of his eyes and a few lifelines across his forehead. She noticed a scar at the corner of his mouth. "What happened there?" she said, pointing to it with her finger, forgetting that she was supposed to be mad at him and that he had hurt her beyond measure. This close to him, she couldn't think clearly at all.

He touched the scar. "Fishing accident. The hook got caught there. It happened shortly after I got to Shipshewana." He shuddered. "Not a pleasant experience." His arm tightened around her waist.

The years melted away as she met his gaze. He still had tiny flecks of brown in his green eyes. And one eyebrow was slightly higher than the other one, but that was noticeable only up close.

"Jemima," he said, his voice husky.

"Everett," his father's voice called from the back of the restaurant.

The two of them jumped apart as Steven walked in. Jemima picked up the mop and slapped it against the floor.

"Be careful," Everett said. "It's slippery over here."

Jemima glanced up and saw Everett looking at her. He winked, then turned his attention to his father.

Her heart fluttered as she gripped the mop handle. She squeezed out the excess water—she wasn't used to such a big and heavy mop—and quickly finished cleaning the floor. Her face was hot, and her pulse ran rampant. But more importantly, the attraction she'd had in the past for Everett had just rammed into her full force. Standing so close to him, his arm tight around her waist, gazing into his eyes—it was like he had never left.

But he had left her. And reminding herself of that made the attraction disappear. Almost. She shoved the mop into the bucket and pushed it back to the supply room. She had just shut the door when she remembered she had to clean out the bucket and mop the way Everett had instructed. She flung open the door to complete the job.

Outside, behind the restaurant, she set the mop against the fence rail to dry, and then she halted, staring at the closed back door, unable to move. She still needed to clock out and get her purse, but she was having a hard time going back inside. She'd been a fool to think she and Everett could work together but not for the reason she'd thought. They hadn't fought or shot any cutting remarks at each other. Instead, they'd worked seamlessly together. Before he'd left Middlefield, their relationship had been easy. The outside influences had made things hard. Today was a reminder of how good it had been between them—and she couldn't handle that.

Jemima forced herself back inside. Everett and Steven were nowhere in sight, and she quickly entered the office to get her purse. She took a pad from the desk and scribbled a note.

I quit.

Jemima

She dashed out the back door of the restaurant, running halfway home before she had to stop and catch her breath, feeling guilty. She hadn't lasted more than a day at her first job, not to mention she was leaving the Wengerd family in a lurch. But at least Sarah was still there. They weren't exactly down a waitress.

That didn't make her feel any better, though. She would apologize to Steven and Lucy—eventually. And as for Everett, she would stay far, far away from him.

~

Everett came back inside after weeding the flower bed in front of the restaurant and watering the flower baskets that hung from the eave. For once he was glad his father had given him a menial task, although it really wasn't that bad. He didn't mind gardening. But that wasn't why he was thankful *Daed* had shown up when he did. If he hadn't, Everett might have taken Jemima into his arms. And if he had, he would have kissed her. *No maybe about it.*

He shook his head, then washed his hands at the

kitchen sink. Jemima would have slapped him for sure if he'd kissed her, and he wouldn't have blamed her. But even now his heart was hammering, thinking about how good it felt to hold her again—even if it was to make sure she wouldn't fall. And because he was so entranced by her, he'd thought he'd seen something in her eyes that had reflected how he was feeling. But he knew that couldn't be true.

Daed stormed into the kitchen, clutching a small piece of paper. "Everett, what did you do?"

What now? "The gardening," he said, drying his hands. "Like you told me to."

"I'm talking about *this*." He shoved the paper at Everett.

Frowning, Everett read it. His brow shot up. "She quit?"

"That's what it says. She didn't even fill out her time card." He shook his head. "I knew it was a bad idea to hire her."

"But she caught on so quickly."

"Not that. I knew she would be a *gut* waitress." He glared at him. "I shouldn't have hired her because of *you*. That's why she quit, isn't it? Something happened between the two of you again." He shook his head once more. "I shouldn't have trusted you."

"Wait a minute," Everett said, fighting the guilt crashing over him. "Nothing happened between us." Then he frowned, thinking about how Jemima had felt in his arms and how he'd almost kissed her. But almost didn't count. Or did it?

"It doesn't matter," *Daed* said. "*Nix* has changed when it comes to you."

"You know that's not true." Everett shoved his hand through his hair. "I've done everything you've asked me to, without complaint. And I'll keep doing it until you understand that I'm serious about working things out between us."

Daed paused. "I don't see how that's possible."

"It's not if you don't try too." Everett's throat constricted. "I made a mistake," he said. "A couple of them, actually. But I'm trying to fix this one."

"Why?" *Daed*'s chin quivered. "We weren't *gut* enough for you ten years ago."

"That wasn't why I left. I left because *I* wasn't *gut* ten years ago. I was selfish. All I thought about was myself. Not *yer* or *Mamm*'s feelings." *And not Jemima's.* "That night I left, you and I had a huge argument. I told you I was going to leave. Remember what you said?"

"I remember *yer* leaving."

"You said *nee* one would try to stop me. Including you."

Daed glanced away. "I remember that too." He blew out a breath and looked at Everett. "I shouldn't have said that to you."

"Maybe not, but I deserved it. I wasn't pulling *mei* weight around here, and I didn't appreciate what you and

Mamm wanted to do for me. I had to learn that the hard way."

His father's shoulders slumped, as if he'd been carrying a burden for years. "You broke *yer mutter*'s heart, you know."

Shame washed over him at the reminder. "I know."

"And I guess I had better own *mei* part in that." *Daed* scrubbed his hand over his face. "And I will. Of course, *yer mamm* forgives you, not only because it's right but because she has a heart of gold." *Daed* sighed. "Can I trust that you won't hurt her again?"

Everett realized his father wasn't just asking for his mother. He had to earn both their trusts. "I promise not to." He moved closer to his father. "And I'm going to back up that promise with action. I just need you to give me a chance. A real chance."

Daed looked at him for a few moments, long enough to make Everett squirm. "All right," he said. "But you'll still have to work *yer* way up. You can't waltz in here after ten years and expect to be assistant manager like you were before."

"I understand."

Daed nodded, then sighed again. "I wish Jemima hadn't quit. I think she would have made a *gut* employee. I'm sorry we had to lose her." He turned and left the kitchen.

Everett looked at Jemima's resignation again. *Me too.* Reconciling with his father was one thing, but what had made him think his ex-fiancée would ever truly forgive him?

⁓

Jemima sat on the swing in the far corner of her backyard, surrounded by flowers, plants, and shrubs. When she was twenty-seven, she built this tiny prayer garden, and then she added the single swing when she was thirty. Growing up, she'd always wished to have a quiet place of her own, and she'd planned to have a similar garden when she and Everett married. When that fell through, it took her a few years to build one here.

She pushed the swing back and forth with her toe, inhaling the sweet fragrance of the flowers and listening to the birds chirping as the sun set. When her mother asked how her first day at the restaurant went, she'd told her parents she didn't work there anymore. As expected, they were relieved. Unexpectedly, neither one of them had given her something to do—which gave her some time in the prayer garden, where she hadn't been since she'd returned from Maine.

Now that she was here, she was struggling with the guilt she felt over quitting her job without notice. And her feelings for Everett didn't make sense. She should be over him—completely. But she wasn't. She felt guilty about him too. She should have forgiven him a long time ago, but she hadn't. Now when she tried to muster the anger and resentment that had fueled that unforgiveness, it was difficult. To say she was confused was an understatement.

She noticed a few weeds by the pink begonias, and she got off the swing and pulled them out. When she stood, she saw Everett striding toward her. Panicking, she dropped the weeds on the ground. No doubt he was here to scold her for walking out on his family. How ironic that the tables had turned.

He stopped a few feet in front of her and glanced around the garden. "Nice," he said. "*Yer* handiwork?"

She nodded, remembering the bite of heartache she'd felt as she planted what was supposed to be theirs together. That steeled her resolve. "If you're here to convince me to come back to work, don't bother. I'll apologize to *yer* parents, but I'm not coming back."

He shook his head. "That's not why I'm here." Then he added, softly, "I know why you quit the job, and it's *mei* fault."

Although he was right, his words annoyed her. "It's always about you, isn't it? Did you ever stop to think that maybe I didn't like the job and that's why I left?" But her words didn't have their usual sharpness.

"*Nee*, because it's not true. I could tell you not only liked the job but were *gut* at it. Much better than I was when I worked there before."

His patience and self-effacing manner were getting to her. "What do you want, Everett?" she said, tired of fighting her feelings, her past, her pain.

"To ask for forgiveness. And to explain why I came back to Middlefield."

"You're forgiven, and you don't have to explain anything." She turned her back to him, a lump in her throat.

He let out a bitter chuckle. "That sounded sincere."

Jemima squeezed her eyes shut. She could never fool him, and apparently that hadn't changed. She turned around, lifting her chin. "Say what you have to say."

He met her eyes. "Jemima, I'm sorry. I know that's not enough for what I did, but I really am. Not long after I got to Shipshewana, I realized I'd made a mistake leaving here . . . and especially leaving you."

Her heart thawed a little, but she froze it again. "It was such a mistake that you stayed away for ten years."

"I'm stubborn. You know that better than anyone. So instead of coming home, I decided to prove I knew what I was doing, which was just as immature and selfish as leaving in the first place." He drew in a deep breath. "But I had another reason for not telling you I was leaving. I didn't want to hear you say *nee* when I asked you to come with me."

"I wouldn't have—"

"*Ya*, you would have. When I brought up moving to Shipshe before, it was clear you were too stuck on *yer familye* to leave them." He looked at her more intensely. "I wasn't enough for you, Jemima. I knew you loved them more than me."

CHAPTER 8

Everett's stomach was in knots. Not only had he confessed his immaturity back then, but he'd admitted something he'd never told anyone until now—even to himself. He finally met Jemima's gaze, expecting her to agree with him. Instead, he saw a spark of anger in her eyes.

"So, I didn't love you enough? That's why you left without a word and broke *mei* heart? You're saying it's *mei* fault?"

"That's not what I meant." But wasn't that it exactly? He hadn't wanted to be stuck working at the restaurant, but the real reason he fled was because the woman he loved more than anything didn't feel the same way about him.

"I don't see how you could have meant it any other way." Her nostrils flared. "I am loyal to *mei familye*, that's true. But when you asked me to marry you, I said *ya*, without hesitation. I wouldn't have agreed to be *yer* wife if I hadn't loved you."

"Just not enough."

"What do you mean by that?"

This was going in an awful direction, and it hadn't been his intention to bare his soul like this. He couldn't explain that when she hadn't tried to contact him, he'd realized their relationship had been lopsided. Yes, he had been wrong to go, especially without telling her he was going to. But if she had loved him more, wouldn't she have at least asked his mother for his address and written to him? Or asked her about him? He knew how ridiculously immature that sounded now, but at the time, the hurt had been real.

He shored up his feelings again. "Look, the main thing is that I'm telling you I was wrong. I'm sorry, and I've spent the last ten years living with regrets."

"And I spent the last ten years living with a broken heart."

Ashamed, he stared at the ground. "Why didn't you marry?" he whispered.

"What?"

He looked at her, a stab of pain in his heart, and all his efforts to protect his emotions dissolved to ash. "You should have married. I expected you'd have a husband and a passel of kids by now. Is it because . . . Is it *mei* fault?"

The wind seemed to drift out of her sails. "*Ya*," she said, her voice low.

"Because I broke *yer* heart." The pain he was feeling was wrenching.

She nodded.

He'd never felt so low. How could he make it up to her for something like that? It was impossible. Tears formed in his eyes. "I never meant to," he said, choking on the words. "All I wanted was for you to be happy. And when I didn't hear from you, I figured you would be."

~

Jemima couldn't believe what she was hearing. She'd always thought he left because his freedom meant more to him than she did. He thought she didn't love him enough. How could they have been so wrong about each other?

"If I could make it up to you, I would," he said, wiping his eyes with the heel of his hand. "But I can't replace ten years. I can't turn back time." He sighed, then gave her a watery smile. "Just know that I realize how badly I messed up everything." He turned and started to leave, only to halt and look back at her. "I never stopped loving you, Jemima. Ever." He turned around again and walked away.

The dam of ice in her heart gave way, and she hurried after him. "Everett," she said, tears pooling in her eyes, "wait. You're not the only one who messed up." She touched his cheek. "I'm sorry I didn't make you feel as loved as I should have."

"It's all right." He removed her hand from his cheek. "I understand."

"I don't think you do. You were right when you said I was angry with myself. I was. I am. I spent years regretting that I didn't get in touch with you. I was too angry to try at first, and I held on to that bitterness for far too long. I always wished I hadn't let you get away from me."

"You did?"

She nodded. "You want to know why I never married? I never stopped loving you either." Tears streamed down her face. "Besides, who could measure up to Everett Wengerd?"

"Plenty of people," he said.

"Not in *mei* eyes." She reached up and put both hands on either side of his face. "How were we so wrong about everything?"

"I'm not sure. Maybe it's proof that neither of us were ready to get married. We were old enough but not mature enough. That's for sure the truth in *mei* case."

Hers, too, she was realizing. Forgiving Everett wasn't about letting him off the hook. It was about healing her heart. She could see that now, and her bitter stubbornness had stood in the way. He'd been right about that too. "What do we do now?"

He took a step closer. "I didn't come back to Middlefield for a short visit. I'm here to stay. Being back in the restaurant, even doing the jobs I didn't like when I was younger, has shown me this is where I'm supposed to be. I even missed the business a little bit, believe it or not."

"I do find that hard to believe."

"God has changed me. I'd like to think he's grown me up a bit." He squeezed her hands. "We can't *geh* back to what we were, but we can start over. Only if that's what you want, though. I know I have to earn back *yer* trust."

"I have to earn back *yers* too." She squeezed his hands back. "If you're willing to try, so am I."

~

When Everett left—after sitting with her on a garden bench to talk and watch the sun set—Jemima went inside the house. The empty, lonely place in her heart was filled in a way she hadn't expected. She and Everett had decided to take things slow, and she was looking forward to discovering the man he had become.

When she stopped in the kitchen to get a glass of water, she found her mother seated at the table, the baby quilt she was making spread out in front of her. *Mamm* took the pins out of her mouth and looked at her. "Was that Everett I saw in the garden with you?"

Jemima nodded, still stunned by everything that had just happened. Stunned but hopeful.

"Did he ask you to come back to work?"

Jemima saw the apprehensive look in her eyes. "*Nee*," she said. "And I won't be going back there."

Relief washed over her features, and she went back to pinning the quilt. "*Gut.* I hope you've got the job idea out of *yer* system."

She stepped closer to the table, hoping her mother would at least try to understand. "I'm going to look for another one, though."

"Jemima, we told you—"

"I know, and I was listening. But I'm thirty-four years old. I need to do something other than housework, mending, and babysitting."

Mamm's chin lifted. "Those are virtuous tasks, Jemima Anne."

It was on the tip of her tongue to ask *Mamm* why she didn't do them if they were so virtuous, but she held in the words. "I know they are. But when do I get time for myself? When do I get a chance to live *mei* life?"

Mamm sighed. "I didn't realize *yer* life was *so* difficult. You don't have any bills or responsibilities, like the rest of us do."

"Maybe I want those things. Maybe I want *mei* own *haus. Mei* own *familye.*"

Her mother sniffed. "There isn't an unattached man of appropriate age in this district." Then she gasped. "You're not talking about Everett, are you?"

"*Nee*, I'm not." She knew better than to jump to that conclusion when they were barely getting to know each other again. "But even if I was, that's not the point. I've always done what everyone in *mei familye* wanted me to do. Am I not allowed to think about a future for my-self?"

"You can thank Everett for ruining that." *Mamm* frowned. "It's not our fault he left you."

"I'm not saying it is." Was her mother being deliber-ately obtuse? Jemima couldn't tell, but then again, some-times *Mamm* didn't seem to realize what was obvious right under her nose.

After a long pause, her mother nodded. "You're right," she said. "You should be able to have *yer* own future. I guess I've just become so used to *yer* help around here." She looked at her and patted Jemima's hand. "I couldn't have raised *yer* siblings without you."

"*Ya*, you could have," Jemima said, sitting down.

"It wouldn't have been as easy." Tears entered *Mamm*'s eyes. "After what happened with Everett, I never imagined you leaving. What am I going to do without you?"

"You and *Daed* will be fine. So will everyone else. And it's not like I won't be around to help. I just won't have as much time to anymore."

Mamm nodded. "I can see that." She put her hand over Jemima's. "You have our blessing. And our apol-ogies that we've held you back. That never was our in-tention."

She hugged her mother, glad that she had finally got-ten through to her. "I want to *geh* back out to the garden for a little while, if that's all right."

"Of course it is. Take all the time you need."

Jemima smiled, then slipped back outside to sit in the swing and pray. She'd forgiven Everett, and she knew she had the courage to start a new life only because of that forgiveness.

Epilogue

Six months later

Jemima locked up the small fabric store connected to Doris Lambright's house, an elderly English woman who'd run the business for almost forty years. When Jemima heard Doris was considering closing her shop, she'd asked to take it over. Doris had eagerly agreed, having known Jemima and her family for a long time. Now Jemima had been running the shop for almost six months, and she'd never been happier.

She buttoned her sweater as she walked down the driveway. As usual, Everett was waiting to pick her up. She could walk home from Doris's, but Everett had insisted on taking her home every day. And he had, without fail. She smiled at him when she climbed into his buggy. "How was *yer* day?" she asked as he tapped the reins on the horse's flanks.

"*Gut.*" But he didn't elaborate.

After waiting a few moments, Jemima frowned. "Is that all? Usually you have a lot to tell me. Who you saw at the restaurant, what *yer* father is planning for next week's specials—"

"You don't want to hear about boring restaurant stuff."

She looked at him, his expression concerning her. "Everett, is something wrong?"

"I wouldn't say wrong." Then he sighed. "*Daed* and *Mamm* are retiring."

Her brow shot up. "What? When did they decide that?"

"They've been thinking about it for months but didn't tell me."

"Are they going to sell the restaurant?"

"That's a possibility." He looked at her again, and then he turned down a road not many people traveled. He stopped the buggy along the side and faced her. "*Daed* asked me if I want to take over the restaurant."

Jemima clasped her hands together. "That's wonderful. You've been managing the place for a while anyway."

"*Ya,* but I've never run it by myself." Doubt entered his eyes.

She reached for his hand. "Everett, you will be a wonderful manager. You love the business now—"

"Which is a miracle in itself."

"God's performed a lot of miracles in our lives lately."

He moved closer to her. "*Ya*. He has." He paused. "Do you think I should take the job? *Daed* said he would sell the diner if I didn't. He already has two people interested in it, so it would continue with or without me."

"What do you want to do?"

He looked down at their clasped hands, then back at her. "It's not just about me. Jemima, I want to marry you. This time I'm ready. And if you say you're still not sure, I'll wait for you. I'm not going anywhere, even if *Daed* sells the restaurant. But I don't want to run it if you don't want me to."

She leaned forward and kissed him. "If you want to run the restaurant, then I support you. Whatever you want to do, wherever you *geh*, I'll be by *yer* side." Tears gathered in her eyes. "And *ya*, I will marry you, Everett. You know how much I love you."

He took her in his arms and kissed her ear. "That I do." He smiled. "I love you too. But are you sure?"

"*Ya*. I'm ready too." Thanks to God, she had another chance at love with Everett—and she wasn't going to let him get away this time.

SECOND-CHANCE LOVE

CHAPTER 1

CHARM AND ASHTABULA, OHIO

Dear Benjamin,

Here is the recipe for the éclair cake you asked for.
I'm still surprised to learn you like to cook and bake!
Marvin, my late husband, did everything he could to
stay out of the kitchen, except when it was time to eat.
For some reason he didn't care too much for the éclair
cake, but it's been requested for a lot of potlucks and
suppers in our district.

I very much enjoyed my time in Charm. The wedding was lovely, as all weddings are. I pray that your
niece and nephew-in-law will have a blessed life and
plenty of children if God wills.

I hope you enjoy the cake. It was nice meeting you at the wedding.

Lora Beth

Dear Lora Beth,

Thank you for the recipe. I've already tried my hand at making it, and while it wasn't as good as yours, it was passable. I took it over to the Bontragers' to share after church this past Sunday. There wasn't a crumb left over. Which is good, since it's just me at home. I probably would have eaten half the cake if left to my own devices.

My late wife, Elsie, was surprised, too, when she discovered I like to cook. She's the one who showed me how to bake. She was a good teacher, not just with me but also with our son. I miss her very much, just like I know you miss Marvin. After her passing, some days I didn't think I could take another breath. But God got me through. It's a hard fact of life that you truly don't know how much you need God until you are in a place where you really need him. I'm not sure if I'm explaining that right or not.

I know Elsie wouldn't want me swimming in sorrow over her, but even though it's been nine years since she died, some days I think she's still here, that I'll wake up and she'll be in the kitchen making buckwheat pancakes and fried ham steaks.

Well, I didn't mean to get all somber on you. I

guess I just had this feeling from our short time of talking at the wedding that you would understand. On one hand, that's relieving. On the other, I wouldn't wish losing a spouse so soon in life on anyone.

Take care,

Ben

Dear Ben,

I'm glad the cake turned out well for you. I thought you might also like an old recipe I found the other day. You'll find it on the back of this letter. It's my grandmother's recipe from the 1930s, and it's surprisingly delicious. She used to call it the Poorman's Meal, and I remember eating it when I was growing up on our family farm. Excuse my bit of nostalgia. I haven't had this dish in a long time, and I think I'll make it for my supper tonight.

I understand what you mean about grief. It sneaks up on you sometimes, even after so many years. When Marvin died six years ago, I also had a hard time moving through life. The pain was so intense at times. Like you, I was in a place where all I could do was lean on God, and he saw me through. He still does. I don't question why Marvin was taken from me at age forty-one, when he was so vibrant and had so much life to live. God's ways are not our own, are they? But I have peace that Marvin is at peace, and that's all that matters.

187

Meanwhile, my daughters sometimes express concern about me living here by myself, but I tell them I'm fine on my own. Even though Marvin left me with savings, they worry about me making ends meet. But God has blessed me with enough part-time work over the years, like cleaning houses and sewing for others, to live comfortably. I'm only forty-seven. I'm not ready to move in with one of them!

Best,

Lora Beth

Dear Lora Beth,

That Poorman's Meal looks really good. I make something similar but with rice instead of potatoes. And I use smoked sausage instead of hot dogs. Nothing better than some good smoked sausage, in my book.

I see you have the same problem with your children as I do with my son. Paul has been after me to move in with him and his family so he can, in his words, "keep an eye on me." I'm perfectly fine living on my own at forty-eight, but talking to him, you would think I was headed for a permanent spot in a rocking chair. I know he's just trying to look out for me, but he says he worries I'm lonely. Which I am, sometimes. Can't lie about that. But that doesn't mean I want to move. It will probably happen eventually, but I'm not interested in rushing time.

Since we've been sharing recipes, I'd like to give you my favorite: yumasetti. I know it's a common meal, but I've played around with it a little and made it my own. The secret is homemade cream of chicken and cream of mushroom soup, plus some provolone cheese on top. You can't beat food from scratch, even though I've been known to cheat a time or two with some premade ingredients.

I pray you're doing well, Lora Beth. I've enjoyed our letters to each other. If it's all right, I'd like to continue writing to you. If you'd rather I not, I understand. And I hope you don't mind me saying this, but your letters have been a bright spot in my life lately.

Best,
Ben

Dear Ben,

I would very much like to continue writing to you too. I've looked forward to hearing from you. I can't wait to try your version of yumasetti. I've made my own casserole a few times, but it's not one of my children's favorites. Maybe they'll like yours better. They're coming over Saturday afternoon, and I'm excited to see my two grandchildren, Rosetta and Katrina. They're twins, which is unusual in both our families but such a blessing. They will be eight months old tomorrow, and they're crawling all over the place. I'll be washing the floors all day before they arrive.

It's nice to talk to someone who understands what I've gone through—and what I'm still going through. Two widows and one widower live in our district, but the women were each married for over forty years, and Lonnie, the widower, was married for nearly sixty. I can't imagine being married that long and losing your partner in life, just like they can't relate to being widowed so young. My children are also concerned that I'm lonely. We're very blessed to have children who care, aren't we? But sometimes that blessing can be a little annoying. Just don't tell them I said that!

How are you coping with the heat wave we're having? Here in Ashtabula, you can fry an egg on the sidewalk. Did you ever try doing that as a youngster? My older brother did, but he just made a mess. Our mother wasn't too happy that day. She didn't like us to waste food. Come to think of it, that was the last time any of us wasted food on something so foolish.

Best,

Lora Beth

Dear Lora Beth,

No, I can't say that I've tried to fry an egg on the sidewalk. Maybe I will one of these hot days, just out of curiosity. If I had tried doing that as a kid, my mother would have had a fit too.

I spend a lot of time fishing when I'm not working

at my accounting job. Summer is slower in my business, but it picks up at harvest time, and then, of course, during the tax season. My fishing trips have been pretty successful. The walleye and trout have been plentiful this year. I've got some fish in my neighbor's freezer, a couple for me and the rest for him and his family. They've always been generous to share freezer space with me, and I try not to take up too much of their room with my food.

I agree that it's good to talk to someone about grief. When Elsie died, I had to put up a brave front for my child. He was in his early teens, and I must admit that I fumbled with him a few times. Paul even left the district for a while. He needed to explore the world outside of Charm. He didn't go very far—just to Akron—and he came back a few days later. I guess he found out pretty quick that the world isn't as great as it seemed to be. He joined the church later that year, but for a while I was wondering if he would. Those days were filled with worry for me, wondering if I could raise him right without Elsie. I spent a lot of time on my knees then. Still do.

How did the yumasetti turn out? I made the éclair cake again. Couldn't help it. I sent most of it home with Paul's wife, Susan. She drops by and brings me treats, offers to do my laundry, and things like that. She's a keeper, and she reminds me a little of Elsie. But I saved three big pieces for me.

Stay cool in this heat, Lora Beth. Make sure you drink lots of water.

Best,

Ben

Dear Ben . . .

Lora Beth Schwartz flinched when she heard the front door of her house open. She looked at the clock. Almost ten already? It was only a little after nine thirty when she sat down to read Ben's latest letter. But then she'd reread it several times and started writing him back, forgetting the plans she'd made with her daughter.

Just as Rachel entered the kitchen, Lora Beth shoved Ben's letter and her stationery into her keepsake box. "Sorry I'm not ready," she said as Rachel set her purse on the table.

Rachel lifted a brow, an expression similar to Marvin's. "You're running late? That never happens."

"I know, I know." Known for her punctuality, Lora Beth was even a little obsessive about being on time. And she'd looked forward to getting out of the warm house for an afternoon with her oldest daughter, who had married last November. They were shopping for fabric to make dresses and a baby quilt for one of Rachel's friends. Lora Beth had made two quilts for Rosetta and Katrina, one pale green and the other pale rose, and Rachel wanted her help with the pattern.

"I got sidetracked," she said as she stood, then took off her apron.

"Oh? With what?" Rachel pulled a pitcher of lemonade from the gas-powered fridge.

"Just things." Lora Beth hung her apron on a peg by the doorway to the mudroom, then grabbed her keepsake box. "I'll be right back and ready to *geh*." She hurried out of the kitchen.

Once inside her bedroom, she shut the door. Normally she didn't hide things from her daughters. But she didn't want them, or anyone else, to find out she'd been writing to Benjamin—or Ben, as he preferred to be called. She ran her fingers over the top of the box. She never thought she'd be writing to a man her age, not only to exchange recipes, which was unusual, but also to talk about the deaths of their spouses.

Lora Beth had always kept her feelings about Marvin's death close to her chest. Her daughters' emotional well-being had been her priority, which meant she had to grieve in private, and that had been difficult. Knowing someone who had traveled this same road gave her some comfort, even after all these years. She wished Ben had never had to go through such pain, but as she'd told him, God's ways aren't their own. She'd been about to tell him she understood how difficult it was to grieve while keeping it from the children, hoping that would give him a little comfort too.

She smiled as she remembered first seeing him in

Charm, at his niece's wedding. She'd agreed to go with a friend she was visiting, although attending a wedding was the last thing she'd wanted to do. Weddings hadn't become much easier for her over the years, even her own daughters' nuptials. She couldn't help wishing Marvin were there, and it was hard to keep that from everyone. Rebecca, Rosemary, and Rachel's weddings had all been beautiful, but after each one, she'd had a long, private cry.

Because of her ambivalence about the wedding, along with not knowing anyone there besides her friend, she was standing off to the side after the ceremony, watching people enjoy themselves. To her surprise, Ben approached her and introduced himself. He'd learned she made the éclair cake she brought, and he raved about it. When he expressed an interest in making the cake—something else that surprised her—she surprised herself by offering to send him the recipe.

Over the past three weeks, they'd been corresponding, and she looked forward to Ben's letters. It was nice to write to someone who not only understood her deepest pain but also had a common interest. She'd never imagined that interest would be cooking, and it had been fun exchanging recipes with him along with commiserating over their losses.

"*Mamm*?" Rachel said from the other side of the door. "Are you all right?"

Her daughter's voice jerked her out of her thoughts, and she yanked open her nightstand drawer. "I'm fine," she called. "Be there in a minute." She deposited the keepsake box in the drawer, then grabbed her purse off the dresser and determined she would put Ben and his letters out of her mind.

"I'm ready to *geh*," she announced when she opened the door, a wide grin on her face.

Rachel frowned. "Are you sure *nix* is wrong?"

"*Ya*. Why?"

"*Yer* face is red."

She touched her cheek. It was warm. "Rachel, it's ninety degrees outside."

"Not that kind of red. It's like you're blushing."

Lora Beth let out a nervous chuckle. "I'm not blushing," she said, slipping past her. What a silly thought. What would she be blushing about anyway? Certainly not Ben. "Are we coming back here for lunch or eating out?"

"I thought we'd eat at *mei haus*," Rachel said, following her.

"Sounds *gut*."

They climbed into Rachel's buggy, and Lora Beth was glad her daughter had dropped the idea that her mother was blushing. She certainly wasn't. But she had to admit that she would be eager to finish her letter to Ben when she got home. He was a punctual letter writer, and she would hear from him soon after he received her latest one. She couldn't help but smile at the thought.

CHAPTER 2

Y ou sure have been making a lot of that éclair cake, Ben."

"It's *gut* cake," Ben said as he looked up at his friend, Menno. Then he took a big gulp of milk. Nothing went better with Lora Beth's cake than milk.

"Oh, I agree. But you've brought it to church dinner and to Vernon's barn raising, and Paul said if he sees another slice of it, he's going to ban you from *yer* kitchen."

"I'd like to see him try." Ben chuckled. Then he shrugged. It wasn't like he'd made this particular éclair cake for his son and daughter-in-law anyway, so Paul didn't have to worry. This cake he wanted all to himself. Maybe he had made it too many times, come to think of it. But it reminded him of Lora Beth.

He smiled as he thought of her last letter. She'd included another recipe, for peach crumble. If he kept making all the delicious recipes she sent him—and he intended to do just that—he'd have to work harder in his garden and yard to avoid putting on a few pounds. More than a few.

"What are you smiling about?" Menno tugged on his graying beard. "Can't be *mei* bank account. That's making me want to cry."

Ben's smile slipped, and he focused on why Menno was visiting him today—to figure out how he could save money. The man was a spendthrift, and over the past several years it had developed into a major problem. "You wouldn't be crying if you weren't going to auctions every weekend."

"You never know when you're going to miss a deal," he said.

"So you've said on more than one occasion." He also knew auctions and flea markets were a social outlet for Menno. He had Amish friends and English friends who attended both, and now that he was getting close to retirement and his kids were busy with their own families, he needed the companionship. "You don't have to buy anything when you *geh*. Especially when you don't need it."

"Never know when you might need something, though." Menno crossed his arms. "It's *gut* to have things on hand."

Knowing that arguing with him right now would be fruitless, Ben shoved the empty plate away and grabbed Menno's ledgers, then put on his silver-rimmed reading glasses. For the next half hour, he tried to convince the man to adopt some ways he could save money. Menno was in his early sixties, and he couldn't work as a farrier forever. He had to start saving now, even though he knew his children would take care of him and his wife when the time came. Ben also knew they wouldn't continue feeding his hoarding habit.

Despite all the facts and suggestions for saving money he'd put in front of this man, they'd made little headway by the time Menno had to return home.

After Menno left, Ben put plastic wrap on the leftover cake and put the pan on the counter. He probably shouldn't make the cake again even though he wasn't tired of it. Maybe he would ask Lora Beth for a salad recipe in his next letter. The Poorman's Meal was pretty good, although he was glad he'd replaced the hot dogs with smoked sausage. Hot dogs just didn't have the same zing sausage had.

He stepped outside to work in the garden. He kept a smaller plot now, but when Elsie was alive and Paul was small, the garden covered almost half his backyard. Now he grew only the essentials—tomatoes, green peppers, a few herbs, zucchini, and summer squash. Later he would plant the root vegetables—carrots, turnips, and potatoes. Just enough for him, with a little to share if anyone needed it. Over the years, when some of his clients couldn't pay his fee, he'd waived it plus sent some canned goods home with them under the guise that he had too much and needed to get rid of it. They had always been appreciative.

As he pulled weeds, he thought about Lora Beth again. He hoped he hadn't been too forthcoming when he told her that her letters were a bright spot in his life. It was the truth, but he wondered if she might read something else into it. Since Elsie's passing, he hadn't been interested in dating or remarrying, and he still wasn't. The fact that Lora Beth was a woman didn't mean anything to him. Friendship was all he was looking for, and she seemed to feel the same way.

But if he was ever in the market for a wife, he'd look for someone like Lora Beth. She was kind, understanding—and pretty. He'd noticed that right off at the wedding. A little on the plump side, she had dark-blond hair, pale-green eyes, nice skin, and a bright smile. He was surprised she hadn't remarried. He figured some single or widowed man would have snatched her up by now.

He put Lora Beth out of his mind as he placed cages around his tomato plants. This evening he would have a simple supper, look over Menno's ledgers again to see if he missed any ways the man could save money, care for his horse, and then read the Bible before he went to bed. A quiet evening, as most of them were nowadays. He didn't mind, but sometimes he missed the bustle of having his son and his friends around. He also missed Elsie the most during those quiet times. He'd always miss her.

The next morning, after he worked out in the garden until the noon sun burned overhead, he went to the mailbox and opened the lid. He smiled when he saw Lora Beth's letter. He appreciated her punctuality in writing him back, and he tucked the letter into his pocket, saving it for later. Not because he had anything pressing to do, but because he wanted to savor the letter later, giving him something to look forward to at the end of the day.

He had to admit that when he read her letters, he was a little less lonely . . . and more than a little happy.

~

"Who wants another piece of blueberry pie?" Lora Beth called above the din of the noisy klatch of her family members as they sat around the huge rectangular table that barely fit into her kitchen. She needed the table only for times like this, when she had her daughters and their families here. Often, she thought about getting rid of it, but she couldn't bear to do that. Marvin had made the oak table after they were married, anticipating a house full of children. They'd had only three, so the table had been too big for them as the girls grew up. But now it was just right.

"Me," Rachel said. "I'll share it with Uriah."

Lora Beth nodded. Figure wise, Rachel took after

her. They both had always struggled with a few extra pounds that refused to drop, but neither of them was bothered by them—although they did try to watch their dessert consumption. To no one's surprise, Uriah nodded in agreement, and Lora Beth set a piece of the flaky, gooey pie in front of her daughter, adding two forks to the plate.

"*Mamm*, may I set up the *boppli*'s playpen in *yer* bedroom?" Rebecca asked, balancing Katrina on her shoulder while her husband, Enoch, cuddled Rosetta.

"Of course. Do you need any help?"

"*Nee.*" Rebecca's voice lowered. "They're falling asleep already."

Lora Beth watched them as they left the kitchen. *If only you could have met the twins, Marvin.* She tried not to have melancholy thoughts when she was with family, but at moments like these, when her heart was full of love and thankfulness, she wished he was at her side, enjoying every moment with her.

"Do you need me to do anything while we're here?" LeRoy, her other son-in-law, asked.

"I can help out too," Uriah added, setting down his fork.

"Are you finished with the pie already?" Rachel asked, looking surprised.

He nodded and pushed the plate toward her with almost half a piece of pie left on it. "Enjoy," he said with a smile.

Lora Beth tapped her index finger against her chin. "The barn can always use some tidying up. I cleaned it out the other day, but it needs another once-over."

"Done," LeRoy said, and then he motioned to Uriah. The men went out through the mudroom off the kitchen and out the back door.

Rebecca came back into the room without Enoch. "All three are fast asleep," she said, grinning. "Enoch sat in *yer* rocker with Rosetta and conked out. He's been tired from working so much overtime on that construction project in Akron."

"*Nee* wonder he fell asleep." She looked at her daughter, checking for the telltale signs of a weary mother of young babies—dark circles under tired eyes, slower than normal movements, frequent sighing. But Rebecca looked fresh and energetic. She took after her father—thin, wiry, and always on the move. She sat down next to Rachel and across from Rosemary, the middle sister, who was a mix of Lora Beth and Marvin.

"Have a seat, *Mamm*," Rosemary said, gesturing to Lora Beth's chair at the end of the table.

"I will, after I finish the dishes."

She was about to turn on the tap when Rebecca chimed in. "The dishes can wait, and we'll do them later."

"We want to talk to you," Rachel said, also pointing to the chair.

Wary, Lora Beth nodded and sat down. She couldn't remember the last time her daughters wanted to have a talk. Now that she thought about it, the three of them had never initiated a discussion with her at the same time, at least not with such serious expressions on their faces.

Rachel and Rosemary looked at Rebecca, who in turn glanced at Lora Beth. Whatever they had to say, they'd designated the youngest sister as their spokesperson. Not a surprise, but it gave Lora Beth pause. Alarm threaded through her. "Something's wrong, isn't it?" she asked, her gaze darting back and forth between her three daughters.

"*Nix* is wrong," Rebecca said. She tapped her fingers on the table, a habit from when she was little. "It's just that the three of us have been talking the past couple of months, and we're concerned about you. Especially because you live alone."

Lora Beth sat back and held in a sigh. "As I've told each of you before, I'm fine and content. Life is *gut*, and I'm grateful to God for it."

"We can tell you're fine," Rosemary added. "But it's been six years since *Daed* died, and this place is too big for you to take care of by *yerself*."

"Then you should all move back in." She laughed, intending her words as a joke. But her girls' expressions remained somber.

"Uriah and I would like you to move in with us," Rachel said.

"Or you could move in with me and LeRoy," Rosemary added.

"Enoch and I have plenty of room," Rebecca injected. "At least we will once Enoch builds on to the *haus*. Or he could build a *dawdi haus* for you—"

"That's enough." She looked at her three daughters, love filling her heart because of how much they cared about her. It was the Amish way to take care of family, but that didn't mean she took their love and concern for granted. "I'm thankful that you're concerned about me, and that you all want me to live with you. But I'm fine here. Truly."

"Don't you get lonely?" Rosemary's voice wavered. "I would be if I had to live in this big *haus* alone."

Lora Beth paused. She couldn't lie to her daughters, but she didn't want to give them any reason to think she wasn't satisfied living on her own. "Sometimes I get a little lonely. But isn't that normal for everyone? Haven't you been lonely in *yer* life?"

"Not since I got married and had the twins." Rebecca chuckled. "I'd like a few lonely moments every once in a while."

"You can always let me know when you want me to watch or keep the *kinner*," Lora Beth said. "I'll be over in a wink."

"I know. But wouldn't it be easier if you were already there? Not that we want you to move in for childcare. Enoch and I are managing fine."

"I can see that you are." Lora Beth didn't know how she was going to explain that while she had her lonely times, she also liked her independence. And she couldn't admit the one major thing that was keeping her here—it made her feel closer to Marvin. Her daughters wouldn't understand, and she prayed they would never experience that kind of loss.

"I don't have any intentions of moving from here," she said, her tone firm. "Perhaps a day will come when I'll need to live with one of you, but that's not necessary right now. I'm still young, although I know forty-seven seems ancient to you all."

"Not really, now that I'm twenty-five," Rachel said. "Time seems to move faster when you're older."

"It certainly does."

She took her mother's hand. "Are you sure about this?"

Lora Beth nodded. "Absolutely sure."

"The offer will always stand. Anytime you're ready to leave here, you'll have a home to come to." Rachel looked at her sisters. "*Ya?*"

"*Ya,*" the other two said in unison.

"*Danki.*" Lora Beth wiped the corner of her eye with her fingers. The Lord had blessed her and Marvin with wonderful daughters.

Enoch came into the room, his gaze going straight to Rebecca. Lora Beth noticed her give him a quick shake of the head, and he returned it with a curt nod, then walked over to her. "You shouldn't have let me fall asleep like that," he said, squeezing Rebecca's shoulder. "Where are LeRoy and Uriah?"

"Working in the barn." Rosemary took a sip of tea. Lora Beth noticed the ice cubes in it had already melted because of how warm it was in the house.

"I'll *geh* help them." He frowned and turned away. "Can't believe she let me sleep while they're working," he muttered as he left the kitchen.

Rebecca popped up from her chair and started clearing the table, Rosemary went to the sink and turned on the tap, and Rachel started scraping leftover food onto a large plate. She'd take it out to the pigs in a few minutes, as her daughters always had while they were growing up.

"*Geh* put *yer* feet up, *Mamm*," Rebecca said.

"We've got the kitchen." Rosemary squirted dish soap into the sink.

Realizing she had to let her daughters do something for her since she'd turned down their offer, she nodded and then went into the living room. She sat down on the couch, the one she and Marvin had chosen during their fifth year of marriage. Then she glanced around the room. Everything was the same as the day he passed away. There was comfort in that, but also, as she admitted to her daughters, some loneliness. But it never lasted for long, especially when she turned to God in those times. No, she had no intention of leaving this place, not anytime soon.

I belong here, and until I have to leave, here I'll stay.

Dear Lora Beth,

I enjoyed your last letter. I know you weren't too happy about your children pressing you to move in with one of them, but it's a testament to their quality of character that they want to take care of you. That's something about the Amish that has always appealed to me—our sense of community. Some of my English clients mention that the rest of the world is losing their community, that even though people are living close together and talk on the phone and on the computer, they really don't know each other. Paul hasn't brought up the idea of me moving in with him and Susan lately, so hopefully he's dropped the subject. If he brings it up again, my answer will be the same as yours—thanks but no thanks.

I wonder if you have more recipes to share. I must admit the éclair cake has already overstayed its welcome at potlucks and church fellowships. If you have any recipes that would be easy to make for those occasions, I'd sure appreciate getting them. Salads are always popular this time of year.

Speaking of vegetables, I worked in my garden this past week. The rain and warm weather sure are making my vegetables grow like wildfire! I should have enough tomatoes to make plenty of sauce. And, of course, I'll can some whole ones along with some diced. I gotta say, though, while I do enjoy growing the food, when it comes to putting it up, I'm not as enthusiastic.

Stay cool, Lora Beth. It's only July—the summer will be getting hotter. Make sure you don't get too much sun. Sunburns are no fun.

Best,

Ben

Dear Ben,

I've included several recipes for potlucks in this letter. I gave you two for salads—potato and macaroni. But I couldn't resist adding one of my favorites—Texas sheet cake. That's always a crowd pleaser. Is there any food you don't like? I don't care for parsnips or turnips, and this might come as a surprise, but I really don't like celery. So many dishes have celery in them, but I just leave it out. No one seems to complain, though!

I'm glad your garden is doing well. Mine is surviving, as it usually does for me each year. I don't have much of a green thumb, but I do enjoy putting up the food. I think it has to do with memories of helping my mother in the kitchen. We had a large garden, and my father was an avid hunter, so we had plenty of food to put up each fall and winter. When my girls were old enough, they pitched in to help their grandmother, then we would can our own crops. I also keep a few extra jars of everything I've canned to give away, just in case. You never know when someone needs a helping hand.

If you'd like any more recipes, I can send more. I've

collected lots of them over the years, and I even have a few Italian, Mexican, and Chinese recipes. It's fun to experiment with seasonings I don't normally use in everyday cooking.

You stay cool, too, Ben. Make sure you drink plenty of water when you're out working in your garden.

Best,

Lora Beth

~

Ben surveyed the crowd at the ox roast in Mesopotamia. He'd agreed to help Menno man his booth—one of among about a hundred, he guessed. He'd managed to convince Menno that he could sell some of his better items at the ox roast flea market, popular with English and Amish alike. Over the past two weeks, Ben had helped Menno sort through one of his hot spare barns, which was filled to the brim with everything from quality antiques to absolute junk. Ben had been impressed, and a little wary, when he first saw Menno's numerous and disorganized collections.

Once everything in the barn was in some sort of order, though, they'd found a lot of unique items to sell. It would take much more time to get everything in the barn categorized and organized, but at least Menno wasn't going to break his neck walking around among it all.

"I'm not sure about this," Menno said, stroking his long, gray beard.

The shopping had just started, and Ben knew that in an hour, the grassy area would be packed. The local fire department was about to roast the oxen that brought crowds from all around Northeast Ohio. Last year, coming as a visitor, he'd stood in line for over an hour for an ox beef sandwich—and it was worth the wait. "What are you concerned about?" Ben asked.

"Selling these things." He ran his thick fingers over an antique glass lamp.

Ben had carefully packed the lamp in a box with newspaper and Bubble Wrap so the yellow-tinted globe wouldn't break. When Menno confessed the lamp had sat in a box in the back of his buggy for over a year, Ben couldn't believe it was still intact. He wasn't sure of the value, but he priced it on the low side since Menno had paid less than two dollars for it at a garage sale. "You want to keep that?"

"I kinda like it."

"It's been sitting in *yer* buggy for a long time." Besides, it was a bit fancy for an Amish home, but Ben figured the English buyers would be interested.

"Then there's this." He picked up a carving of a bear standing on its hind legs. "I don't think I want to sell this either."

Ben inwardly groaned. He'd been afraid of this. Convincing Menno to sell these items had been a chore. Now all the work he'd done could be for nothing if Menno decided to pack everything up and head home.

"Remember our goal, Menno," he said. "You're selling these things to put some money into savings."

Menno frowned and looked at the merchandise on the table in front of him, then began rubbing the back of his neck. "*Ya*, about that. I think I've changed *mei* mind—"

"Are you hungry?" Ben said, grasping at something that might distract him. "I thought I saw a donut stand a few yards away." He dug in his pocket for his wallet, then gave a few dollars to Menno. "Do you mind getting me a cup of *kaffee* and two donuts? Get *yerself* some, if you want to."

Menno nodded and took the money. "Be right back."

Ben leaned against the table and let out a long sigh. Menno might be nervous about selling, but he was also an amiable man who liked to help folks out at any opportunity. Getting him away from the booth gave Ben some time to think—although he wasn't sure what he was going to do. He couldn't force the man to sell his things. He'd learned over the past couple of weeks that easing Menno into an idea was better than strong-arming him. Ben said a quick prayer, asking God to help Menno not change his mind.

Twenty minutes later, Menno hadn't returned, but the shoppers had started to arrive, and Ben had already sold three items. He hoped when the old man saw how much money he'd made in a short period of time, he'd realize he'd made the right decision to sell. But where was he?

It shouldn't have taken him this long to buy coffee and donuts.

He sat down in one of two metal folding chairs behind the table and started to unwrap plain brown paper from two more items—an old kitchen knife set from the 1930s and a windup toy car made of metal that had to date to at least the 1950s. He wrote prices on two stickers, placed them on the items, then put them on the table. Then he stood and smiled at people as they passed the booth.

Two Amish women, both with dark-brown hair and similarly shaped faces, paused in front of the booth. "Rosemary," one of them said, "don't these look like the knives *Grossmutter* had?"

The woman peered at the set. "I think so. They sure are similar."

"I'm sure *Mamm* would want them." The woman turned around and waved her hand. "*Mamm!*" she called. Then she turned to Rosemary. "I'll be right back. I see *Mamm* taking the twins to the gazebo."

Rosemary nodded, then moved on from the set and looked at the lamp. "How old is this?" she asked.

"Honestly, I don't know." He explained that the items belonged to Menno, and he had tried to price them fairly. "We didn't have much time to have anything appraised, and Menno doesn't worry about value. He just buys what he likes."

"It is pretty. And fancy." She glanced in the direction

of the gazebo. "I better see if they need help with the *bop-pli*." She turned to Ben. "*Danki* for *yer* time."

Ben nodded as Rosemary walked away. He would have been surprised if she'd bought the lamp, but he hoped one of the women would return to purchase the knife set. He stepped outside the booth and looked across the crowd toward the gazebo, but all he saw were people huddled all around him. It would be a busy day, which he prayed would translate to selling everything. It would be nice to go back to Charm with empty hands.

A few minutes later, Menno finally showed up. "Sorry it took me so long," he said. Instead of carrying donuts and coffee, he held a cardboard box. "You wouldn't believe how many booths are here," he said, his eyes bright. "I picked up this box for next to nothing."

Oh no. "What's in it?" Ben grimaced.

"Nails." Menno tipped the box so Ben could see inside. "Hundreds of nails."

Ben shook his head. This was the last thing he'd wanted to happen. "You already have thousands of nails, Menno."

"But you never know when you'll need a particular one." He set the box down behind the table. "I'll be back."

"Where are you going now?"

"To check out the rest of the booths. It's a gold mine here." Menno disappeared into the crowd.

Ben plopped into his chair. He hadn't thought about Menno taking off on him to buy more stuff. He rubbed his forehead. What he thought would be helpful to Menno had turned out to be the worst thing possible. When Menno returned—hopefully without buying out the entire flea market—Ben would have to put a limit on him. *Or a leash.*

He looked at the items on the table. At least he could do his best to sell what they brought. And he'd learned a lesson—never, ever take Menno Yoder to a flea market again.

~

"I think they're hungry," Lora Beth said as she held Katrina close. The baby had been crying almost from the moment they'd arrived at the ox roast. She'd been headed to a booth when both twins started wailing at the top of their lungs, and she immediately took them to the gazebo and tried to calm them down. Rebecca had soon joined her, then Rosemary.

"I fed them before we came," Rebecca said.

"Their diapers are dry." Lora Beth rocked Katrina back and forth while Rosemary picked up Rosetta. "They are a little hot, though."

"I was afraid of that." Rebecca pulled two bottles of milk out of her diaper bag.

Lora Beth had put a cold pack next to the bottles before they left Rebecca's to come to the ox roast. Enoch and LeRoy were also here, and the van they'd hired to bring them to Mesopotamia had dropped them off a little while ago. The men were checking out the booths that interested them, and the women were supposed to do the same. But the twins had other plans.

Rebecca handed the milk to Lora Beth and Rosemary. Rosetta took her bottle immediately, but Katrina shoved hers away. Her face was bright red, and she was perspiring. A few seconds later, Rosetta was also refusing the milk, as if she were taking cues from her sister, who was older by five minutes.

"Maybe I should take them back home," Lora Beth said. She didn't want to drag two crying babies all over the flea market on this hot day. That wouldn't be good for her granddaughters or their parents.

"I'm sure they'll calm down in a minute." But Rebecca looked doubtful.

Lora Beth smiled at her daughter. "It's all right. I can manage them at home. You and Rosemary *geh* find Enoch and LeRoy and enjoy the day."

"But we want you to enjoy it with us," Rosemary said, Rosetta now leaning on her shoulder.

"I'll enjoy being with the *boppli*."

Rebecca and Rosemary exchanged a look, then Rebecca nodded. "I'll find Enoch and have him call a taxi. He said he and LeRoy were going to check out the ox roast first and see the progress. I'm sure they're still there talking with the firefighters if they haven't already found some friends." Rebecca took off, and Rosemary sat down next to Lora Beth on the bench.

"This is a little disappointing," Rosemary said above the crying babies.

But Lora Beth wasn't disappointed at all. She'd been to this flea market many times over the years, and while she enjoyed the ox beef sandwiches and being around friends from different districts, she would rather be at home taking care of her grandchildren. She had reluctantly agreed to come because Rachel had been so persuasive, as usual. "There's always next year."

"True. And I don't want the *bopplis* to be upset." Rosemary patted Rosetta's bottom, which seemed to calm her. "Rebecca and I found something we thought you might like, though."

Katrina had also settled down a little bit, but the poor baby was sweating through her light-purple dress. "What was that?" Lora Beth said as she sat Katrina upright on her lap, then bounced her on her knee.

"A knife set, just like *Grossmutter*'s. I remember you liked using it when we went to visit."

Lora Beth nodded. She had liked her mother-in-law's set, which had been her own mother's set back in the thirties. The set had gone to her sister-in-law, as it should have. "I don't need a knife set," she said. "The ones I have are *gut* enough."

"I know. We just thought you might want it as a keepsake."

Smiling, Lora Beth's heart warmed. "I appreciate the

thought, but it seems the older I get, the fewer things I need around me—including knives."

Rebecca hurried toward them. "*Yer* ride will be here in a few minutes."

"That was quick," Lora Beth said, standing to put Katrina in the double stroller while Rosemary put Rosetta in too.

"Enoch flagged down a taxi driver he knew." She knelt by the stroller. "You be *gut bopplis* for *Grossmutter, ya?*" She looked up at Lora Beth. "We'll bring you a sandwich or two."

"One will be fine."

As they waited for the taxi, Lora Beth looked around the flea market. Both English and Amish were teeming up and down the lawn where the booths were set up. The scents of roast ox and other foods permeated the hot, steamy air, and she had to admit she was glad she was going home. She wasn't missing out on anything. She knew that for sure.

CHAPTER 3

Dear Lora Beth,

Thank you for the recipes you sent. I plan on making the cake right away. I apologize for not writing sooner. I've been busy helping a friend sell some of his "collectibles," which has kept me on my toes. He's a good man, and he's becoming a great friend, but he does have a problem buying things—as in buying too many things. Three weeks ago, we had a booth at the ox roast in Mesopotamia, and he ended up buying more than he sold, which was my fault. I should have known he would be like a rooster in a hen house at a flea market. We did sell a few things, but not enough to offset his purchases.

Now that it's almost August, I'll be spending more time canning. I've already harvested a good crop of peppers and tomatoes, and I've begun drying my herbs. I'll also be helping another friend of mine put a small deck over his concrete patio. I'm not as good with a hammer as I am with numbers and gardening, but I do like to lend a hand when I can.

Speaking of that, I'm expecting my friend with the spending problem any moment. His wife told me he snuck out to another auction this past weekend. I'd laugh, except this is looking serious.

Best,

Ben

Dear Ben,

I was surprised to hear you were at the ox roast. I was there, too, although just for a little while. My granddaughters were cranky that day, so I took them back to their house while their parents spent the day at the roast, along with my other daughter, Rosemary, and her husband, LeRoy. They enjoyed themselves, and the grandbabies were much happier out of the heat. It's hard on babies when the weather is so hot. I did see that a lot of people were at the roast, so I'm not sure we would have seen each other even if I had stayed. I'm a little disappointed that we didn't.

As far as your friend who spends too much, I wish I had some good advice. It sounds like he might even have a hoarding problem. Both Marvin and I never felt the need to have a lot of things around us, and the older I get, the less use I have for clutter. But I do remember one of my father's friends had three huge barns full of items he'd bought, and he let us kids pick out one item each every once in a while. That stopped when I was a teenager, because the barns were so over-filled they were dangerous, and by that time I was old enough to realize that he had mostly junk and trash stored in there.

When he passed away, his family had a huge sale, then moved to another district. I can offer my prayers, though, asking for wisdom for you as you talk to your friend and for God to open his ears to listen to your advice.

I will also be canning soon. The green beans and okra are abundant this year, as are the tomatoes and peppers, of course. I also planted green onions. Have you ever had a green onion and cheese sandwich on fresh, soft bread? It's delicious—but you can't breathe on anyone afterward!

Take care,

Lora Beth

Ben finished reading Lora Beth's letter and smiled. He appreciated her prayers for him and Menno, who had promised he wouldn't go to any more auctions or flea markets. Ben was positive the man had good intentions, but he also knew the urge to shop always seemed to win out. Before Menno left after his last visit, they'd prayed together, asking God to give him the strength to not only resist the urge to buy but to be willing to let go of some things.

He folded the letter and stuck it in his pocket, thinking about the green onions. He didn't like any kind of raw onions. He only liked cooked ones, so the idea of a green onion and cheese sandwich didn't appeal. But he was tempted to try one just on Lora Beth's recommendation. Only tempted, though.

He went into the kitchen, and even though he didn't want an onion and cheese sandwich, the thought of food made him hungry. He made himself a ham and swiss and poured a glass of iced tea, then sat down to eat.

After praying, he picked up the sandwich, then stilled. Normally he didn't pay attention to the silence in his house, but for some reason it was affecting him now. How many meals had he eaten alone since Paul left home? Of course, he could go to Paul and Susan's for supper anytime he wanted to. He had an open invitation to visit, and he stopped in to see his granddaughter, Lillian, every few days. But he limited showing up for a meal to two or three times a month. His son and his family had their own life to live, which was another reason he'd refused to move in with them.

But right now, he was feeling lonely. And for the first time, he didn't think about Elsie. He thought about Lora Beth.

The back door was open, and he was about to take a

bite of food when Paul knocked on the screen door. Ben motioned for him to come inside. "*Yer* ears must be burning," he said as his son sat down at the table.

Paul frowned. "What do you mean?"

"I was thinking about you, that's all. Want a sandwich?" He got up from the table.

Paul shook his head. "Susan's making supper. You're welcome to come if you want."

"Just don't bring éclair cake, *ya*?" Ben chuckled as he sat back down.

Paul's cheeks turned red. "I think we've all had our fill."

"I understand." Ben sipped his drink. "What brings you by?"

"Well, I want to let you know"—Paul started to grin—"We're having another *boppli*."

Ben knew he was beaming. "How wonderful. Another blessing from the Lord."

"*Ya*. Susan is about three months along. She's had a lot of morning sickness, though, and I didn't want you to worry if you didn't see her at a church service or two."

"I understand." He sat back in the chair. "That's great. I'm really happy for you both. I hope she gets over the sickness soon."

"So do I." Paul rubbed his thumb against the edge of the table, his smile dimming slightly. "Susan asked me to talk to you about something else too."

"Oh?"

"With the *boppli* coming, she could use *yer* help with the cooking and canning this fall. It was difficult to do it last year with Lillian under her feet, and she's been tired lately."

Ben recalled that Elsie had been tired the first months when she was pregnant with Paul. "I'll be happy to help."

"Susan said it would be easier if you were there more often. As in all the time."

He met his son's gaze. "Moving in, you mean."

Paul nodded. "She'd like that. So would I."

"We've gone over this before," Ben said. He remembered what he'd written to Lora Beth, about how he hoped Paul had decided to drop the idea of him moving in. Apparently his son had only put the idea on pause.

"I know, but the situation is different now. Susan could really use *yer* help. It's not easy for her mother to come from Kentucky because she still has children at home. She plans to help out for a few weeks after the *boppli* is born, but she can't up and leave just for cooking and canning."

Ben paused. He didn't have a problem with Paul and Susan asking him to help her with typically female-oriented chores. He'd never had a hang-up about women's and men's roles, and he would pitch in with any job when he was needed, something he'd always done with Elsie. But moving in? A minute ago, he'd felt the sting of loneliness, but that didn't mean he wanted to leave his home.

It was because I was missing Lora Beth.

The words had just popped into his head, surprising

him. Then he realized it was true. But how could he miss someone he'd met in person only once? Yet through their letters, he felt like he'd known her for a much longer time.

"*Daed?*"

Ben came out of his thoughts to see Paul frowning. "Sorry. Can I have time to think about it?"

Relief crossed his son's face. "Take all the time you need." He let out a puff of air. "I have to say I'm surprised. I thought you would say *nee* as soon as I asked."

"That wouldn't be fair to you and Susan. I'll think and pray on it. It's a big decision for me."

"I know." Paul rose from his chair. "I better get home, and I'll let Susan know what you said. She'll be glad you're taking the idea under consideration."

Ben walked Paul out, then returned to the kitchen. He stared at his sandwich, his appetite dulled. If it had been just Paul asking him to move in for the dozenth time, he would have immediately dismissed the idea. But this was different. Susan needed his help. It would be nice to spend more time with his granddaughter, too, as well as the new baby after it was born. *At what expense, though?*

He closed his eyes and asked God for wisdom and direction. When he finished praying, he'd almost had what he was going to do settled in his heart. But he wanted to get one more person's advice.

He went to the desk in his living room, pulled out a pad of paper and a pen, and began a letter to Lora Beth.

~

Lora Beth set Ben's most recent letter on the kitchen table and frowned. He'd explained his son's offer and had asked for her input. She glanced at the last paragraph again.

> I don't mean to put my dilemma on you, Lora Beth. But I do value your opinion, and I know you understand how I feel about leaving my home. What would you do if you were in my situation?

She got up from the table and went to the sink, intending to get a glass of water. Instead, she stared out the window, her gaze drifting to the oak tree in the middle of the front yard. She and Marvin had planted it right after they were married, and it had grown a few feet every year. It had a lot more growing to do before it reached the size of the surrounding trees, but that didn't matter to her. Each year she planted the prettiest annuals she could find around the base of the trunk, then added red mulch, Marvin's favorite.

She looked at the pink and coral impatiens, the purple pansies, and the red begonias that made a full and vibrant ring around her tree. *Our tree.* It was one of many things about her home she didn't want to leave.

But if one of her children needed her, she wouldn't hesitate. Quickly, she turned around and strode back to the table, then sat down to write.

Dear Ben,

I do realize how difficult a decision this is for you. But I also know how much you care about your family. I think you already know what you need to do—the same thing I would do.

She continued to write, asking him questions about his possible living arrangements at Paul's and suggesting that he take from his house everything most important to him. When she finished, she added,

If it will make things easier for you, I can come to Charm and help you with your move . . .

She paused. Was this a little too forward? Would he get the wrong idea if she made this offer? Her heart went out to him, and perhaps that was why she had written those words. But she didn't want to complicate their relationship. They were friends—technically only pen pals. Just because he asked her for advice about something so important didn't mean he wanted her to help him move.

Thankful she was using a pencil, not a pen, she erased the last sentence. Then she signed her name before putting the letter in an envelope. Once she'd placed a stamp in the corner, she stepped out to her mailbox. She said a quick, heartfelt prayer for Ben, then set the letter inside and lifted the flag.

As she was walking back to the house, an unfamiliar

buggy turned into her driveway, and she paused as it pulled to a stop. An Amish man about her age exited the vehicle and approached her.

"Are you Lora Beth?" he asked, stopping a few feet short of her.

"*Ya*," she said, on her guard. "And you are . . ."

"Ivan Nissley." He extended a beefy hand. "Wow," he said as she tentatively shook it. "*Mei schwester* was right. You sure are pretty."

Lora Beth released his hand and took a few steps back. "Do I know *yer schwester*?"

"*Ya*. She's Rosemary's mother-in-law."

She frowned. "I don't understand. I met Brenda's whole family at the wedding."

"You did." He grinned, the wrinkles around his gray eyes and above his full cheeks deepening. "Everyone but me."

CHAPTER 4

I'm sorry you had to meet him that way, *Mamm*."

Lora Beth diced potatoes as Rosemary tried to explain why Ivan Nissley had shown up out of the blue. She gripped the handle of the knife, still thrown by his arrival and forward demeanor. Shortly after he arrived, Rosemary had pulled into the driveway and scrambled out of a buggy Lora Beth realized moments later was Rachel's.

"LeRoy needs *yer* help at home, Ivan," Rosemary said while giving her mother an apologetic look. "He didn't realize you were heading over here right away."

"Couldn't wait to meet this pretty *maedel*." Ivan grinned, and while he had a nice smile, something about him was a little off. He seemed too eager. Eager for what, she had no idea. Fortunately, he left right after Rosemary asked him to, and now her daughter was trying to explain what was going on.

"Is he here to visit LeRoy?" Lora Beth asked, fumbling with the cutting board as she slid the potatoes into a colander. She set down the knife. She needed to settle down before she hurt herself. Turning to Rosemary, she said, "Or is there another reason he's in Ashtabula?"

Rosemary threaded her fingers together, averting her gaze. "Um, he wanted to visit *familye*." Then she looked up at Lora Beth. "And he wanted to meet you."

Lora Beth had been afraid of that. "Why?"

"I might have told him about you." Rosemary shifted her eyes again. "In a letter . . . or two."

She leaned against the kitchen sink. "I can't believe you would do that without telling me. Why didn't you say something?"

"Because you would have told me not to." She got up from the table and walked over to her. "*Mamm*, you discount everything Rachel, Rebecca, and I say to you."

"I do not—"

"There you *geh* again." Rosemary sighed. "*Mamm*, we worry about you rattling around in this *haus*. *Daed* has been gone a long time, but you're not moving on."

"I'm fine with *mei* life the way it is. And I'm definitely not ready to *meet* anyone." But her mind suddenly drifted to Ben. Her daughters had no idea she'd been corresponding with him, and she planned to keep it that way. Ben was only a friend, though. Rosemary—and she was sure by extension Rachel and Rebecca—wanted her to date, something she wasn't ready to do or was even interested in doing. "I'm too old for courtship."

"*Nee,* you're not. But you're using *yer* age as an excuse."

"Excuse?" Lora Beth rarely lost her temper, but she could feel anger rising. "You're making a lot of suppositions about me. Unfair ones, at that."

Rosemary nodded, glancing down at her feet. "I'm sorry. You're right. But would you at least consider meeting him again, this time properly? We planned to have you over for supper with Rachel and Rebecca's families this Friday. You never know, *Mamm.* You might end up liking Ivan. But you'll never know unless you give him a chance."

Lora Beth wasn't sure what to say. She knew her daughters well enough to know that if it wasn't Ivan, they would find some other single man to fix her up with. The only thing she had in her corner was that very few Amish men in their forties and fifties were single. She needed time to think about it. "I'll let you know. That's all I can agree to right now."

"All right." Rosemary smiled. "We just want what's best for you, *Mamm.* I hope you know that."

She opened her mouth to speak, then shut it. She was tired of having this conversation, and she wished her girls would drop this idea. But they seemed intent on forcing the issue.

"I have to get back home," Rosemary said. She gave

Lora Beth a quick hug. "*Danki* for at least thinking about it after what happened today. And if Friday doesn't work, we can do it another time. Ivan will be here for three weeks, at least. He and his *bruder* run a logging company, and he's been wanting to come to Ashtabula to check out the woods here in the northeast part of Ohio."

When Lora Beth didn't respond, she added, "I'll talk to you later."

Rosemary slipped out the back door, and Lora Beth slid onto one of her well-worn kitchen chairs. She had no idea what to do. For some reason she hadn't been able to convince her children that she was fine. But she had to do something, or they would be fixing her up with every single man her age within a fifty-mile radius.

After thinking about the situation, she decided she could turn to only one person. He, of all people, would understand. She had to write to Ben.

~

A few days later, Ben stared at Lora Beth's letter, then reread it again. What he thought would be one of her pleasant and enjoyable letters was much different, and it inexplicably filled him with anxiety.

Dear Ben,

My daughters are trying to set me up with one of LeRoy's relatives. I met him briefly earlier today, and

I don't know much about him except he's in the logging business. The girls have planned this out, and they want me to come to supper on Friday to get to know him better. Even if I turn them down for this time, Ivan will be here for three weeks. I know they won't stop until we've met—and possibly have a date.

I don't know what to do. They're worried about me being lonely, and I can't tell them that I'm not, because sometimes I am. I guess since I refused to move in with one of them, they're trying to marry me off. I'd laugh at the idea, except they're serious. Even if I do refuse to meet Ivan, they'll find someone else. I'm sure of it.

I'm at a loss. What do you think I should do?

Lora Beth

Ben lowered the letter and put one palm over his heart. He frowned as it pounded. But why? Why did learning that Lora Beth's daughters were determined to see their mother remarry make him feel so unsettled? Lora Beth didn't want this, but he knew there was something more to it, something lurking below the surface of his feelings. Because the thought of her dating Ivan or any other man was making him angry.

A knock sounded on the screen door, and Menno walked into the living room. "Hey, Ben. I want you to know that I went to an auction last week, but I bought only one thing." He sat down on the couch across from

Ben's chair. "Isn't that an improvement? Fannie didn't think so, and I want you to set her straight." He paused. "Ben? Are you okay?"

Ben blinked, and Menno came into focus. "What?"

"You're white as a sheet, like you've seen a ghost or something. Not that I believe in ghosts, of course. But something has you way out of sorts."

He nodded, barely hearing Menno's rambling. He looked at the letter again. Lora Beth wanted his advice, and she needed to hear from him right away. It was Tuesday, and if he wrote her right now and went straight to the post office, she would get his letter by tomorrow, Thursday at the latest.

"All right," Menno said, tapping the heel of his work boot on the floor. "Tell me all about it."

Ben shook his head. His letter-writing relationship with Lora Beth was private. "I'm fine," he said, waving his hand and shoving the letter into his pocket. "What did you say about Fannie?"

"Never mind Fannie." Menno's gaze bore into him. "You're upset about something. I want to know what it is. You've been a *gut* friend to me, and I'm here to return the favor."

He started to shake his head again, then blew out a breath and told Menno about Lora Beth. "We're just friends," Ben said. "I want to make that clear."

"Uh-huh." The older man's expression was unreadable. "*Geh* on."

Ben explained about her daughters' intention to marry Lora Beth off. "It's not right," he said. "She's explained she's fine with living alone."

"Just like you are."

"*Ya*. Just like me. But that's about to change. I'll be moving in with Paul soon."

"Really?" Menno's bushy brows shot up. "Didn't see that coming."

"Me either. The *kinner* need *mei* help, though."

"To do what?" After Ben told him why he was moving in, Menno shook his head. "You got duped, I see."

Ben frowned. "What?"

"You think a *maedel* like Susan isn't capable of handling two *kinner* and keeping *haus* at the same time?" He chuckled. "It's a ruse. I'm surprised a bright *mann* like *yerself* didn't see it."

"They said they needed me," Ben muttered. Now that Menno had pointed it out, though, he could see the man was possibly right. "I wanted to help."

"They do need you. And I'm sure they would appreciate any help you offer. But their idea of you moving in? They think that's more for *yer* benefit than theirs." He leaned back on the couch and tugged at his beard. "Now, about this Lora Beth. You need to *geh* after her."

Ben's jaw dropped. "Why would you say that?"

"Because if she marries Ivan or someone else, that's the end of *yer* friendship . . . if indeed that's what it really is between you two."

234

"It is," Ben said, insistent. But Menno was right about one thing. He'd lose Lora Beth's friendship if she remarried. There would be no more letters, and he couldn't stomach the idea of not writing to her anymore. But his hands were tied. "I can't stop her from marrying someone if she wants to."

"True. But it's clear from what you're saying that she doesn't want to date Ivan or anyone else. I reckon she's a lot like you, though, and she'll put her own feelings aside to make her *kinner* happy."

"Or to get them off her back." Ben didn't believe Lora Beth would go as far as getting married to appease her daughters, but she would go on a date or three if it would make them happy. He rubbed the sides of his fists over his pants.

"I can see that idea sticks in *yer* craw." Menno grinned. "Seems like you've taken more than a friendly shine to her." Before he could deny it, the man added, "Doesn't matter, though. Lora Beth needs someone in her corner right now. It's three against one."

Ben nodded. Menno was right. It wasn't fair that her daughters were ganging up on her, even though their intentions were good. He stood and started for the door.

"Where are you going?" Menno called.

Ben answered over his shoulder. "To make a taxi reservation and then ask *mei* neighbors if they'll care for *mei* horse and water *mei* garden."

Lora Beth needs me. And he would be there for her.

235

~

Lora Beth wrung her hands as she sat in her buggy near the end of Rosemary's driveway. She wished her daughters had let her host tonight's supper. Her house was larger, and she could use the excuse of being busy to keep from having to make small talk—or any kind of talk—with Ivan.

But she couldn't sit out here forever. She said a prayer, asking God to make the evening go well—and quickly. A bit of guilt pricked her. She wanted little to do with Ivan. He could be a nice man, for all she knew, but that didn't make her any more enthusiastic about this.

She had hoped to hear from Ben by now, but then she realized that unless he'd replied to her letter right away, she wouldn't have. Maybe she would get a letter from him tomorrow, but that did little good now. Still, once she got through tonight, she wanted to know what Ben thought she should do in the future if her children continued their matchmaking. His opinion meant a lot to her.

She took a deep breath and got out of the buggy, then looped the reins over the hitching post near the barn before retrieving the plate of chocolate whoopie pies she'd made that morning. The sun was low in the sky, but the temperature was still high enough that perspiration broke out on her forehead. *Or maybe it's because of* mei *nerves.*

She'd just headed for the front door when a car whipped into the driveway. She watched as an Amish man scrambled out of the front passenger door, slung a back-pack over his shoulder, then quickly waved off the driver. As the man neared, her heart started to thrum. "Ben?" she said, hurrying toward him. They stopped in the middle of the driveway and gaped at each other.

Finally, Lora Beth found her words. "What are you doing here?"

Ben shoved his hands into his pants pockets. "I, uh, came to help you."

"I don't understand."

Wariness entered his eyes. "In *yer* letter, you said you didn't want to have supper with Ivan tonight. That *was* tonight, wasn't it?"

She nodded. "*Ya.* But I didn't expect you to come here. How did you find Rosemary's address?"

"*Mei* friend Menno—he's the one with the spend-ing problem—has at least ten years of Amish directories stashed in one of his barns. He'd picked up the latest one last month. For once I was happy he made an impulse purchase."

The screen door of the house opened, and Lora Beth turned around to see Rosemary and Rebecca stepping outside. "*Mamm?*" Rosemary said, frowning as she stood at the top of the porch steps.

"Is everything all right?" Rebecca asked.

"*Ya,*" Lora Beth said, then swallowed hard. "Every-thing is fine." She turned to Ben. "What are we going to do?" she said in a low voice.

He frowned. "Uh, I kind of hadn't thought this far."

"I can see that." She glanced over her shoulder and saw her daughters walking toward them. She had to come up with something fast. She spun on her heel and forced a smile. "Would it be all right if we had another guest for supper?"

"Sure," Rosemary said, her voice friendly but her expression wary. "There's always plenty extra."

"Rosemary, Rebecca," Lora Beth said, gesturing to Ben, "this is Benjamin Troyer. I met him at that wedding I attended when I was in Charm a while back. His niece was getting married."

"You look familiar," Rebecca said, her expression a bit confused.

"Weren't you at the ox roast in Mespo?" Rosemary asked.

"Right," Rebecca said, nodding. "You were selling that knife set."

"And the pretty lamp," Rosemary added. "We wanted to buy the knife set for *Mamm*, but she said *nee*." She glanced at her mother. "*Mamm* hasn't mentioned you."

Lora Beth's face heated as she looked at Ben, hoping he didn't feel insulted. Rosemary wasn't being rude on purpose, but her words weren't all that kind either.

"That's all right," he said, his expression cheerful. "We haven't known each other that long." He glanced at Lora Beth, a knowing look in his eyes.

"And I'd forgotten that I'd invited him to visit me

this weekend." Lora Beth slapped her forehead with exaggeration. "Silly me."

Ben nodded. "And when she wasn't home, I . . . I . . ." Panic entered his eyes as he tried to come up with an explanation for how he'd known he'd find her at Rosemary's.

The screen door burst open, and Ivan came out. "What's the holdup?" he said, coming down the stairs with heavy steps. "The men are hungry."

LeRoy trailed after his uncle, looking almost apologetic. "We were wondering what was taking you so long."

"A man could starve waiting on you hens to finish talking." Ivan's eyes locked on the platter Lora Beth had tucked in the curve of her arm. "Are those whoopie pies?" He reached for them.

Shocked that he would invade her personal space like this, she took a step back.

"Oh, you're shy, then," Ivan said, then guffawed. "That's all right. I like a shy *maedel*."

Ben stepped in front of her and extended his hand to Ivan. "Hello, I'm Benjamin Troyer. I'm a friend of Lora Beth's."

Ivan looked at his hand, then gave it a hard shake while obviously noting his backpack. "Ivan Nissley. Nice to meet you. Where are you from?"

"Charm. I hear you're in the logging business. I'm an accountant. How's business going for you these days?"

Lora Beth's mouth dropped open as Ben smoothly

guided Ivan back to the house. Then she turned to Rosemary and Rebecca, who stared after the two men, both looking dumbfounded. "I'm sorry," she said.

Her daughters both turned toward her, Rebecca crossing her arms. "You've got some explaining to do, *Mamm*."

"But first," Rosemary piped in, "I have to apologize." She let out a long sigh. "I had *nee* idea Ivan was like this. LeRoy tried to warn me . . ." She leaned forward. "He's been driving me crazy all week. I can see why he's still single."

Lora Beth couldn't help but laugh, which broke the tension. "I'll explain about Ben later." She looked at the house. "Right now, I think he might need saving."

"Oh, I don't know." Rebecca grinned. "He seems able to manage Ivan all right. But I'm dying to know the real reason he's here."

Lora Beth said nothing as they walked toward the house, but she was dying to know the real reason too.

CHAPTER 5

After supper, Ben privately offered to drive Lora Beth home in her buggy, ignoring the inquisitive stares of her three daughters, who, he had discovered, were just as kind and sweet as their mother. Fortunately, Lora Beth agreed to let him. And when Ivan suggested she take a little walk down the road with him, she'd said, "I already told Ben he could take me home."

Ben felt a little sorry for the guy at that moment, as he'd looked genuinely disappointed. But he was also relieved that Lora Beth and Ivan hadn't hit it off. He couldn't imagine her with someone so loud, large, and a little too ignorant when it came to personal space. Ivan was a good guy, but he was just too . . . much.

And he still didn't like the thought of Lora Beth with

any man, and that feeling had intensified when he helped her into the buggy. It was dusk, and the fading sunlight illuminated her face, which was just as pretty as he remembered. But he was also feeling something different that both pleased and unsettled him. He cleared his throat as he put his backpack behind the buggy seat and stepped inside.

"Well," she said, glancing at him, "that was an interesting meal."

"It definitely was." He guided the horse out of Rosemary and LeRoy's driveway. "I enjoyed meeting *yer* daughters. They're fine people, as are their husbands."

Lora Beth smiled, and his heart skipped a beat. That had to be because he'd been able to help her tonight. Helping a friend. Yes, that was all it was.

"I hope you're not too upset that I dropped by unexpectedly," he said.

"*Nee*. It's *gut* to see you again. I'm just confused."

So am I. He cleared his throat again. "I listened to Menno, and I probably shouldn't have."

"*Yer* friend with holes in his pockets."

Ben chuckled. "The very one. Anyway, after talking to him, I thought you might have needed a little more help than just some advice in a letter."

"It turns out I did." She looked at him. "I can't believe you came all the way here just to be a buffer between me and Ivan."

"You're only a couple of hours away by taxi," he said.

"That's still a long ride." She paused. "Where are you staying tonight?"

"At a bed and breakfast in Harpersfield."

She nodded. "It's a *gut* one." Then she didn't say anything for a long moment.

"I'll be leaving in the morning," he said.

She nodded, but she still didn't say anything. Now that they were away from Ivan and the matchmakers, he wondered if she was uncomfortable with him being here. He had surprised her out of the blue, and now he realized he'd overreacted a bit. This was the last time he was taking Menno's advice.

She gave him directions to her house, and when they arrived, he pulled into her driveway and steered the buggy to the barn. "I'll be glad to put the horse up for you," he said.

"That would be nice."

"And when I'm finished, I'll call a taxi to take me to the B and B." He started to get out of the buggy but stopped when she put her hand on his arm. He looked at her, and the expression on her face made his heart race again.

"Would you mind staying for a little bit?" she said, her voice almost timid. "I can make some tea. Or *kaffee* if you'd like."

"*Kaffee* sounds *gut*."

She smiled. "See you in a little bit." Then she climbed out of the buggy, taking her empty platter with her.

Ben's heart thumped harder. *Oh nee.* He recognized

this feeling. Attraction. The same feeling he'd had with Elsie but different. Much different. Menno had been right after all . . . and that was a problem.

～

Lora Beth's hands shook a little as she poured two mugs of coffee. She hadn't felt like this since Marvin. But although she'd had intense feelings for her husband, they'd been different from her attraction to Ben. Ben had been a lively conversationalist at supper, and he'd kept Ivan occupied with more questions about his business and the various people they were both acquainted with in Holmes County. She'd discovered two new things about Ben as well—he enjoyed doing crossword puzzles and playing ping-pong.

But what had really touched her was that he'd come all the way from Charm to help her. She'd expected only his advice, never imagining he would go to the trouble of coming in person. Although her dilemma had been a big deal to her, she never thought it would be a big deal for Ben. Yet she was so thankful he'd been here. She wouldn't have to worry about Ivan again.

Ben knocked on the screen door, carrying his backpack. She let him in, butterflies flittering around her stomach.

He smiled. "Where can I wash up?" he asked.

She showed him where the bathroom was, then put the coffee mugs on the table along with a bowl of sugar and a small pitcher of milk. She didn't even know how Ben took his coffee. There was so much to learn about him, yet she felt like she knew him well.

When he returned, he sat down at the table and set his pack on the floor. "*Danki*," he said, lifting his mug and taking a sip.

"You take *yer kaffee* black, then?"

"Sometimes. Depends on *mei* mood. I'm not opposed to a little sugar."

"I like mine with lots of sugar and milk." She added three teaspoons of sugar and a large pour of milk to her mug. Then she took a sip and looked at him. He was staring at the coffee mug, looking pensive. She frowned as the awkward silence stretched between them. "You'll like the bed and breakfast," she said, grasping for anything she could think of to get the conversation going.

"So you told me." He looked at her, concern in his eyes.

She realized that, while these burgeoning feelings she was experiencing were new, she was too old to be coy. "Ben, is something wrong?"

"I . . . I don't know." He lifted his gaze and met hers. "When we first started writing to each other, I didn't think it would lead to anything. But I've been grateful for *yer* friendship. When you said you didn't want to be forced into dating anyone, I had to come here. I didn't want you going through that hardship. But now I'm wondering if something else is happening . . . between us."

A lump formed in her throat. "Me too."

He leaned forward. "Then you're also feeling something?"

She nodded, her heart rate increasing. "*Ya*. I'm confused, too, Ben. I also value *yer* friendship, and I don't want to lose that."

"I don't want to lose yours."

"But now that you're here"—she lowered her gaze, her cheeks heating—"And I'm seeing you in person . . ."

"Things are different."

"*Ya*." She looked at him. "In a *gut* way."

He grinned. "What should we do?"

"I don't know."

Tentatively, he took her hand in his. "Is this okay?"

She nodded. His hand wasn't work-worn like Marvin's had been. But Ben worked hard in a different way. He was a successful accountant, an accomplished gardener and cook, and he helped others at the drop of a hat. "Elsie was a lucky woman," she said, the words slipping out. Yet they were the truth.

"And Marvin was a lucky man." He released her hand. "I've got to be honest. This is throwing me for a loop. I'm not going to move in with Paul after all. They don't need me like I thought they did. But I've got a *grandboppli* and a new one on the way too."

"I'm settled in *mei* life here as well."

He ran his finger over the mug's curved handle. "But I can't see things between us going back to the way they were."

Lora Beth clasped her hands together, already missing his touch, but knowing he was right. "Me either. I think we both need to pray about what our next step is."

"*Ya*," he said softly. "We do." He paused, his gaze intently holding hers. "I should *geh* now."

"I think that's a *gut* idea. I'll *geh* to the phone shanty and call a taxi for you."

"*Danki.*"

Lora Beth got up from the table and resisted looking at Ben again. Her chest squeezed as she hurried to the phone shanty at the end of her driveway. She didn't want him to leave so soon, but she also knew it was the right thing to do. They both had thinking and praying to do—and lots of it.

When she returned to the house, Ben was at the sink washing out the coffee mugs. "I hope you don't mind," he said, putting the last one in the dish drainer. "Force of habit."

She couldn't help but smile as he dried his hands. He was so courteous. "The taxi will be here in a few minutes."

"I'll wait for it outside." He lifted his backpack and looked at her. "I'd like to drop by in the morning and say good-bye, if that's all right with you."

"Of course."

He nodded. "*Gute nacht*, Lora Beth." He hesitated, then walked out of the kitchen to the front of the house. A minute later she heard the door shut.

When she stepped into the living room to make sure

the door had latched closed, she looked out the window and saw the taxi pull into her driveway. Ben got into the car, and she watched as the driver made his way to the end of the driveway, then onto the road.

What am I going to do, Lord? A simple friendship, begun with a recipe for éclair cake, had just become very, *very* complicated.

~

As soon as Ben returned home from Ashtabula, he saw Menno sitting on the front porch of his house, carving a bar of soap. Ben paid the taxi driver and slung his backpack over his shoulder. He was tired from not sleeping a wink last night, and when he told Lora Beth good-bye this morning, it had taken everything he had to leave her. His mind and emotions were still whirring after the car ride. Dealing with Menno was the last thing he had the energy to do.

Still, he managed to smile as he approached the older man. It wasn't his fault Ben was tired. Then again, maybe it was—partly. If he hadn't listened to him, he wouldn't have gone to Ashtabula. He wouldn't have these feelings that both thrilled and terrified him. One minute his life was set, and the next it was upside down. He didn't like that one bit.

"How'd it *geh*?" Menno asked without looking up.

Ben sat down on the top porch step. "Confusing,"

he said. There was no reason to hide anything from his friend now.

"As expected." Menno set the soap in his lap. "Women are confusing creatures. Can't live with them, can't live without them."

"I think Fannie would say the same thing about you," Ben mumbled.

He chuckled. "That she would. So, tell me what you're confused about."

Ben closed his eyes and rested the back of his head against the wood pole holding up the front porch awning. "Everything. I never thought I would have these feelings again."

"What feelings are those?"

Ben opened one eye. "Do I really have to tell you?"

Menno picked up the soap again. "I guess not. You've fallen in love, eh?"

"Not love. That takes time and proximity. You can't fall in love with someone through just a few letters and two meetings in person."

"Who says?"

"Common sense does."

"And common sense has what to do with love?" He scraped a thick slice of soap from the bar, and suddenly the soap started to look like a duck. "Fannie married me. That right there is a reason to question her common sense."

From the twinkle in Menno's eye, Ben knew he was joking. But that didn't ease his mind. "I have family here.

She has family there. We're in our forties, for Pete's sake. Neither one of us likes change very much."

"Well, there's *yer* answer. End the relationship."

Menno's words felt like a stab to the heart. "I can't do that."

"Why not? You just laid out why a future relationship is moot."

"Because . . ." Ben hung his head. "I like her, Menno. I like her a lot. I feel more alive since meeting her than I have in a long time. But there are too many complications."

"If you're meant to be together, God will make it so, even if there's a mountain separating you." Menno closed his penknife and stuffed that and his soap in his pocket. "You'll figure it out, with the Lord's help. Now, how about we talk about me? Fannie's threatening to move in with her *schwester* in Millersburg."

"Really?"

Menno nodded, and Ben realized he was really worried for the first time. "I can't let that happen. I don't know what I'd do without her."

Ben sat up and looked at him. "Then you have a decision to make. It's either *yer* stuff and *yer* shopping, or it's her."

"I know, I know. But when I think about getting rid of *mei* things, I get anxious. And I know I shouldn't be anxious for anything, but I am when it comes to this. I've made an idol out of *mei* possessions, Ben. I don't know how it happened, but it did."

Ben tapped his finger on his chin. "Maybe we're going about this the wrong way. We've been focusing on you stopping *yer* spending and selling *yer* things to get you out of the red and some savings. You have to stop spending. That's nonnegotiable. But what if you gave away *yer* things? What if you figured out who can benefit from what you have?"

"I'm not sure that will work. *Mei kinner* don't even want *mei* things."

"Just because they don't doesn't mean other people wouldn't. There are always needs that need to be met, Menno. You just have to open *yer* eyes to them. For example, Andy Kaufmann can use a few more milk cans, and I saw several in the back of that spare barn I helped you with. You can clean them up and give them to him. I know he'd appreciate it."

Menno lifted one bushy brow. "That just might work. I should have thought of that before." He looked at Ben. "I could use *yer* help figuring out who needs what, though."

"On one condition."

"What's that?" he said, sounding suspicious. "Last time I agreed to one of *yer* conditions, I ended up buying a box of nails."

"That wasn't *mei* fault," Ben said, laughing. Then he sobered. "*Mei* condition is simple. You don't buy anything else, not one single thing, until both barns are cleaned out. Then you'll tear them down and donate the wood. If you don't have room to put things, you won't buy them."

Menno groaned and put his hand over his chest. "You're driving a hard bargain, Benjamin Troyer. You know that?"

"I do. But if you want to keep Fannie with you, you have to make the sacrifice. Besides, this is *gut* for *yer* soul. You said it *yerself*, *yer* things are *yer* idol, and you and I both know we're not supposed to have any of those in our lives."

Menno got up from the chair. "You're right on both counts. Can you come to *mei* place Monday morning so I can get started? Unless you'll be busy with work."

"I don't have to see any clients until the afternoon, so I'll be there." Ben rose from the step. "You won't regret this, Menno, even though it will be hard."

"Humph."

"See you tomorrow," Ben called, grinning as Menno descended the porch steps.

"*Humph.*"

Ben watched as Menno got into his buggy and left, then he sat down in the porch chair his friend had just vacated. The day's heat was already rising, and he could use a cool drink. But his mind drifted to what Menno said. He and Lora Beth had agreed to pray about their relationship, but did he really believe God could overcome all the obstacles in front of them? He'd been so doubtful on the ride home, which wasn't helping. But doubting was the exact opposite of what he should be doing—and not just because he cared for Lora Beth.

He closed his eyes and put all his trust and belief in the Lord. If it was meant to be with him and Lora Beth, God would make a way. And if he and Lora Beth didn't have a future together, he would accept that too.

CHAPTER 6

I can't believe you didn't tell us about Ben," Rachel said when she and her sisters all burst into Lora Beth's kitchen.

"*Gute morgen* to you too." Lora Beth sat down with the bottle of syrup in her hand, the syrup she intended to pour over the short stack of pancakes she'd made for her late breakfast. She rarely had sweets for her morning meal, but after telling Ben good-bye and not knowing if she'd see him again, she'd immediately gone to the pantry for the sweet stuff.

"How long have you known him?" Rebecca demanded.

"Have you been writing letters?" Rosemary said. She gasped. "Don't tell me you two have been talking on the phone. That's against the *Ordnung*, you know."

"What are his intentions?" Rachel said, crossing her arms.

"One question at a time." Lora Beth looked at the pancakes, then pushed them away. Glad they didn't already have the syrup on them, since she'd have to heat them up later. "First, let me remind all three of you that you didn't mention Ivan to me."

All three women shrank back a bit. "We said we were sorry about that," Rosemary said.

"I know. And I forgive you. I'm also sorry I never told you about Ben, but there wasn't much to tell."

"That's not what I saw last night. You two couldn't keep *yer* eyes off each other." Rebecca smirked. "Even when Ben was talking with Ivan, he was still casting glances at you."

"Which is romantic, when you think about it." Rachel sighed.

"There's *nix* romantic between us." But that wasn't true, and she knew it. From the doubtful look all her daughters were giving her, they didn't believe it either.

Rosemary scoffed. "*Mamm*, he wouldn't have come all the way from Charm to rescue you from a date with a man if he didn't have romantic intentions."

"So last night was a date? I thought I was just supposed to get to know Ivan."

"Rebecca might have implied to Ivan that it was something more," Rosemary said, grimacing at her sister.

"Great, put the blame on me. He's *yer* relative, remember?"

"*Maed*, that's enough." Lora Beth put her fingertips to her forehead. She was tired, having tossed and turned the night before, and when she had slept, she'd dreamed about Ben. One minute, he was there, holding her hand. The next minute, he had disappeared, and she couldn't find him. Then she woke up and couldn't get back to sleep. "If you ever decide to match me up with anyone again, please give me advance notice."

"I don't think we have to anymore." Rebecca smiled.

"Are you moving to Charm? Or is he moving here?" Rosemary asked.

Rebecca's smile dimmed. "I didn't think about that." She turned to her sisters. "Obviously, he'll move here."

"Or maybe *Mamm* wants to move to Charm," Rachel said.

"I'm not moving anywhere." Lora Beth sighed. "Look, Ben and I are . . . We're *gut* friends." That was the truth. Maybe not the whole truth, but she didn't want to go there with her daughters. "At the wedding in Charm, he asked me for the recipe for my éclair cake, and I sent it to him. Now we write to each other occasionally." More like every few days, but she didn't want to add more fuel to the fire the girls were already stoking. "As two people who've lost their spouses and like to cook and bake, we have something in common. That's all there is to it."

All three girls pinned their gaze on her. "Right. Just friends," they said in unison.

Lora Beth hesitated. How could she lie to her children? "Maybe a little more," she squeaked.

"I knew it," Rebecca said, her face beaming.

"But we have a lot to think and pray about when it comes to a relationship. At our age, it isn't easy to just start over." Her chest squeezed. "We can't just think about ourselves. We both have *kinner* and *grosskinner*. He has a job. I have *mei* life here. *Yung* people can be impulsive. We can't."

Her daughters, for once, were silent.

"*Mamm*," Rebecca finally said, "don't let us keep you from Ben. Charm isn't that far, and there would be plenty of visits."

"We haven't had one date yet," Lora Beth said. "That's jumping ahead a bit, don't you think?"

"You know we want you to be happy." Rosemary had tears in her eyes. "That's all we ever wanted."

Rachel nodded. "If Ben makes you happy, then you can't let that slip away. *Daed* wouldn't want you to."

Tears trailed down Lora Beth's face. "*Danki*," she said. "It's *gut* to know that I have *yer* blessing if the time comes."

"Or *when* the time comes." Rebecca grinned.

"Don't pressure her," Rosemary said.

"I'm not pressuring her."

As the sisters bickered, Lora Beth smiled. She was happy to have such wonderful *kinner* who gave their support so willingly. But that didn't make her decision any easier.

A short while later, her daughters left, with Rachel leaving last. She hugged Lora Beth. "Remember what you said to me before *mei* wedding?"

She shook her head. "What was that?"

"You said time moves fast and to cherish every moment with Uriah. Which I do."

"I had forgotten all about that."

Rachel smiled. "If Ben is *yer* second chance, you shouldn't waste a minute, *ya*? That's what you would tell me and *mei schwesters*."

Lora Beth didn't answer, but after Rachel left, she thought about her daughter's words and about all her daughters' support. Perhaps that was God's way of telling her she was free to move on.

She spent some time in prayer at the kitchen table, then got out her stationery.

~

By the end of Tuesday, Ben and Menno had managed to sift through a third of Menno's barn. Fannie was excited about the idea of giving things away, and she'd pitched in. She'd also gathered some items to take to a friend of hers. Before she left, she pulled Ben aside. "*Danki* for being a *gut* friend and helping Menno with this."

"*Nee* need to thank me," Ben said.

Fannie pushed up her glasses, tears in her eyes. "But I do. I don't think anyone else would have the patience to help him work through this. I know I ran out of patience long ago. He's always been creative, picking up things here and there and coming up with ideas for how to use them. But when Brian passed away five years ago, things began to get out of hand."

Ben nodded. Menno and Fannie's grandson had died in a drowning accident. It had been tragic for everyone in the community. Menno had held his feelings close to his chest, but now with Fannie's explanation, Ben thought he understood why the man had struggled so much with spending and hoarding.

"He even said last night that he was going to have everything cleared out by the end of the summer." Fannie smiled. "I didn't think I'd ever hear those words. It seems the key was to focus his attention on something else— giving instead of hoarding."

As Ben walked home from Menno's house, he felt satisfied that he'd been able to help his friend who was struggling more than he imagined. But that satisfaction hadn't fully replaced his thoughts about Lora Beth. Working through Menno's stash had been a distraction, but now that he was alone, she came instantly to mind. He missed her. He couldn't deny that. And he had prayed for wisdom over the past few days. More than once he'd started a letter to her but couldn't finish it. Now his fear wasn't of starting the relationship—it was of being rejected. What if she decided it couldn't work out between them?

He grimaced as he stopped by the mailbox. This was one reason he'd steered clear of getting involved with a woman again. He couldn't go through the heartache a romantic relationship could cause. He'd suffered enough when Elsie died.

He opened the mailbox and pulled out its contents. On top of his gas bill was a letter from Lora Beth. His heart began to pound, and he tucked the bill under his arm and opened the letter.

Dear Ben,

I hope this letter finds you well. I've been thinking and praying a lot about our situation.

Ben's heart fell, and he stopped reading. She sounded so formal, so distant. He folded the paper and went into the house, where he set the letter on the table, then sat down and stared at it. He could hear the pounding of his heart in his ears. He knew what she was going to say. After a long time sitting in silence, he picked up the letter with dread.

I know things are complicated, not just between us but also in our individual lives. But I believe God brought us together for a reason, and it wasn't just because you liked my éclair cake. I'd like to keep writing to each other and see where things go.

I miss you, Ben. I miss your letters, and I miss seeing you.

Warmly,
Lora Beth

Ben stood and let out a whoop, then looked around and felt foolish because he was alone. He reread her letter, unable to stop smiling. She hadn't cut him loose after all. She was open to what the future might hold for them, and so was he.

He scrambled to get pen and paper, and then he started to write.

EPILOGUE

ONE YEAR LATER

L ora Beth and Ben entered their home for the first time
as a married couple, holding hands. Their wedding
had been a week ago, and they'd spent the time since visiting family in both Ashtabula and Charm. But their new
house wasn't in either town. They'd decided to move to
Middlefield, which put them between Lora Beth's family
and Ben's.

The furnishings were a combination of belongings
from their old houses, which were both waiting to be sold.
The new house was small, but with three bedrooms, they
had enough space for their children and grandchildren to
visit. And they were both excited to make new friends in a
new community while staying in touch with their former

communities. Ben led Lora Beth to the couch, and they sat down.

"I'll get the suitcases in a minute," Ben said. He ran his thumb over the back of Lora Beth's hand and leaned his head against the couch back. "It's been a long week."

"That it has, but a *gut* one." She shivered at her husband's touch. They had taken their courtship slow, so both they and their children could adjust to such a big change. Lora Beth had spent time in Charm, and she especially enjoyed getting to know Menno and Fannie, and, of course, Paul's family. And her daughters had welcomed Ben with open arms, especially when he didn't hesitate to play with Katrina and Rosetta on the floor.

But after all the visiting and family time, it was nice to be alone. She sighed and closed her eyes.

"Happy?" Ben said.

"Very." She turned to him and smiled. "I never thought I would be this happy again."

"Me either." He turned toward her and cupped her chin in his hand. "I didn't believe in second chances, Lora Beth. Until I met you." He leaned forward and kissed her sweetly. "I love you."

She leaned her head on his shoulder, eager to start their new life together. "I love you too."

NEVER TOO LATE

CHAPTER 1

‿

Elva Gingerich set her blueberry pie on the table and glanced around the area, feeling her nerves on edge and perspiring a little despite the cooler fall air. She wished her friend Regina hadn't talked her into participating in this pie-baking competition, especially since she was only visiting this small community in Millersburg.

"It's all in fun," Regina had said yesterday as she pinched the crust around her rhubarb and strawberry pie. "It's more about eating the pies than awarding a prize—a blue ribbon."

"But you do determine a winner, *ya?*" Elva forced herself to stop wringing her hands to stir her blueberry filling.

"*Ya.* The ribbon gets passed from last year's winner

to this year's winner. Then we slice all the pies and share them. Everyone has a great time."

Right now, as she waited along with the other women who'd entered the contest—most she barely knew—she wasn't enjoying herself like they were. They were eagerly waiting for the judges to approach the table while she fought to quash her anxiety.

Over the years, she and Regina, a childhood friend, had kept in touch through letters. But when Elva's husband, Henry, passed away two years ago, Regina paid her a visit. Elva was now returning the favor, a decision she'd made on the spur of the moment, just happening to come when Regina's community had their annual fall picnic. She'd enjoyed her visit with Regina and her husband, Nelson, so far. Except for today. She should have stood her ground and said she wasn't going to enter the contest. But Elva wasn't used to standing her ground, and it hadn't taken much persuasion from Regina for her to capitulate.

"I'm sure *yer* pie will win," Regina said, leaning over and whispering. "When you gave me a taste of that filling yesterday, I knew the rest of us didn't have a chance."

"But I don't want to win." *I don't even want to be here.*

Regina looked at her, adjusting her glasses. Her gray hair peeked out from beneath her *kapp*. She might be sixty-five, but Regina had always been young at heart, and she looked much younger, with very few wrinkles on her smooth skin. "I knew you were going to say that."

She patted Elva's hand. "Relax and enjoy this." Then she paused. "Uh-oh."

"What do you mean, uh-oh?"

"I thought he was in Kentucky visiting his relatives." Regina frowned. "Hold on to *yer kapp*."

"What are you talking about?" Now wasn't a good time to feel bewildered.

A short man with a balding head, a little older-looking than Elva and Regina, approached. He smiled across his clean-shaven face, revealing teeth that were a little crooked. But his blue eyes held a pleasant twinkle. "Hello, Regina," he said, eyeing her pie.

"I thought you were visiting *familye*, Jerald," Regina said, her tone a little curt.

"Now, you know I wouldn't miss judging the pie contest for anything. Planned *mei* visit short just to be here." He licked his lips and looked at Elva's blueberry pie. "Oh, that looks scrumptious." He lifted his gaze, and when he met hers, surprise entered his eyes. "Who are you?"

"Elva's a friend of mine." Regina moved the blueberry pie back an inch. "She's here visiting."

"I see." Jerald held out his hand. "Jerald Byler. Pleased to meet you." He eyed her pie again. "Can't wait to taste that delicious-looking dessert."

"You'll have to cool *yer* heels, because the judging hasn't started yet." Regina sighed and waved her hands at him. "Now shoo! You'll get *yer* taste in a little bit."

Jerald rolled his eyes, then looked at Elva again. "I

don't know how you put up with her bossiness," he said in a loud whisper while pointing his thumb at Regina.

"I heard that, Jerald."

Ignoring that remark, he took a place at the end of the table, where the rest of the judges were lining up.

"He can be such a pest sometimes," Regina said. "Nelson has been friends with him since they were *kinner.* That's the only reason I put up with him."

Jerald was in the middle of the line, but he was hard to see because of his height. "He looks harmless to me."

"He is, for the most part. But whenever food is concerned, he's like a fly on honey. You'd think with him being single all his life he would have learned to cook, but he's content to invite himself to our place for supper every Tuesday." She shook her head. "All right, that's not fair. He does have a standing invitation. But he always shows up early and hovers in the kitchen."

Elva couldn't help but chuckle. "Does he put in his two cents?"

"*Ya,* unfortunately."

"Then *nee* wonder you think he's a pest." She poked her on the arm. "*Nee* one tells Regina Raber what to do."

Regina laughed. "This is true. It's a *gut* thing Nelson is so easygoing. Oh, they've started judging." She looked at Elva. "Now the fun begins."

Elva had experienced a short reprieve from her nerves thanks to Jerald, but now they ramped up again. *This is not mei idea of fun.*

~

Jerald rubbed his hands together as the contest got underway. They had fifteen contestants, more than any other year, and he couldn't wait to dig in to so many pies. He'd left his niece and nephew's house early yesterday morning just so he could be back for the contest he'd judged for the past twenty-five years, ever since their community had started the annual picnic. He'd never missed a pie contest, and he didn't intend to.

This year he was one of five judges, and he tapped his foot as he waited his turn for a bite of Carol Yoder's cherry pie. Good, as usual, but nothing special. He tasted three more pies—banana cream, buttermilk, and pecan—and they were all satisfactory. But so far, he hadn't been wowed by any of them.

The line moved quickly, and before he knew it, he stood in front of Regina. He gave her a blank look, which he knew would bother her. She was a pip to tease, and he enjoyed every minute of it. As he waited for Mose Plank to taste her pie, he looked at Elva again. The pinched expression on her face made her look like she'd rather be anywhere but here. He was sure Regina had convinced her to enter the contest. The woman usually got her way, although Nelson knew when to keep her in line. Or try to.

He felt a little sorry for Elva, but at least the contest never took very long. He had to admit she was rather pretty, especially for a woman her age. Her pale-green eyes were her most striking feature, along with the light-brown eyebrows arching above them. She had a trim figure, in contrast to Regina's plump one. In fact, Elva was the prettiest woman near his age he'd seen in a long time.

"Here." Regina's sharp voice pulled him out of his thoughts. She thrust a small sliver of her rhubarb and strawberry pie, which was always excellent, at him.

"Passable," he said, handing back the plate with one bite left—although he'd had to resist the urge to eat every crumb. He held in his laugh when she scowled. Regina Raber was nothing if not predictable.

Then he landed in front of Elva. "Enjoy," she said in a quiet voice, handing him a piece.

He examined it for a quick second. Flaky crust, packed with filling, the plump berries covered in a thick, sweet, dark-purple sauce. He took a bite. "Oh *mei*," he said as the fresh flavor filled his mouth. He quickly took another bite.

"*Gut, ya?*" Mose said, pointing to Elva's pie. "Best one I've tasted so far."

"Agreed." Jerald scraped the filling and crust crumbs off the plate and then set it on the table. "Well done, Elva."

Her cheeks blushed as she looked down at her pie.

He moved on, but he knew no other pie would match Elva's. Then he reached the last contestant. *Oh boy.* Unfortunately, Wilma Jean Raber, one of Nelson's cousins, had entered again this year. He wished her husband, Willis, would tell her to stop entering her pies. Or to stop baking altogether. Jerald forced a smile. "Hello, Wilma Jean. What have you baked for us this year?"

"Pumpkin." She shoved a plate with a jiggly piece of pie toward him and then tapped her finger on the table behind it. "Fitting, since it's fall."

"Very fitting." He picked up the plate and saw chunks in the pie's filling. He was no cook—actually, he didn't cook at all—but he knew pumpkin pie filling was supposed to be smooth. And the pie's crust looked like rubber. But he took a bite and forced it down. "That was very . . ." A pumpkin chunk was stuck in the back of his throat, and he coughed to pry it loose. "That was something, all right."

Wilma grinned, looking as pleased as she always did. No one had the heart to point out that her pies were terrible. Of course, she never won the contest, but she had entered every year since its inception. Strangely enough, her perfect losing streak didn't seem to deter her.

A few minutes after Jerald choked down Wilma Jean's questionable interpretation of pumpkin pie, he and the rest of the judges gathered to the side and unanimously chose a winner. Mose, who had the loudest voice, not to mention the longest beard, which was currently sprinkled with pie crumbs, made the announcement. "This year's winner is Elva Gingerich."

Jerald looked at Elva, whose pretty eyes were wide with surprise. Regina nudged her, and she came around the table to accept the ribbon, which was faded and frayed at the edges. She nodded to the crowd, then hurried back to stand next to Regina, who, along with the other ladies, congratulated her. Everyone looked genuinely happy for her, which was the case every year when it came to the winner. The contest was all in good fun, and no one, not even Wilma Jean, was ever a sore loser.

His mouth watered as the women cut their pies into small slices. Since he had already tasted the pies, he waited with the other judges until everyone else had a sample. If any slices were left, the judges could have more. Elva's line was the longest, and her dessert was long gone before any of the others.

Jerald glanced at Wilma Jean, who with a smile on her face, watched everyone pass her pie. He walked over to her. "Cut me a big old piece, will *ya*, Wilma?"

Her eyes sparkled. "*Ya*, Jerald. I'd be happy to." She sliced almost a quarter of the pie and plopped it on a paper plate, then gave him a plastic fork. "Here you *geh*. Enjoy."

He glanced at the mess of pumpkin and crust and nodded his thanks, trying to keep an even smile on his face.

Wilma Jean looked over at Elva, who was wiping pie crumbs from her area on the table. "I'm happy she won."

"You are?" Jerald picked up his fork and held it over the pie. He'd have to take at least one bite in front of her before discreetly getting rid of the rest.

"*Ya*. She's had a tough time of it, losing her husband

two years ago. Regina said she's still trying to recover. They were married for forty-five years, you know."

He didn't know, and usually when a bit of gossipy info passed his way, he either ignored it or just pretended to listen. Not that Wilma Jean was gossiping right now. But for some reason, this information made him look back at Elva. He'd never been married, so he couldn't empathize with her. Yet he did sympathize. Imagine living with someone, loving them and having a family together, then dealing with that kind of loss. It would be hard on anyone.

Nelson came over, and as he saw Wilma Jean's pie oozing on Jerald's plate, his eyes grew nearly as big as Elva's had been a short while ago. "Uh, we've got a game of horseshoes started," he said, glancing at the pie, then at Jerald, then at the pie again. Jerald thought he looked a little green around the edges. "I, uh, thought you might like to partner up."

Jerald nodded and crammed a bite of pie into his mouth, forcing it down and thankful nothing got stuck this time. "Mm," he somehow managed, even though he was certain old shoe leather would have better flavor. "*Danki*, Wilma Jean."

She grinned, and he walked away, Nelson at his side.

"How can I get rid of this?" he asked his friend as they headed for the horseshoe pit.

"Don't ask me. I'm not sure pigs would even like it."

They might not. But tossing it into a pigpen might be the best way to dispose of the nearly inedible pie. In the meantime, he set the plate and fork down on a tree stump near the horseshoes game as Nelson headed for the pit.

Jerald turned around and looked at Elva, who was now talking to Wilma Jean. He couldn't see their expressions clearly—even with his glasses his eyes weren't what they used to be—but when he saw Wilma cutting a piece of her pie for her, he grinned. Elva was in for quite a surprise.

CHAPTER 2

"Nelson and Jerald should be here pretty soon."

Elva glanced up from setting the table and saw Regina's annoyed expression. "If you don't like him coming over here, why don't you tell him? Or Nelson? I've never known you not to speak *yer* mind."

"Because I won't interfere with nearly sixty years of friendship. Besides, even though Jerald is irritating, I'd miss him if he didn't come. But only a *tiny* bit. And don't you dare tell him I said that."

Nodding and hiding her grin, Elva placed cloth napkins by the four plates on the table. The picnic had been three days ago, and she'd attended one church service since then. She really liked Regina's community, and she wished she'd visited her sooner. The women had made her feel welcome, and their sincere congratulations when she won the pie contest had touched her. In her own district back in Michigan, where Regina was from originally, not everyone was so gracious.

She was puzzled by one thing, however. At the picnic, she'd seen Jerald take a huge slice of the pumpkin pie Nelson's cousin made. Thinking the pie must be good, she'd also asked for a slice. But it was the worst thing she'd ever tasted, bad enough that she wondered if Jerald's taste buds weren't working properly. She'd forced herself to eat it, since Wilma Jean had seemed so pleased that Elva had wanted a piece. Desperately pleased, now that she thought about it.

Regina pulled the roasted potatoes and meat loaf from the oven just as Nelson and Jerald walked into the kitchen. "What have you two been up to today?"

"Auction at Broomfield." Nelson peeked at the food over Regina's shoulder. "Smells *appeditlich*, as usual."

"Did you add garlic salt?" Jerald said, sitting down at the table like he was a member of the family.

"*Ya*, Jerald. I did."

"And did you peel the potatoes completely? You know I don't like any skin on *mei* roasted potatoes."

Elva frowned, thinking Jerald was being rude. He and Nelson might be longtime friends, but that didn't excuse his behavior. Then he glanced at Elva and winked.

"What about the apple strudel?" He crossed his arms over his chest. "That crust better be tender and flaky."

Regina spun around, storm clouds in her eyes. "If *mei* cooking isn't up to *yer* standards, Jerald Byler, feel free to eat somewhere else."

Jerald met her gaze. "I just might."

"Ugh!" Regina turned to Nelson. "Put the drinks on the table."

Nelson smirked as he did what he was told. He and Jerald exchanged a knowing look, and it was clear to Elva that the two of them were enjoying this immensely. She had to admit she was even a little entertained. It was unusual to see Regina so flummoxed.

Elva helped Regina take the food to the table, and then she sat down across from Jerald. He nodded at her as Regina and Nelson sat down, and they all closed their eyes for silent prayer. When she opened her eyes, Jerald was already reaching for the basket of fresh-baked Parker House rolls Elva had made earlier that day. He really did make himself at home here.

"The auction was a bust." Nelson put a slice of meat loaf on his plate, then handed the platter to Elva.

"Sorry to hear that," Elva said.

"I'm not." Regina snatched the basket from Jerald. "We don't need a single thing," she said, dropping a roll on her plate.

"Except maybe a muzzle," Jerald quipped, glancing at Regina. Then he took a bite of one of the rolls. His eyes widened. "Who made these?"

"Me," Elva said softly.

"They're scrumptious." He took another large bite. "This doesn't even need butter."

Regina glared at him. "You don't say that about *mei* rolls."

"Because they're not as *gut*."

Nelson took a roll and bit into it. "He's right, Regina. Elva's are better."

"You both should be glad I accepted long ago that Elva is a better cook, or the two of you would be eating *yer* supper in the barn tonight."

"I'm not that *gut* of a cook." Elva put her napkin in her lap, uncomfortable with the compliments. Her late husband, Henry, had been a man of few words, and he'd rarely said anything complimentary during their forty-five-year marriage. She wasn't used to someone fawning over her cooking, and now she had experienced this twice. "The rolls are *mei mamm*'s recipe. She was an excellent baker, and she taught me everything I know."

"That's true," Regina said, piping up. "I remember eating supper at *yer haus* when we were *kinner*, and every single thing she made was yummy. I really liked her chicken and noodles."

"You learned well." Jerald grabbed another roll from the basket in the middle of the table. Then he took a bite of the meat loaf. "Adequate," he said, glancing at Regina.

Regina smirked. "Elva made the meat loaf too."

Jerald hung his head, then lifted it again, chuckling.

"You got me this time. It's very *gut*, Elva." He glanced at Regina. "So is *yers*, but you already know that."

For the rest of the meal, Elva listened as the three of them talked about the auction, Nelson and Jerald mentioning people they'd seen in Bloomfield whom Regina also knew. Then their talk turned to the community. "Wilma Jean is hosting a quilting bee tomorrow evening," Regina said. "Elva and I are planning to *geh*."

"Let me guess," Jerald said, looking at Elva. "You quilt circles around all the ladies too."

She shook her head. "I'm terrible at quilting. I don't have the patience for it. But it will be fun to socialize and get to know the ladies better."

"A quilting bee is really just a glorified hen party," Nelson said, dabbing his napkin at the corner of his mouth.

"That's not true. Every quilt we make at our bees is donated to the Haiti auction. You both know that." She shook her head and stood. "I don't know what I'm going to do with you two."

"You say that every Tuesday," Jerald said.

"And we're both still around," Nelson added.

Regina gave her husband a harsh look, and Nelson returned it. But Elva also saw both expressions change and soften. As it happened, more often than she liked over the years, a familiar lump formed in her throat. How blessed Regina was to have such a wonderful husband who was with her during her golden years. "If you'll excuse me,"

Kathleen Fuller

Elva said, getting up from the table, "I don't think I'll have dessert tonight." She looked at Regina. "Do you mind if I sit on the patio for a while?"

"Of course not. Stay out there as long as you wish." Regina gave her a concerned look.

Elva slipped outside through the mudroom off the kitchen, then sat on one of the plastic chairs on the patio. A dull ache spread in her chest. Sometimes being out in the fresh air helped, and she looked at the pale-yellow and pink sunset streaking the sky. A soft breeze rustled through the trees, and she felt her emotions settle. Except for one. Now she was embarrassed that she'd excused herself before supper was over, leaving Regina to do the dishes. What kind of guest was she to do something so rude?

"Mind if I join you?"

She looked up to see Jerald. Surprised, she nodded, and he sat down on the chair next to her.

"Regina's giving Nelson a *gut* talking-to." He leaned back and ran his hand over the top of his balding pate. "He didn't mean to upset you, Elva."

"Oh, I know." She clasped her hands in her lap. "And this is *mei* fault. I've always been a little too emotional. That's what Henry used to say."

"He's *yer* late husband?"

Elva nodded. "I suppose he was right. I do get teary at the drop of a hat."

"You're not crying now."

282

She looked at him. "*Nee*, I'm not." She paused, a little worried that he pointed that out. "Does that make me a bad person? That *mei* heart doesn't hurt when I think about *mei* husband?"

～

Jerald looked at Elva. How could this gentle woman possibly think she was a bad person? "I don't think so. I've never had a wife, but I have lost people. You don't live to be seventy years old and not gone to a fair share of funerals. I think it's healthy to grieve but not hold on to it forever, if that makes sense."

"It does." She looked at him again, uncertainty in her eyes. After a long moment, she said, "Do you mind if I ask you a personal question?"

"You want to know why I never married."

She nodded. "I hope I'm not being too nosy."

"Not any nosier than the dozens of other people who've asked me that same thing over—and over—the years." He shrugged. "But *mei* answer has never changed. I never married because I never found the right woman. It's as simple as that, although I'll admit it would have been easier to marry someone, especially in an Amish community. That's the usual expectation."

"But you're not usual."

He lifted one brow. "You noticed, that, *ya*? *Nee*, I'm a little unique—or *seltsam*, depending on who you talk to. I never fell in love, thus I never married. And while I do love plenty of people, I've never loved anyone in that way."

"Then you don't regret being single?"

"At one time it didn't sit all that well with me. It can be hard, even now, seeing couples and families together. I end up being on the outside looking in a lot of the time. But I came to terms with it in *mei* forties, when I realized God meant for me to be single."

"Henry and I married when we were seventeen," she said, her gaze pinned to the sunset. "Before that I lived with *mei* family, which was large. I never knew what it was like to live alone until after Henry died." She glanced down and murmured, "It wasn't as hard as I thought it would be." Then she shook her head so hard the strings on her *kapp* swung. "I'm sure I'm making quite an impression on you. Here I am a widow, and I'm not filled with grief, and I don't mind being alone."

She was making an impression all right. A good one. But he wasn't going to admit that. Her response, though, was unexpected. Why wasn't she still grieving her husband? He was also surprised to hear that she liked living alone. That hadn't been his experience in talking with other widows and widowers. Not that they were all eager to remarry, but they had family surrounding them, keeping some of the pain at bay.

Something about Elva was different. He sensed she was like a flower caught up in a summer breeze—stronger than she seemed but still fragile. "How you feel is how you feel," he said. "Everyone handles loss differently. You shouldn't compare *yerself* to other folks."

"But I do."

"Even to Regina? Because if you do, you're in more trouble than I thought." He chuckled, hoping she would get the joke.

"*Nee*," she said, laughing. "Regina is one of a kind."

Relieved that she did understand, he said, "That she is." Then he paused. "I hope you don't think I'm being hard on her for real. She knows I'm teasing, and I think she gets a kick out of it as much as I do."

"She does. Although she probably won't let you live down that meat loaf comment."

"I'd be disappointed if she did." He settled back in the chair, and the two of them sat in silence, watching the sunset. At his age, he'd seen lots of sunsets, many of them by himself. But sitting in the quiet with Elva as the sun disappeared below the horizon, leaving dusky colors in the sky, was extra nice.

"I should probably see if Regina needs any help." Elva got up from her chair and pulled her navy-blue cardigan around her slim body. "I might have a bite of that strudel after all."

Jerald smacked his forehead with his palm. "I completely forgot about that. Elva, you're witnessing a rare occasion—me forgetting dessert." He stood and looked at the house. "Hope she has vanilla ice cream to *geh* with it." He glanced at Elva. "Only vanilla ice cream will do. Homemade, at that."

Elva smiled. "I agree. And you're in luck. She made some last night."

He smiled and let Elva go inside first. As the screen door closed behind them, Jerald stopped and turned, looking at the pale sky now fading to twilight. For some reason he wanted to savor this moment. He couldn't deny that he'd just witnessed the most beautiful sunset he'd ever seen—and being in Elva's company had been a big part of the experience.

CHAPTER 3

The next evening, Elva and Regina sat in the buggy, waiting for Nelson to take them to Wilma Jean's for the quilting bee. Regina told Elva the ladies had been working on this quilt for several months, and they were starting on the top stitching now.

"We hope to have it finished two weeks from today," she said. "That's cutting it close since that will be just before the auction. But that's usually how it goes. I can't think of a time when we finished a quilt any earlier. Could have something to do with us talking more than sewing."

"A hen party, then," Elva said, smiling.

Regina smirked, then grinned. "Just don't mention it to Nelson or Jerald."

Elva nodded, and she was silent in the back seat of the buggy as Nelson climbed in. Soon after they were on their way to Wilma Jean's, Nelson and Regina bickering about what time he should pick them up. He was going over to Jerald's while they were at the bee since Jerald lived only a few houses down from Wilma Jean. Elva tuned them out as she thought about her conversation with Jerald the night before.

She'd been surprised he'd joined her, even though she had to admit she was glad for the company. Jerald was an easy man to talk to, the opposite of Henry. She hoped Jerald didn't get the wrong impression of her when she said she didn't hurt when she thought about Henry. His response had been kind, and for some reason she'd felt a spark of warmth in her heart, something she hadn't felt in a long, long time. Or maybe she was overreacting to a listening ear. But being on the receiving end of such kindness from a man was foreign to her—and a fact she didn't want anyone else to know. She hadn't even admitted how empty her marriage had been to Regina.

Nelson pulled into a driveway Elva assumed was Wilma Jean's. Regina picked up her bag of sewing notions and turned around to look at Elva. "Nelson will pick us up in an hour and a half," she said, then gave a pointed look to her husband.

"Right," he said. "An hour and a half or so."

"An hour and a half on the dot." Regina climbed out of the buggy, and Elva followed. Regina waved at Nelson, who backed out the buggy and headed for Jerald's. "You'd think those two hadn't seen each other in years. But they're like this every time they get together. I didn't think Jerald would ever leave last night. I finally told Nelson I was going to bed, and the two of them kept right on talking. I was asleep by the time he turned in for the night."

Elva had turned in early, too, leaving the two men in the kitchen to their second helpings of strudel. "I think it's nice they have such a close friendship."

"They're like *bruders*. I think it's because Nelson never had a *bruder*, only *schwesters*. The other reason is Nelson always included Jerald in everything, even after we were married. Well, *almost* everything," she said, laughing. "That's what cemented their relationship."

Elva nodded. Since Henry's death, she was experiencing what Jerald and other single Amish people experienced— being on the outside looking in when it came to couples and families. But it didn't bother her as much as she'd expected it would. She liked being single, something she hadn't meant to reveal to Jerald, even in a roundabout way. But he'd understood that too. *How you feel is how you feel.* No one had ever told her that, and it sparked something positive and hopeful inside her.

Regina looked at her. "Before we *geh* inside, I have a question for you. Since Nelson was hanging around all day, I didn't get a chance to ask you. What did you and Jerald talk about last night?"

"*Nix* important."

"I hope you don't think I'm being nosy—"

"Regina, you're always nosy."

Regina sniffed. "I suppose you're right. But in this case, I have a reason to ask. Jerald has never, to *mei* knowledge, sat with a single woman and talked."

"That can't be true." Elva frowned. "Surely he's been on dates before."

"When he was younger, *ya*. But he's been *firmly* single for the last thirty years. And although right now we don't, in the past we've had some widows in our community. Yet he's never taken any kind of interest. Both Nelson and I were surprised that he went out and sat with you for so long."

"We were watching the sunset. And just making small talk." She looked at Regina. "Oh *nee*. I recognize that look."

"What look?"

"You know what I'm talking about." Elva waved her hand. "Don't even think about it. I'm serious."

"What? You and Jerald?" Regina laughed. "That never entered *mei* mind. Jerald would be the last person I'd ever think of setting you up with—or any other woman. That man is never getting married." She paused. "Are you thinking about remarrying?"

She shook her head. "*Nee.*"

"Why not?"

"Being married to Henry was enough." More than enough. She squirmed, not wanting to delve further into the topic, even with one of her closest friends. "We should probably get inside, or the ladies will wonder what's keeping us."

"They don't know we're here. Wilma Jean has the tables set up in the basement. But you're right. Time is ticking." She put her hand on Elva's arm. "If you ever decide you're open to remarrying, let me know. I'm sure I can find just the right man for you."

"*Danki.*" But Elva knew she would never take advantage of her friend's offer. Just like Jerald, she was also firmly single. Nothing was going to change that.

~

"I see you've taken a shine to Elva."

Jerald rolled his eyes as he and Nelson sat on his front porch and watched the Mast children play across the street. The family had moved in two years ago, and they were *gut* people. They had six kids ages ten to two, and they loved to play catch and chase one another around the front yard, which was expansive. Jerald always enjoyed watching the kids' antics. "I don't know what you're talking about," he said, taking a sip of lemonade. Loretta Mast had brought over two pitchers of it yesterday to thank him for helping her husband, Maynard, pick corn the week before.

"You and her on the patio last night. You were out there a long time."

"I couldn't bear to listen to Regina giving you another

lecture, that's all." He turned to Nelson and smirked. "You're a saint, you know that?"

"Don't act like you don't think the world of her." He pointed his finger at him. "I know you better than that. Although sometimes I think you're right."

The men laughed as a buggy made its way down the road, the horse's hooves clip-clopping against the asphalt. How many times had he sat out on his porch over the years, taking in the peace of the area as he wound down the day? He could name only a handful of times when he'd wished he'd had a companion to share those times with, other than when Nelson and other friends dropped by. He was mostly content with himself. Yet for some reason, last night he couldn't stop thinking about watching the sunset with Elva.

Still, that didn't mean he'd taken a shine to her. They barely knew each other, for one thing. "How long is she planning to stay in Millersburg?"

"Why? You going to court her?" Nelson chuckled, the skin around his brown eyes wrinkling at the corners.

"*Nee.*" He pushed back his hat. "I'm just curious, that's all."

Nelson nodded. "I'm not sure. I thought it was going to be only a week, but it's been longer. Not that I mind. I know Regina has enjoyed her visit. I think Elva has too."

"You think? Does that mean you're not sure?" That concerned him—and made him think about how concerned Elva was about her reaction to her husband's death.

"She's a lot different from Regina." Nelson looked at the lemonade in the mason jar glass he was holding. "Quiet and reserved. I can't really tell what she's thinking or feeling. Regina's an open book."

Jerald nodded. Normally he would crack a joke about Regina, but he wasn't in a joking mood. "Elva does keep things close to herself."

"You noticed too."

"*Ya*. But I also think she's a fine lady. It's got to be hard to lose a lifelong partner."

"*Ya*, I'm sure. I don't know what I'd do without Regina."

Jerald knew what would happen to Nelson if Regina passed before he did—he would be lost for a long time. That was one other benefit to singlehood. He didn't have to worry about grieving a spouse. "Enough of this depressing talk. What are you thinking about donating to the auction?"

"Probably a cord of firewood, like I usually do. Those seem to *geh* fast. I thought I'd offer some carpentry services too." He stretched out his hands and bent his fingers back and forth. "Since I partly retired, I haven't had too many jobs lately."

"Which is *gut*, considering *yer* arthritis."

"*Ya*, but I can still donate some work." He looked at Jerald. "What about you? Other than a casket, obviously."

Jerald chuckled. He'd been making caskets for most of his adult life, and unfortunately, he'd had enough work that he'd never had to branch out into anything else. "I've got a few breadboxes I made when I had some free time. I'm going to donate those."

"They should *geh* quick and catch a *gut* price from the English visitors."

"That's what I thought."

The men talked for a little while longer, but like many of their visits, they also sat in silence, enjoying the peace of the evening. When they were younger and spent time together, they would usually be doing something in their workshops. But now, more often than not, they passed the time just sitting and enjoying nature. It was a relaxing way to end the day.

As dusk descended, Nelson got up from the hickory rocking chair. Jerald had two of them, both of which had belonged to his parents. They were old and worn from time and elements, but they were still sturdy. "Guess I better get the women," he said. "Lord knows I'll have to listen to Regina gripe if I'm more than a minute late."

Jerald took Nelson's glass and nodded. "You better hurry, then. Surprise her with being early."

"She'll probably fuss at me about that too." Nelson grinned, then waved good-bye and made his way down the steps to his horse and buggy.

Jerald watched him leave. The Mast children had already gone inside, probably to get ready for bed since they had school in the morning. After caring for his horse, Jerald went into the house, then washed the mason jars before settling in his favorite living room chair. He turned on the gas lamp next to it, then slipped on his reading glasses and opened his Bible, preparing to read a few chapters before turning in for the night. This was a habit he'd had since he was a child.

He suddenly looked at the empty chair opposite from his. He had that chair and a couch just so his visitors had a place to sit. All he needed was his own well-worn recliner. But a shiver came over him as he looked at that empty spot, as if someone was supposed to be sitting in it. He glanced down at the Bible open on his lap. *Therefore shall a man leave his father and his mother, and shall cleave unto his wife: and they shall be one flesh.*

Jerald frowned. His parents had died thirteen years ago, and this verse had never applied to him. But his gaze went back to the chair. He'd had it for over three decades, but it was practically new since only visitors sat in it. He stilled. Was God trying to tell him something? Jerald suspected he was, but it couldn't possibly be what Jerald was thinking. Because what he was thinking was 100 percent *ab im kopp.*

He turned to the book of James, where he found no verses about marriage or anything like that. After a few minutes of reading, he felt more at ease. The nonsense that had popped into his head was gone, thank the Lord for that. He didn't need to be thinking about marrying Elva—ever.

CHAPTER 4

"Are you sure I'm not overstaying *mei* welcome?" Elva asked the following week.

She'd asked Regina if she could stay a little longer, because she'd been thinking about the auction the community was having to raise money to help the people of Haiti. The more she thought about it, the more she wanted to be a part of it. Her own community had fund-raisers for missions, and she was very involved in them. Henry had thought they were a waste of time, although he always showed up to eat and visit. He put on a good front in public. In private, however . . . Elva fought off a shiver.

"Of course not."

"But I've been here so long already."

Regina flipped over the pancakes bubbling in a

cast-iron pan. "Nelson and I would love for you to stay as long as you want, whether that's a month or six." She turned and smirked. "I'm surprised our bickering hasn't run you off yet."

Elva shook her head. "I can tell it's all good-natured." During her time here, she'd seen the loving way the two of them looked at each other when they didn't think anyone else was watching. And when their children and grand-children came for supper last Saturday, even she had felt the love the whole family shared. Pain had pricked her heart, though. This was the way married life was sup-posed to be. *But it wasn't for me.*

Elva set all that aside and hugged her friend. "*Danki*," she said.

Regina nodded. "You're welcome." She frowned a little. "Are you all right? You're usually not this demon-strative."

"I'm just happy to be here." She stepped to the pantry and pulled out the syrups, then placed them on the table. Raspberry for Nelson and maple for Regina. Elva liked a little of both.

"I'm glad." Regina turned down the gas burner under the pancakes. "I was a little worried about you when you first got here."

"Oh?" She put the glass-covered butter dish on the table.

"Pardon me for saying so, but you still look a little . . . haggard." Regina took a plate out of the cabinet and set it next to the stove. "But I shouldn't have been surprised. Grief can do that to a person."

What if it isn't grief? What if it's just the way I've looked for years and years, but mei *other friends just assumed I worked too hard?*

Elva shook off the thought and nodded. "It can. But I'm glad I had a chance to get away and visit."

"You're not in any hurry to get home, then?"

She paused and shook her head. "There's not much for me there, other than *mei* friends. They mean a lot to me, but so do you."

Regina gave her another hug. "I'm sorry things have been so hard for you."

"It's all right. Hard times come on everyone, don't they?" But when her friend nodded, Elva understood she was referring to something that didn't happen for all couples.

She and Regina had never discussed her and Henry being childless. As they finished preparing breakfast, she thought about the emptiness that had always been there because of it. She had wanted children, and so had Henry. They'd tried for years, but she'd never become pregnant. Henry had blamed her, and she had blamed herself—until she saw a doctor when she was thirty.

"There's no reason why you can't have children," the doctor had said before going over her test records and results.

Elva had saved money without Henry's knowledge

to pay for the expensive ultrasound in cash. She had felt guilty about that, but she had to know for sure. "There isn't?" A ray of hope dawned.

"You're perfectly healthy. Very healthy, I might add." The doctor took off her reading glasses. "What about your husband?"

"Henry? You think there's something wrong with him?"

"There could be. We would have to run some tests like we did with you to know for sure."

Elva shook her head. "He would never agree to tests."

The doctor nodded. "I understand. But sometimes even patients who are healthy and normal have trouble conceiving. Thirty is still young. You can keep trying."

She pretended to agree with the doctor, but she knew there was no point. And she would never tell Henry what she'd learned. He was convinced she was barren, so telling him about the doctor's appointment would anger him. And when Henry was angry, she was the one who suffered.

Nelson walked into the kitchen, sniffing the air. "Those pancakes smell *gut*. Can I get them to *geh*?"

"What do you mean?" Regina asked, looking confused.

"Last night Jerald gave me an idea for the auction. He's made a few breadboxes, and I thought I'd make a couple of those lazy Susans I used to build years ago."

"You haven't done that in a while." Regina smiled. "I

think that's a great idea. You've been missing working out in the shop."

"*Ya*, but I don't have much time to make them before the auction." He looked at the plate of pancakes on the table, then grabbed two plus a cup of coffee. "I'll be in the shop if you need me."

Elva had expected Regina to scold him for rushing off, but when she looked at her friend, she saw she was still smiling.

"He hasn't been excited to work in the shop in months," she said. "I know it hurts for him to build cabinets, especially if they're detailed. But the jobs he's been getting have been too easy, which is *gut* for his pain but not so much for his creativity. His arthritis has been hard on him."

Elva looked out the window of the kitchen's back door and saw Nelson taking big strides toward the shop. "He does seem excited."

"Which means he'll also be busy all day, praise the Lord." She chuckled. "I love *mei* husband, but sometimes he does get underfoot." She paused, her mouth forming an O shape. "Oh, Elva, I'm sorry. We can't seem to keep our feet out of our mouths."

"It's all right."

"But we're being insensitive." Regina pressed her lips together. "Henry hasn't been gone that long."

"Regina, I'm fine. I really am." And she was, now that she was in Millersburg with her friend. And Nelson.

And she had to include Jerald in that, even though they didn't know each other well. She'd also gotten to know the women in the community better. It amazed her how easily she fit in here compared to back home. But she wasn't trying to hide a broken marriage now—only the fact that it had been broken. "You don't have to watch everything you say."

"All right." Regina's eyes pleaded with her. "But you make sure to tell Nelson and me if either of us says something that hurts *yer* feelings. Promise?"

"I promise." Elva smiled, her heart filling. It was so good to be around people who cared.

After breakfast, Elva and Regina baked three loaves of bread for the week. "How about making another blueberry pie?" Regina asked as they worked.

"I'd love to."

"I bet Henry asked you to make them all the time."

Elva shook her head, focusing on punching the bread dough. "He preferred cake."

"Oh. Then I bet you make an excellent cake."

"Not according to him." The words slipped out, and Elva bit her tongue. "Maybe I'll make an extra pie for Jerald," she said, hoping the mention of Regina's partial nemesis would distract her friend from asking any questions.

"He'd like that, I'm sure. The *mann* does enjoy his desserts. You can take it over to him if you want to."

"Me?"

Regina lifted a brow. "It was *yer* idea."

"I can't do that."

"Why not? Lori is coming over this afternoon to work on some curtains she's donating to the auction," she said, referring to her oldest daughter. "She says she's behind and asked me to help. Unless you'd like to do some more sewing?"

Elva paused. She had enjoyed the quilting bee, but only for the company, not the actual stitching. Yet she didn't like the idea of taking a pie over to Jerald either. "That seems a bit bold, don't you think?"

"Elva, it's Jerald. You don't have to worry about that. You can take our buggy too."

"All right," she finally said. She also had to admit it would be nice to see him again, if only because she knew he would appreciate her pie.

She and Regina spent the rest of the morning baking. After lunch, Lori, who was the spitting image of her mother down to the dark eyes and plump figure, arrived. Then after asking for directions to Jerald's, Elva decided she'd walk to his house instead of taking the buggy. It was a nice fall afternoon, not too cold or windy, which would make for a pleasant stroll. She put the pie in a picnic basket, making sure it was securely placed.

As she made her way, she questioned what she was doing. Why had she decided to bake Jerald a pie? Or to agree to take it to him? Although Regina had mentioned Henry, which had alarmed her, Elva could have distracted her friend with a number of topics. But for some reason, baking a pie for Jerald was what popped out of her mouth. And as she neared her destination, she couldn't explain the flittering feeling she had inside. It was more than just a desire to see someone enjoy eating a dessert she'd made. Surely she wasn't *excited* about seeing Jerald again. Was she?

~

Jerald sanded down the top of the casket he was working on. This one was for an Amish man thirty minutes away in a nearby community. He'd lived to the ripe old age of ninety-seven. Jerald couldn't imagine living that long. Some days he even felt ninety-seven. But if the Lord wanted him here for more than nine decades, Jerald would make sure he made the most of his time serving him.

He thought about Nelson. Unlike his friend, Jerald didn't have crippling arthritis, and he would keep working until he couldn't work anymore. He blew on the sawdust that covered the lid of the casket, and a cloud of dust flew into the air. He was almost finished with this one.

"Hello."

He looked up at the soft feminine voice, and his brow lifted. Elva was standing at the opening of his workshop door. He dusted his hands and walked over to greet her. "Hi," he said. "I'm surprised to see you."

"I'm surprised to be here," she mumbled. Then she

lifted the picnic basket in her hands. "I brought you a blueberry pie," she said, her speech rushed. "But not for any reason other than I thought you'd like it."

He would have laughed except he saw how uncomfortable she was. "I appreciate that. And don't worry, it never would have crossed *mei* mind that you would have any other motive." He glanced at the sawdust on his shirt and pants. "I'm a little messy, though. Give me a few minutes to clean up. You can wait in the kitchen if you want." Then he paused. "That is if you want to stay. I should have asked you that first."

"Regina's busy helping Lori," she said. "So *ya*, I can stay."

Jerald's heart took a leap. He almost put his hand to his chest, the feeling was so surprising. "Uh, then you should probably follow me."

Now he was the one who was uncomfortable. No, that wasn't the right word. *Awkward* definitely worked but *anticipating* was more like it. When he realized he wasn't even thinking about the pie, his heart leaped again. Yet another time when he was presented with a dessert, but his mind was on something else. And both times he'd been with Elva when it happened. Did that mean something?

Of course it didn't. He shook off the thought as they entered his mudroom, where coats and boots and other items were strewn around in messy fashion. He quickly picked up a few things. "Sorry," he murmured as he lifted one of his jackets. "The place is a bit untidy. I don't have company too often, and it's been nearly a year since I hosted church."

"Don't apologize. I'm not offended by a little mess." She smiled, and he realized how much it transformed her face. She was a pretty woman, but when she smiled, she nearly took his breath away.

"Uh, *gut*," he said, trying to stay on an even keel. But as they walked into the kitchen, he remembered he'd forgotten to clean up after breakfast that morning—and after supper last night too. He held up his hands. He'd never worried about neatness very much, even though he wasn't a slob. "I'm not the best housekeeper, that's a fact. I would have gotten to the dishes tonight, though."

She glanced around the room. "It doesn't look too bad to me."

He knew she was just being nice. Clean and tidy was the Amish way, and while his house wasn't dirty, it wasn't remotely tidy. He started clearing the table of what was left of his toast and two boiled eggs while Elva set the pie on his counter.

"Jerald, why don't you wash up, and I'll cut the pie?"

"Well, all right."

In the bathroom, he decided to not only put on clean clothes but also wash his hands and face and run a comb through what little hair he had left. All that primping took longer than he thought, so he hurried to the kitchen, not wanting to keep Elva waiting.

He found the table cleaned off, and he heard water swirling down the drain. Elva was at the sink, wiping the rim of the metal basin with a dishcloth. Then she draped it over the side of the sink to dry before drying her hands on a towel. When she turned and found him just standing there, she said, "There you are. Do you want tea or *kaffee*?"

"I should be making that offer, not you. And you didn't have to do this," he said, gesturing around the room. His kitchen was sparkling clean.

"I didn't mind. Where are *yer* plates?"

"Upper cabinet to the right. I don't have that many," he said, feeling a little pathetic. "Don't really have a need."

"I gave a lot of things away after Henry died." She pulled two dessert plates out of the cabinet. "I don't like a lot of clutter."

"Well, we have that in common." He went to the stove. "I'll be the one making the *kaffee* or tea. Which do you prefer?"

"*Kaffee*, please. Black."

Another thing they had in common. Jerald smiled as he prepared the percolator.

A short while later, they were enjoying the coffee and blueberry pie. "This is really *appeditlich*," he said, finishing off a second piece. "Is it a special recipe?"

She shook her head. "Just one *mei mamm* gave me. She always said it's not the ingredients or how you put them together but the love that goes in."

Jerald grinned. "There must be a whole lot of love in that pie, then."

Her cheeks turned red. "I do enjoy cooking."

Uh-oh. He hadn't meant to embarrass her. She poked at a few crumbs on her plate with her fork, but she didn't look at him.

After a stretch of awkward silence, he said, "I hope I didn't say something that bothered you."

She glanced up at him. "Oh, *nee*. Just thinking."

He wanted to ask her what was on her mind, but he knew he shouldn't be nosy like Regina was. He also realized this was uncharted territory for him. He and Elva weren't on a date, but he also didn't spend time socializing alone with women. Or socializing anytime with them, for that matter. Not to mention he still sensed Elva kept something carefully guarded below the surface.

"I'll wash the dishes," he said, starting to get up from his chair. "You're probably eager to get back to Regina's."

Before he stood, she put her hand on his forearm. "*Nee*, Jerald. I'm not."

CHAPTER 5

Elva looked at her hand on Jerald's forearm. His well-muscled forearm, which had come from decades as a woodworker. She knew she should move her hand, but she couldn't. Just like she couldn't stop herself from telling him she wasn't in any hurry to leave.

She pulled away and hung her head. "Sorry," she whispered.

"There's *nix* to be sorry for." He frowned, confusion in his eyes. "Elva, are you all right? I hope I'm not overstepping, but I sense you're upset about something."

Elva almost laughed. She'd been upset for forty-five years. She almost couldn't remember what it was like not to be upset, not to hide herself from everyone. Except for when she arrived in Millersburg. Regina and Nelson had been so welcoming, along with the community. But something about Jerald was special. Or maybe she was just starving for some kindness. "*Nee*," she said, rising from her chair. "I'm fine. And you're right. I should be getting back to Regina's. Besides, I don't want to keep you—"

This time his hand touched hers. "You can stay as long as you want, Elva."

Oh bother. Tears formed in her eyes, and she turned away. "Sorry," she said again. Apologies were second nature to her, and she had said them so often during her and Henry's relationship.

"Don't be."

"Henry used to hate when I cried." She bit her lip. She shouldn't have said that. But it was out there, and she couldn't take it back.

"I don't mind a few tears. Been known to shed some of *mei* own." He paused and let go of her hand. "Like I said, people grieve in their own way, and their own time—"

"I'm not grieving." She put her hands over her face. "I don't know why I can't stop saying these things." She started to cry.

After a long moment, Jerald got up and left the kitchen. She removed her hands and wiped her tears on the back of her hand. When he returned, he silently handed her a handkerchief, and she wiped the rest of her tears with it.

He sat back down and looked at her, kindness and concern in his eyes. What she wouldn't have done to get the same expression from Henry. "I'll be okay," she said.

"I know. I have a feeling in *mei* gut that you're a strong

woman, Elva Gingerich. And I'm usually not wrong about my gut feelings."

She shook her head. "I'm not strong at all. At least I don't feel like it."

"And that's when we turn to the Lord, *ya*?"

Elva started to nod, only to shake her head. "But what if he doesn't answer? What if he remains silent, for years, while every prayer you've ever uttered is ignored?" Her eyes grew wide. Why couldn't she keep her mouth shut? She was edging closer to telling him the truth about Henry after spending forty-five years of keeping the truth to herself. Maybe that was the problem. She could hold in the pain for only so long.

The compassion in Jerald's eyes changed to concern. "I take it *yer* marriage to Henry wasn't easy."

She popped up from her chair and grabbed their plates. "I shouldn't speak ill of anyone," she said, hurrying to the sink. "Especially a man who isn't here to defend himself."

Jerald gasped. "He did things that need defending?"

"That's not what I meant." She put the dishes in the sink and turned around. She'd made a mess of this, and she had to set things straight before Jerald jumped to conclusions. "My marriage was complicated. I'd known Henry since he was twelve and I was eleven. He told me on the playground he would marry me, and I believed him. We dated when we were old enough to, and we married at seventeen. For the first two years, our life was wonderful. We were waiting on God to bless us with a child. When he didn't . . . That's when things changed."

Jerald didn't say anything, just continued to look at her with kind, encouraging eyes.

She twisted the kitchen towel in her hands, spurred by Jerald's expression and silence, and continued. "He blamed me for us not having children, and he took his frustration out on me. I had always known he had a temper, even when we were *kinner*. But that temper grew worse as the years passed. Every difficulty in our lives made him angrier and angrier at home. Somehow he was able to hide that anger around others." She sighed, but no tears came this time. In fact, she felt a little relieved. "I've never told anyone this. Not even Regina."

He got up from the table and came toward her. "What did you and Henry do for fun?"

"Fun? What do you mean?"

"Did you ever *geh* camping? Or hiking? Or on a vacation to Florida or Pennsylvania or anywhere else? Did you have picnics or walks by the lake or friends over?"

She shook her head, bewildered that he would ask her this after what she had just revealed. "Other than hosting church, we didn't have anyone over. I did *geh* over to *mei* friends' *hauses*, though. Henry liked to keep to himself, however."

"You were pretty isolated, then."

"You could say that." She frowned. "What are you getting at, Jerald?"

His mouth tightened, and she saw his beefy hand form a fist. "I know I shouldn't ask this question, and you don't have to answer it. But I can't help myself. Elva, did Henry ever hurt you?"

~

Jerald couldn't remember ever being this angry. As he heard Elva's story, he had a harder and harder time keeping his feelings in check. Now her question about being a terrible person that night they watched the sunset at Nelson and Regina's made more sense. She blamed herself for the wrongs in her marriage, because her husband had always blamed her. And as he was asking the most personal of questions, it dawned on him that if he had more experience with women, he might know better than to bring up something so horrible. But all he cared about now was whether his suspicions would be confirmed. He just wasn't sure what he was going to do if she said yes.

Fear entered her eyes. "I—I—"

"He's not here anymore." Jerald approached her but kept a good-sized distance between them. She looked like a scared rabbit, and he didn't want to frighten her. "But if you don't want to say—"

"*Nee*. He never hurt me. Not physically."

"But words can cut just as deep."

"*Ya*." She nodded, her gaze locking with his. "They can."

He clenched his fists again. He'd never been a jealous

man—or a violent one. But that didn't keep him from wishing Henry were still alive. Because if he were, Jerald would give him a piece of his mind and probably more. *Forgive my terrible thoughts, Lord.* Those thoughts weren't helpful to Elva, and they were pointless. Henry was gone, and Jerald could do nothing to make up to Elva what she'd suffered from her late husband. He also couldn't stand here not saying anything. But for once in his life, he was at a loss for what to say.

Then a strange idea occurred to him. "Do you like to fish?"

She shrugged. "I've never been fishing. *Mei daed* wasn't interested, and Henry never took me."

"I've got some poles in the shed, and there's a pond two houses down with some pretty *gut* fishing. The English family there owns it, but they give me free rein. Would you like to *geh* for an hour or so?"

Elva nodded. "I would like that very much."

"Let's *geh*, then."

As he got the poles and gave one to Elva, he realized he had made the right decision. She couldn't go home looking like she had just attended a funeral, and she seemed genuinely interested in fishing. He hadn't known too many women who liked to fish, but he enjoyed the hobby very much. If she ended up not liking it, he would come up with something else to distract her. He'd do anything to keep her mind and heart off the man who had hurt her so much.

~

A few hours later, Elva stood in the dark and watched Jerald's buggy disappear down the driveway and then down the road. She turned and looked at Regina's darkened house. A slash of guilt penetrated her otherwise sense of peace. She should have let Regina know she'd gone fishing with Jerald instead of just taking off with him. But she'd been so surprised when he asked her to fish—and because talking about Henry had upset her—that she'd been eager for the diversion. It was as if Jerald had known that, and somehow, he chose the right activity.

For someone who'd never fished before, she'd caught quite a few, surprising herself and Jerald. "You sure you've never done this before?" he said, giving her a side eye as she awkwardly cast her line back into the water after nabbing another smallmouth bass.

"*Nee*, never." She grinned. "But it's so much fun!"

They'd caught so many that she'd helped Jerald put some of the fish in freezer bags, although she had let him scale and gut the catch on his own. She was brave enough to fish but not to clean the fish. They'd kept out four trout for supper, and she'd coated the fish with cornmeal and fried them in a cast-iron skillet as well as roasted a couple of large red potatoes in the oven and boiled green beans on the stove. After they finished eating the meal Jerald proclaimed "scrumptious," they split another piece of blueberry pie.

During their time together, they'd talked nonstop about everything. He wanted to know about her community in Michigan, and since she was now relaxed, she was able to tell him the good things about her district— how she picked cherries with her friends and their families in the fall and that Henry always tapped the maple trees in winter so she could put up maple syrup. Her community also held several activities to support Haiti and other missions, which Jerald was very interested in. She realized that, all in all, living in Michigan, while it had been difficult because of her relationship with her late husband, wasn't all bad.

Jerald had talked about Millersburg and the surrounding Amish counties in the area. She hadn't known there were so many Amish in Ohio. He told her about his family, his niece and nephew in Kentucky with whom he was close, and that he'd made caskets almost his entire life.

"It's an important job," she'd said. "I imagine it isn't easy."

He nodded, pressing his thumb against the top of the table. "You're right about that. But it's a necessary job, and I'm glad I can take care of it for people so they can have one less thing to concern themselves with when preparing for a funeral." He waved his hand. "Enough depressing talk. Tell me more about the mission programs back home."

It was well past sunset when Jerald offered to take her

home in his buggy, and she accepted. Now she couldn't stop smiling as she approached her friend's front porch, her steps sure under the light of the moon. She had never met a man like Jerald. He wasn't handsome, like Henry had been, but his charm and kindness made him good-looking in her eyes. He could converse on a variety of topics, and he'd asked her opinion on every one of them, something Henry had rarely done.

She hadn't felt this full and happy in years, not since she and Henry dated. Her late husband had been kind at one time, or perhaps it was all an act. She wasn't sure, and right now she didn't care. She'd had a wonderful time with Jerald, and she hoped he'd enjoyed being with her.

Fortunately, the front door wasn't locked, and Elva quietly opened it. She closed the door and clicked the lock in place, then tiptoed toward the stairs.

The gas lamp in the living room hissed to life.

"Sneaking into the *haus*, I see." Sitting in a chair, Regina crossed her arms over her chest. She was still wearing the blue dress she'd had on earlier, but she'd taken off her *kapp*. Her hair was twisted in a long gray braid over her shoulder.

Elva cringed at Regina's stern expression, feeling like a toddler caught escaping her crib. "I hope I didn't worry you."

"Were you with Jerald all this time?"

She nodded and looked down at her feet. She'd never

been scolded for being out with a boy in her life, and now at sixty-four, she was getting dressed down by her friend. A woman who had become her best friend. Just another unusual event in a very unusual but very pleasant day. "I should have let you know I was staying longer."

"*Ya*, you should have. Jerald has a phone shanty." Regina pressed her lips together. "I started to get concerned when you were gone so long."

"But you knew I was with Jerald."

"That's why I was getting worried." She sighed, but her expression relaxed slightly. "I thought about sending Nelson out after you, but the poor *mann* was so exhausted from working in his shop that he fell asleep in his chair right after supper." She paused. "I also realized that I'm not *yer mamm*. I can't exactly chase you down and demand that you come home."

Elva chuckled at the idea. "*Nee*, you can't. But it's nice to have someone be concerned about me." Jerald came to mind again.

Regina sat up in the chair and pointed to the couch. "You can't *geh* to bed until you tell me all about what happened today. I can't believe you spent that much time with Jerald. How did he not drive you crazy?"

"He's a nice *mann*." Elva felt a little protective of Jerald. "We went fishing."

"Fishing? That was his idea, I'm sure. The *mann* probably wants to be buried with his fishing pole."

"I'd never been fishing, and I've always wanted to *geh*."
She told Regina how many fish they caught and about
their delicious supper.

"And after dessert?" Regina's brow lifted.

"We talked."

"For a long time, I see." Regina had a sly grin. "I can't
believe it."

"Believe what?"

"That you've accomplished the impossible. The eternal bachelor Jerald Byler is sweet on you."

Elva shook her head. "*Nee*, he's not. Not in the way
you think." But she remembered how gentle his touch
had been on her hand. The shiver that had gone down
her back. The warm, secure feeling she'd had in his company that she'd never experienced with Henry. Did that
mean Jerald liked her? Or just that he was being nice? She
couldn't tell, and she was woefully out of practice when it
came to determining romantic intentions. Henry had been
her only boyfriend, and she'd been married to him for
ages. All she knew was that she'd been lonely for so long,
and this afternoon, she hadn't felt lonely at all.

Regina's smile faded. "You've got that look again."

Elva's gaze shot up. "What look?"

"The one that worries me. You know how much I like
to tease. If talking about you and Jerald that way bothers
you, I won't do it."

She looked at her friend, and once again almost started
to cry, this time from her friend's kindness. "There's *nee*

reason to tease," she said, her voice a little thick. "Jerald and I had a pleasant day together, that's all. It wasn't a date. There is *nix* romantic between us."

Regina nodded. "Then I won't tease you about him again." She yawned. "Are you ready for another quilting session tomorrow afternoon? This time the bee is at Ada's *haus*."

"Um, about that." When Regina gave her a questioning look, she said, "I've made plans to *geh* to Jerald's. He suggested I make pies to sell at the auction along with the other food and baked goods that will be available. He said I can make them in his kitchen, and he would keep them there and then take them to the field house."

"Why don't you just make the pies here?"

Elva paused. "I already told him I would make them there."

"I see." Regina looked at her. "I have to say I'm a little confused."

You're not the only one.

"But if you want to bake pies at Jerald's, you have *mei* blessing." She yawned again and stood up. "It's past *mei* bedtime. I'm not a night owl like you." She winked and made a hooting sound. "See you in the morning."

"*Gute nacht.*" After Regina left, Elva sat in the quiet of the living room, the hissing of the gas lamp the only sound breaking the silence. If Regina thought she was confused, she had nothing on Elva. *Lord, give me clarity when it comes to Jerald.* But God hadn't answered any of her prayers about Henry or about having a child. Why would he listen to her now? Yet despite that, she had never lost her faith. Everything in her life had happened for a reason, even if she'd been hurt and disappointed. This time, she hoped it would be different.

CHAPTER 6

Jerald clasped the horse's reins in his hands as he and Elva drove to the local scratch-and-dent salvage store to pick up ingredients for baking pies. Elva had agreed to bake them at his house this afternoon, the day before the auction. He didn't know what had gotten into him by suggesting that she make the pies at his house when she could have prepared them at Regina's. He'd been more surprised when she said yes.

He'd also been happy. Another day with Elva. He hadn't been able to stop himself from smiling until it was time to pick her up. Then he tempered his expression. He might be unique, but he didn't want her to think he was *ab im kopp.*

Now they were riding in the buggy together, the fall leaves starting to change color and the air a cooler temperature, and it all felt right, as if they had been riding in a buggy together for years. Even the silence between them was comfortable. Last night after he took her home, he'd been jittery but in a good way. The feelings swirling inside him were still foreign—and still confusing. But when he was in Elva's presence, the confusion melted away.

"What do you think about me making a few chocolate pies, instead of just all fruit?" Elva asked.

His mouth watered at the thought. "I think that's a great idea. I also think you're making me hungry."

"Didn't you eat lunch?"

"I grabbed an apple before I picked you up."

Her brow furrowed. "That's not lunch. *Nee* wonder you're hungry. It's just going to get worse when we get to the store."

He hadn't thought about that, and he wasn't about to tell her that he'd been so excited to see her again that he could barely choke down the apple, much less any breakfast. But she was right. His stomach was rumbling a little.

"I'll make you a *gut* meal when we get back home. Uh, I mean to *yer haus*."

He glanced at her. A light blush was spreading across her cheeks. He wasn't going to point out her verbal slip or tell her how it made him feel for her to refer to his house as home. He'd spent some time in prayer last night and listened for God's still, quiet voice, trying to figure out what was going on between him and Elva. He didn't get many answers, only the sense that he needed to enjoy their growing friendship.

"I received a letter from *mei* friend Deborah this morning," Elva said as he turned on the road where the store was.

"Oh? How are things back in Michigan?"

"They're fine. She asked me when I was coming back home."

Jerald gripped the reins. "What are you planning to tell her?"

Elva paused. "I'm returning the day after the auction, so instead of writing her back, I'll just see her at home."

The leather reins bit into his hand. "That soon?" he blurted.

"I've been at Regina's for weeks. I don't want to overstay *mei* welcome."

"I understand. And I'm sure you have things you need to take care of."

She turned her head and looked out at the passing landscape. "Not really," she said, her voice so low he barely heard her.

Yesterday they had talked a lot about different things, but he noticed that other than admitting Henry had verbally abused her, she mentioned him very little when she talked about her life in Michigan. He was glad to hear her life hadn't been all bad, and she had really perked up when she talked about her community's involvement with missions.

Still, he sensed she was holding back more personal things, though he had no idea what. He didn't blame her. Of course, he was curious, but he didn't have the right to be nosy. He was finding it hard not to be, though, and his keen and sudden interest in her unsettled him more than he expected. He wanted Elva to be happy, especially knowing she'd been so miserable for so many years.

They reached the store, and Jerald put aside his thoughts as he hitched up the buggy. He and Elva walked inside together, and while Elva shopped for the pie ingredients, he looked at the tools in the back of the store. The owner, Isaac, and his wife, Linda, were longtime friends, so he wasn't surprised when Isaac walked over and started a conversation. After they chitchatted about the weather, Isaac said, "Well, I gotta be straight with you, Jerald. Linda wants me to find out something."

"About what?"

"About you."

Jerald rolled his eyes. "Why doesn't she ask me herself, then?"

"Why do women do anything they do?" Isaac shrugged. "She saw you walking in here with Elva."

Jerald frowned. "And?"

"She was wondering if . . ." Isaac rubbed the toe of his work boot against the concrete floor. "I know this isn't any of our business . . . but are you and Elva . . . together?"

Jerald scoffed, but he should have known questions

would start once he was seen with Elva in public. This wasn't the only time people had talked about him after spotting him with a single woman, but the last time had been years ago, when he was younger. Maybe he should rescind his offer to take Elva to the auction. He didn't want to put her in an awkward position. But he was old enough not to let other people's nosiness and suppositions get to him anymore, and if Elva had seemed uncomfortable with his offer, she hadn't let on.

"Elva and I aren't together," he said. "She's baking pies for the auction, and I drove her here to get ingredients. That's all it is."

Relief crossed Isaac's face. "*Danki* for not being put out by the question. You know I'm not one to pry into personal business."

That was true, but Linda, along with a few other people in the district, was. Just like any community, he supposed, Amish or English. He frowned as Isaac walked away. Maybe he should warn Elva about this.

He went looking for her in the baking section of the store, and as he passed one of the aisles, he saw Donna Yoder and Marie Miller together, whispering. They suddenly stopped when they saw him. *Oh nee.* He'd forgotten about those two, who were always whispering to each other whenever they were together. Surely the gossip had already begun if these two middle-aged airbags were talking about him.

He quickly found Elva, who was placing two bags of

flour into a cart half filled with other ingredients. "Ready to *geh*?" He glanced over his shoulder to see if anyone else was watching them.

"In a minute. I saw some almond extract and thought about making a pistachio pie too. But I can't find any pistachios."

"We can ask Linda to fetch a bag when we check out." Without thinking, he tugged at her arm, just as Donna and Marie turned down the aisle. They gave each other a knowing look. "Hi, Jerald and Elva. How are you two doing?" Marie said. Jerald wanted to wipe off the foolish grin both women had on their faces.

"Peachy," Jerald said. When they started walking toward him and Elva, he said, "We were just leaving."

"We were?" Elva said.

"You two have a lovely day, then," Donna said.

"*Ya*," Marie added. "Both of you. *Together.*"

"Bother," Jerald muttered under his breath. He glanced at Elva, who looked confused. "We should *geh*," he whispered. "Now."

"Will we still get the pistach—"

"Make an extra blueberry!" His voice rang out in the store, and when he looked over his shoulder at Donna and Marie, their eyes were wide.

So were Elva's. "Why are you in such a hurry?" she said, as they rushed to the checkout counter at the front of the store.

Jerald didn't respond and started tossing Elva's ingredients onto the counter before Linda had even positioned herself behind the manual cash register.

"Hi, Jerald and Elva." Linda smiled. "Fancy seeing you two here together."

Jerald fought the urge to roll his eyes. "Just ring up the groceries, Linda." He was frustrated, but he had only himself to blame. He never should have driven Elva here.

~

Elva climbed into the buggy as Jerald unhitched his horse from the post with such quick movements you'd think his pants had caught fire. He'd been behaving strangely ever since she'd seen him talking to Isaac. She had come to know most of the residents of the community, and this was her third trip to this particular store, although the other two times she'd gone with Regina. She'd also thought Linda had given her several strange looks as she checked them out. Then once she'd rung up the total, Jerald practically threw the money at her and ushered Elva out of the store.

She frowned as Jerald got into the buggy. "Is there a problem?" Elva asked as he guided the horse at a quick pace out of the parking lot.

He didn't say anything until they were a short distance from the store. "Possibly. But I wouldn't worry about it."

"How can I not worry? You're acting *seltsam*, and now you're saying there might be a problem?" She twisted the hem of her apron. "Tell me what's going on, Jerald." She normally wouldn't have spoken so firmly, especially to a man, but she needed to know what he was talking about. Maybe Regina was rubbing off on her a little.

He sighed. "This is *mei* fault. I should have realized that if we were seen together in public, people would draw conclusions."

"What conclusions . . ." She blanched. "Oh. *Oh*. I can see how that is a problem."

"Not for me." He waved his hand. "I don't care what people think. The folks here have been talking about me for decades. I'm immune to gossip. Except . . ."

"Except what?"

"Except when someone else is concerned." He glanced at her. "Someone who doesn't deserve to be gossiped about."

Her heart warmed again. "*Danki*," she said, looking at her lap, touched by his thoughtfulness once more. "You don't have to worry about me, Jerald. I won't be here much longer anyway. But if you're bothered by us being out together—"

"*Nee*, of course not." He turned down a road she wasn't familiar with. "I . . . I like spending time with you, Elva."

She turned and looked at him. He was staring straight ahead, but she saw his Adam's apple bobbing, and that made her smile. "I like spending time with you, too, Jerald."

He turned and grinned. "I'm glad we straightened all that out." He chuckled. "You gotta laugh at people's imaginations sometimes. Us being together . . . How wrong could they be?"

Although she managed an awkward laugh, his words struck her. Was it really such a foreign concept, the two of them together? Then she shook her head. Of course it was. She was going home in two days, and he was a dyed-in-the-wool bachelor. Nothing was between them except some great conversation and good times spent together. She turned and looked out the buggy, then frowned. "Where are we?"

"We're on our way home."

"This road doesn't look familiar." She'd always had an excellent sense of direction.

Jerald glanced at their surroundings. "For the love of . . ." He let out another laugh, although this time he was the one who sounded awkward. "Would you believe I made a wrong turn?"

Elva smiled. He was clearly rattled, and she didn't want him to be off-kilter. "It's all right. I like sight-seeing."

"We're not going in the wrong direction, but it will take us longer to get back to the *haus* this way. Is that okay?"

"That's fine."

"You're easy to please, you know that?" Then he paused. "That's not because of Henry, is it?"

She understood what he meant. "*Nee.* I did have to

watch what I said and did around him, but I don't have to do that around you."

"*Gut.* I don't want you to ever feel like you can't be *yerself.*" He glanced at her again. "Because the real Elva Gingerich is a great person to be."

Elva smiled as she leaned back against the seat, taking in the rolling hills surrounding them, true happiness flowing through her. If only she wasn't leaving and if only Jerald wasn't set on being single . . .

Lord, why am I even thinking about this? After Henry died, she vowed she'd never be involved with another man. Yet here she was having romantic thoughts about a seventy-year-old lifetime bachelor. *How foolish.* Her prayers from last night hadn't given her any more clarity, and she realized that she couldn't keep taking advantage of Regina's hospitality. She needed to go home and get her thoughts and feelings in order. Even though leaving was the last thing she wanted to do.

Then another thought went through her mind. *Enjoy the moments.* She didn't need to spend what little time she had left with Jerald, and with Regina and Nelson, mired in confusion. She wasn't going to waste any more moments in her life. She'd wasted plenty enough.

CHAPTER 7

The next morning, Jerald took Elva's pies to the fairground building where they were holding the auction. After making them a big lunch, she'd spent all afternoon baking, then stayed for a light supper. They played cards, too, and when he returned from taking her home, his house—and his heart—had felt emptier than ever.

He met Elva at a long table at the back of the building, where the rest of the food was being sold. "Here's one batch," he said, three of her pies loaded into his hand wagon. They were carefully wrapped, lying in a large shallow box.

Elva smiled, and his heart flipped. He couldn't count how many times yesterday he'd been affected by her smile, the sparkle in her eyes, the sweetness of her voice. Or how many times he'd thought that if he had met her as a young man, he wouldn't be single. And if that were the case, she wouldn't have been married to a man like Henry.

He pushed the thoughts out of his mind and unloaded the pies while Elva laid them out on the table. Just as he brought in the next three, Regina arrived.

"Wow," she said, looking at the half-dozen pies. "You really were busy."

Jerald waited for Regina to say something scathing, as she usually did, but she just smiled at him as well as at Elva. As he went for the last batch, he thought about how much had changed, including his sparring with Regina. Regina was being downright nice to him. He wasn't sure what to make of that.

"I'll get the rest," he said.

Back at his buggy, Nelson approached him just as he set the last pie in the wagon. "Those are going to sell fast," he said, looking at the desserts. "Each crust is perfectly golden."

"Elva has the magic touch, all right," he said, then quickly added, "when it comes to baking and cooking."

"Just those two things, *ya*?"

Jerald looked at Nelson, his guard up. "What else would I be referring to?"

"You tell me. Something is different about you since you and Elva met."

He rolled his eyes. "Not this again. I'll tell you like I told everyone else. There is *nix* between me and Elva."

"But you wish there were."

He stilled, taking in Nelson's quiet words. One of the downfalls of having a lifetime best friend was that friend knew him inside and out. Still, Jerald shrugged. "Doesn't matter. She's leaving tomorrow."

"I know. Regina's been upset about it. I didn't realize how close those two were, and they've become practically *schwesters* now. I already have extra clean handkerchiefs on hand for Regina when Elva gets on the bus in the morning."

Jerald paused. "I thought she was leaving in the afternoon."

"Nope, bright and early. The taxi is already booked for six thirty."

He reeled from the news. He'd planned to stop by Nelson's tomorrow and tell Elva good-bye. He could still do that in the morning. She'd be in a hurry to eat breakfast before she left, but he couldn't let her go without a farewell.

"We should get these pies inside," Nelson said. "People are filing in, and the auction starts in an hour."

"I know," Jerald snapped. "It's not like I haven't been here every single year."

Nelson held up his hands. "It was just a reminder. Do you need any help?"

He shook his head. "Sorry. Didn't mean to snap at you."

"It's all right." Nelson's eyes filled with understanding. "I'm going to miss her too."

Not as much as I will. As his friend walked away, Jerald just stood there. It had hit him now—Elva was leaving. There would be no more pies, no more talks, and no more fishing with her. He would continue to live his single life, the one he had always been settled and comfortable with—until he met her.

And now he realized he couldn't just let her leave.

~

"Where is Jerald with those pies?" Elva glanced at Regina, then at the open door at the back of the building where people were bringing in items for the auction. He should have been back by now with the last load. Not that they were going to run out in the next few minutes, but it was strange that he hadn't come back. "I wonder what's keeping him."

Then she saw him coming in, dragging his wagon. She smiled, only to have it fade when she saw his face. Was he upset? As he neared, she could see he was. Without hesitation, she went to him. "What's wrong, Jerald?"

He met her gaze, and what she saw in his eyes made a shiver go down her spine. Attraction. She'd felt it before, in smaller waves, but right now it nearly knocked her off her feet.

Without saying anything, he took her hand and led her back to the pie table. "Do something with these," he barked at Regina as he halted the wagon behind the table.

Then he led Elva to the bleachers that had been pulled out for the auction. She followed as he stepped behind them, the only place where they'd have any privacy.

"Don't *geh*," he said, still holding her hand. "Stay here a while longer."

The desperation in his eyes touched her. "I already made *mei* reservation," she said. "I'll be back to visit—"

"That's not enough." He moved closer to her. "I don't want you to visit, Elva. And I don't want to visit you. I want you here, with me. Will you marry me?"

CHAPTER 8

"Marry you?" Elva couldn't believe what she was hearing. "I . . . I don't understand."

"I want you to be *mei* wife. And if you're worried I'll treat you like Henry—"

She shook her head. "I know you wouldn't." But marriage? "Where is this coming from?"

He let go of her hand and ran his palm over his balding head. "I don't know. I mean, I do know." He put his hand over his heart. "It's coming from here. I love you, Elva. I've never thought I would fall in love, but I have. And I don't want to let you *geh*."

She could barely process what he was telling her. She heard the crowd on the other side of the bleachers, and people were already sitting in the stands.

"We can't stay here," Jerald said, his gaze still locked

with hers. "Just think about it. I'll meet you at *mei* buggy after the auction." He leaned over and kissed her on the cheek, then took off.

Elva touched her face where he'd kissed her. Her mind raced, and her heart hammered. What was she going to do? Did he expect an answer from her today?

For the rest of the auction, she was barely present as she sold pies with Regina's help. When she counted someone's change wrong for the third time, Regina told her to take a break. She stepped outside and breathed in the cool, crisp air. *Lord, what do I do?* She cared for Jerald, but love? That happened over time. It had taken her years to fall in love with Henry, only to have that love destroyed in much less time.

Jerald isn't Henry. But that didn't mean she loved him. She put her face in her hands, perilously close to tears.

"Are you all right?"

She looked up to see Nelson standing there. She nodded, wiping her damp eyes. "*Ya.* I'm fine."

He peered at her through his glasses, then frowned. "I don't believe you. Do I need to get Regina?"

"*Nee.* I really am okay." She couldn't imagine telling Regina about Jerald's proposal. Her friend would undoubtedly point out how nonsensical the idea was, as well as that Jerald was out of his mind. Elva wasn't in the mood for that.

"You're thinking about Jerald," Nelson said.

"How did you know?"

"Because he had the same bewildered look on his face you do. And when I asked him what was wrong, he said the exact same thing you just did. But it's clear neither one of you is fine."

Nelson paused. "I don't know what's going on between the two of you, and it's none of *mei* business. But as someone who knows Jerald better than anyone, I can tell you he's never acted this way about another woman. He thinks you're special, there's *nee* doubt about that. And I'll tell you what I told him—it's never too late." He turned and walked away.

Never too late. For what? Love? Marriage? Neither of those had crossed her mind until she met Jerald. But those thoughts and the feelings that accompanied them didn't mean she and Jerald were meant to marry.

She plodded back inside, forcing herself as best she could to focus on the rest of the auction. After all her pies were sold, she watched as several items were auctioned off, including Jerald's breadboxes and Nelson's lazy Susans, which all fetched good prices. But while she'd seen Nelson hovering near the auction stage, she hadn't seen Jerald since he'd proposed. Had he changed his mind? She wouldn't be surprised if he'd realized how impulsive his proposal was and wanted to take it back—even though the thought of that caused a twinge of pain in her heart.

She couldn't do anything about it now, and she forced her dilemma out of her mind while she helped clean up when the auction ended. It helped to have the distraction, but not much. When everything in the building had been put back in order, Regina asked, "Are you ready to *geh*?"

She looked at the doorway that led to the now nearly empty parking lot. Was Jerald waiting for her there? Or had he changed his mind and left?

~

Jerald paced in front of his buggy as people left the auction building under a dusky sky. He nodded to a few men and women he knew, but he barely noticed them. His heart was pounding so hard he thought it might explode. Would Elva meet him? He doubted she would, but still he held on to a thin thread of hope that he hadn't scared her off.

What had he been thinking, proposing to her? Declaring his love after they'd known each other such a short time. But now that the words were out, he would never take them back. He'd spoken the truth, every word of it. He did love her, and he wanted her to be his wife. But how could she accept that when he'd never so much as hinted that he cared about her other than telling her he liked her? Even with his lack of experience with women, he realized he'd taken a giant leap of faith, and it wouldn't be long before he knew if he had landed smack on his face.

He pressed his lips together as he spotted Regina and Nelson's buggy leaving. Although surely Elva was with them, he waited until the parking lot was empty, still grasping hope. But then he saw the lights in the building turning off one by one. *She's not coming.* His chest ached with a pain he'd never experienced. This was what a broken heart felt like, then. Still, he didn't wish to take back what he'd said, despite the rejection. He turned and started to climb into his buggy.

"Jerald."

He closed his eyes at the sound of her sweet voice, his aching heart speeding up again. He stepped down and turned. The parking lot had lights, and he could see her beautiful face. But he couldn't read her expression.

"Elva," he said softly as she approached. When she was standing in front of him, he said, "I didn't think you'd come."

"I almost didn't. But I want you to hear what I have to say."

~

Elva gripped her hands until her knuckles ached. She had almost gone home with Regina and Nelson. It would have been the easy choice, running away from Jerald. But she couldn't run away from her feelings. "You surprised me when you proposed," she said.

"I know." He looked down at the ground. "It was stupid of me to say that without giving you some kind of warning." Then he met her eyes. "But I meant every word."

"I believe you did. But I need to be honest with you too. I'm not ready for marriage, Jerald."

His head hung, and she wished she'd been a little less blunt. "I understand," he said. She started to speak again, but he interrupted her. "I just hope I haven't ruined our friendship."

"You haven't." She took a step toward him. "I might not be ready for marriage, but I am ready to explore the future. Nelson told me it's never too late, and I'd like to believe him. I care about you, Jerald. More than I ever thought I could care for a *mann*. I've decided to stay in Millersburg and see what the future holds for me here."

Jerald smiled. "That's probably more than I deserve, considering how I sprung a proposal on you." He paused. "Is it all right if I drive you to Nelson's?"

Elva chuckled. "I should hope so. I don't want to walk there this late at night."

As he drove her to Regina and Nelson's, neither one of them said much, but it was a companionable silence. When he pulled into the driveway, he turned to her. "I'm new to this relationship stuff," he said. "What do we do next?"

"I think another fishing trip would be nice."

"Me too."

They made plans to meet the next afternoon, and she went inside the house. The light was on in the living room, and Regina was sitting in her chair, reading a cooking magazine. She set the magazine aside. "Out late with Jerald again, I see. Is this going to be a regular thing?"

Elva sat down on the couch and took a deep breath. Then she explained about Jerald's proposal, and Regina's jaw dropped.

"He proposed?"

"*Ya.* But I turned him down." Before Regina could ask another question, she said, "I like Jerald a lot. He's a special *mann.*"

"You can say that again. Although I think *yer* definition of special and mine are quite different in this case." Regina smiled. "It's *gut* to see you happy, Elva. I've been worried about you. I know you're still grieving Henry, but until you and Jerald became friends, you seemed sad."

"I was, but not for the reason you think." She looked at her hands and clasped her fingers together. "Henry and I had a difficult relationship," she said.

For the second time, Regina looked stunned. "I had *nee* idea."

"*Nee* one did. We were *gut* at hiding it. But he blamed me for not being able to have *kinner.* Because of that, our relationship changed—and it got worse as the years went by." She averted her gaze. "He . . . he wasn't a nice *mann.*"

"I see." Regina's expression turned cold. "I wish I would have known that. I would have given him a piece of *mei* mind."

"It wouldn't have done any *gut.*" She met her friend's eyes again. "But when Henry died, I was certain I didn't want to get involved with anyone ever again."

"But you feel differently now."

Elva hesitated, then nodded. "I don't want to impose on you again—"

"Elva." Regina moved to sit next to her on the couch. She took her hand and squeezed it. "You can stay here as long as you want to. I already told you that. We love *yer* company." Her eyes took on a watery sheen. "As long as we're being honest, I was missing you already. I'm glad you're staying."

She hugged Regina, then pulled away. *"Danki."*

"Just don't rush things with Jerald. From what you've said, this is new territory for you both. Make sure this is God's will."

"I will."

"Oh, and one more thing." Regina smirked. "Tell him that I won't be making him supper on Tuesdays anymore."

"Oh?" Elva said, surprised. "Why not?"

"Because I'm sure he will prefer you making him a meal instead. Then he can hover over *yer* shoulder instead of mine."

They both laughed, and a short time later, after she'd said her prayers for the night, Elva climbed into bed. She lay there, staring into the darkness, wondering if she was doing the right thing. Then a still, quiet voice spoke to her heart. *Yes, beloved. You are.*

EPILOGUE

Elva stood in Regina's kitchen with a stomach full of butterflies. "I can't believe I'm doing this," she said. Then she began pacing the length of the room filled with food for the reception after her wedding ceremony.

"Marrying Jerald?" Regina lifted her chin. "I can. I knew you two would get married."

She stopped pacing and looked at her friend. "You did?"

"I had *mei* reservations, obviously. But after you decided to stay here, I knew you'd tie the knot." She grinned. "And I couldn't be happier."

"Because we found love?"

"That, and now I don't have to worry about him coming over for supper!"

They both laughed, and Regina gave her a hug. "You'll both still come over every once in a while, *ya*?"

"*Ya.*" Elva patted away the tears in her eyes, and Regina, who was always stalwart, had tears in hers too.

"I'm glad you're happy," her friend said, dabbing Elva's cheek with a white handkerchief. "But you can't get married crying *yer* eyes out. What will Jerald think?"

"He's used to it." Over the past three months, she'd been able to let down her guard with him, and more than once she'd cried in his arms, finally giving in to her grief over the children she didn't have and for the marriage that had been so hard. Each time he had made her feel loved and cherished. She looked at the clock, and her heart skipped a beat. "It's time."

Regina smiled. "*Geh* get married, *mei* friend."

As Elva walked into the living room of Nelson and Regina's home, she looked at the small gathering of friends huddled there. Normally weddings were an all-community affair, but while Elva now felt a part of this community, she and Jerald had wanted something small. She took her place beside him, and he winked at her, looking handsome in his black pants, black vest, and crisp white shirt. But what meant the most to her was the love in his eyes, love she'd never thought she'd experience. *Danki, God.*

"Are you ready?" Jerald whispered as the bishop took his place.

"*Ya.*" She gazed at him, forcing herself not to cry. "Never too late, *ya?*"

He winked at her. "*Ya.* It's never too late."

ACKNOWLEDGMENTS

Thank you to my editors, Becky Monds and Jean Bloom, for their editing expertise, which is always top notch. And thank you, dear reader, for coming along this journey of generations with me. Happy reading!

DISCUSSION QUESTIONS

YOUNG LOVE

1. Fern didn't want to tell anyone but her family about her rheumatoid arthritis. Do you think that was a wise decision? Why or why not?
2. After Fern's date with Dan, her mother asked her, "How will you know if you give up before you even try?" What other advice would you give to Fern?

LONG-AWAITED LOVE

1. Jemima admitted that she tended to keep grudges. How can keeping grudges cause problems for people?
2. Do you agree with Jemima's assertion that she could still be humble without being a doormat? Why or why not?

Second-Chance Love

1. Ben and Lora Beth are drawn together because of their shared grief over losing their spouses. How has tragedy in your life brought you closer to someone else, and to God?
2. Both Lora Beth's and Ben's children thought they knew what was best for their parents. Do you agree with them and what they did? Why or why not?

Never Too Late

1. Do you agree with Jerald when he says, "Everyone handles loss differently. You shouldn't compare *yerself* with other folks"? Explain your answer.
2. Do you agree with Nelson's statement that it's never too late? Has there been a time in your life when you thought an opportunity had permanently passed, only to appear again much later? How did you respond?

AMISH BRIDES

of

BIRCH CREEK

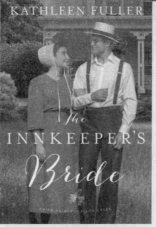

AVAILABLE IN PRINT
AND E-BOOK

About the Author

With over a million copies sold, Kathleen Fuller is the author of several bestselling novels, including the Hearts of Middlefield novels, the Middlefield Family novels, the Amish of Birch Creek series, and the Amish Letters series as well as a middle-grade Amish series, the Mysteries of Middlefield.

Visit her online at KathleenFuller.com
Facebook: @WriterKathleenFuller
Twitter: @TheKatJam
Instagram: @kf_booksandhooks